diamond dogs, turquoise days
tales from the revelation space universe

Ace Books by Alastair Reynolds

alastair reynolds

diamond dogs, turquoise days

ACE BOOKS, NEW YORK

THE BERKLEY PUBLISHING GROUP
Published by the Penguin Group
Penguin Group (USA) Inc.
375 Hudson Street, New York, New York 10014, USA
Penguin Group (Canada), 10 Alcorn Avenue, Toronto, Ontario M4V 3B2, Canada
(a division of Pearson Penguin Canada Inc.)
Penguin Books Ltd., 80 Strand, London WC2R 0RL, England
Penguin Group Ireland, 25 St. Stephen's Green, Dublin 2, Ireland (a division of Penguin Books Ltd.)
Penguin Group (Australia), 250 Camberwell Road, Camberwell, Victoria 3124, Australia
(a division of Pearson Australia Group Pty. Ltd.)
Penguin Books India Pvt. Ltd., 11 Community Centre, Panchsheel Park, New Delhi—110 017, India
Penguin Group (NZ), Cnr. Airborne and Rosedale Roads, Albany, Auckland 1310, New Zealand
(a division of Pearson New Zealand Ltd.)
Penguin Books (South Africa) (Pty.) Ltd., 24 Sturdee Avenue, Rosebank, Johannesburg 2196, South
Africa

Penguin Books Ltd., Registered Offices: 80 Strand, London WC2R 0RL, England

First American edition: January 2005
Previously published in Great Britain in 2003 by Gollancz.
A slightly different version of *Diamond Dogs* was first published in 2002 by PS Publishing.
A slightly different version of *Turquoise Days* was first published in September 2002 by Golden Gryphon
Press.

Library of Congress Cataloging-in-Publication Data

Reynolds, Alastair, 1966–
        Diamond dogs; Turquoise days / Alastair Reynolds.— 1st American ed.
        p.   cm.
        ISBN 0-441-01238-8
        1. Life on other planets—Fiction. I. Reynolds, Alastair, 1966– Turquoise days. II. Title.

PR6068.E95D53 2005
823'.92—dc22

2004052578

PRINTED IN THE UNITED STATES OF AMERICA

10   9   8   7   6   5   4   3   2   1

Thanks to Peter Crowther of PS Publishing and Marty Halpern and Gary Turner of Golden Gryphon Press for giving me the opportunity to write these novellas.

diamond dogs

one

I met Childe in the Monument to the Eighty.

It was one of those days when I had the place largely to myself, able to walk from aisle to aisle without seeing another visitor; only my footsteps disturbed the air of funereal silence and stillness.

I was visiting my parents' shrine. It was a modest affair: a smooth wedge of obsidian shaped like a metronome, undecorated save for two cameo portraits set in elliptical borders. The sole moving part was a black blade which was attached near the base of the shrine, ticking back and forth with magisterial slowness. Mechanisms buried inside the shrine ensured that it was winding down, destined to count out days and then years with each tick. Eventually it would require careful measurement to detect its movement.

I was watching the blade when a voice disturbed me.

'Visiting the dead again, Richard?'

'Who's there?' I said, looking around, faintly recognising the speaker but not immediately able to place him.

'Just another ghost.'

Various possibilities flashed through my mind as I listened to the man's deep and taunting voice – a kidnapping, an assassination – before I stopped flattering myself that I was worthy of such attention.

Then the man emerged from between two shrines a little way down from the metronome.

'My God,' I said.

'Now do you recognise me?'

He smiled and stepped closer: as tall and imposing as I remembered. He had lost the devil's horns since our last meeting – they had only ever been a bio-engineered affectation – but there was still something satanic about his appearance, an effect not lessened by the small and slightly pointed goatee he had cultivated in the meantime.

Dust swirled around him as he walked towards me, suggesting that he was not a projection.

'I thought you were dead, Roland.'

'No, Richard,' he said, stepping close enough to shake my hand. 'But that was most certainly the effect I desired to achieve.'

'Why?' I said.

'Long story.'

'Start at the beginning, then.'

Roland Childe placed a hand on the smooth side of my parents' shrine. 'Not quite your style, I'd have thought?'

'It was all I could do to argue against something even more ostentatious and morbid. But don't change the subject. What happened to you?'

He removed his hand, leaving a faint damp imprint. 'I faked my own death. The Eighty was the perfect cover. The fact that it all went so horrendously wrong was even better. I couldn't have planned it like that if I'd tried.'

No arguing with that, I thought. It *had* gone horrendously wrong.

More than a century and a half ago, a clique of researchers led by Calvin Sylveste had resurrected the old idea of copying the essence of a living human being into a computer-generated simulation. The procedure – then in its infancy – had the slight drawback that it killed the subject. But there had still been volunteers, and my parents had been amongst the first to sign up and support Calvin's work. They had offered him political protection when the powerful Mixmaster lobby opposed the project, and they had been amongst the first to be scanned.

Less than fourteen months later, their simulations had also been amongst the first to crash.

None could ever be restarted. Most of the remaining Eighty had succumbed, and now only a handful remained unaffected.

'You must hate Calvin for what he did,' Childe said, still with that taunting quality in his voice.

'Would it surprise you if I said I didn't?'

'Then why did you set yourself so vocally against his family after the tragedy?'

'Because I felt justice still needed to be served.' I turned from the shrine and started walking away, curious as to whether Childe would follow me.

'Fair enough,' he said. 'But that opposition cost you dearly, didn't it?'

I bridled, halting next to what appeared a highly realistic sculpture but was almost certainly an embalmed corpse.

'Meaning what?'

'The Resurgam expedition, of course, which just happened to be bankrolled by House Sylveste. By rights, you should have been on it. You were Richard Swift, for heaven's sake. You'd spent the better part of your life thinking about possible modes of alien sentience. There should have been a place for you on that ship, and you damned well knew it.'

'It wasn't that simple,' I said, resuming my walk. 'There were a limited number of slots available and they needed practical types first – biologists, geologists, that kind of thing. By the time they'd filled the most essential slots, there simply wasn't any room for abstract dreamers like myself.'

'And the fact that you'd pissed off House Sylveste had nothing whatsoever to do with it? Come off it, Richard.'

We descended a series of steps down into the lower level of the Monument. The atrium's ceiling was a cloudy mass of jagged sculptures: interlocked metal birds. A party of visitors was arriving, attended by servitors and a swarm of bright, marble-sized float-cams. Childe breezed through the group, drawing annoyed frowns but no actual recognition, although one or two of the people in the party were vague acquaintances of mine.

'What is this about?' I asked, once we were outside.

'Concern for an old friend. I've had my tabs on you, and it was pretty obvious that not being selected for that expedition was a crushing disappointment. You'd thrown your life into contemplation of the alien. One marriage down the drain because of your self-absorption. What was her name again?'

I'd had her memory buried so deeply that it took a real effort of will to recall any exact details about my marriage.

'Celestine. I think.'

'Since when you've had a few relationships, but nothing lasting more than a decade. A decade's a mere fling in this town, Richard.'

'My private life's my own business,' I responded sullenly. 'Hey. Where's my volantor? I parked it here.'

'I sent it away. We'll take mine instead.'

Where my volantor had been was a larger, blood-red model. It was as baroquely ornamented as a funeral barge. At a gesture from Childe it clammed open, revealing a plush gold interior with four seats, one of which was occupied by a dark, slouched figure.

'What's going on, Roland?'

'I've found something. Something astonishing that I want you to be a part of; a challenge that makes every game you and I ever played in our youth pale in comparison.'

'A challenge?'

'The ultimate one, I think.'

He had pricked my curiosity, but I hoped it was not too obvious. 'The city's vigilant. It'll be a matter of public record that I came to the Monument, and we'll have been recorded together by those float-cams.'

'Exactly,' Childe said, nodding enthusiastically. 'So you risk nothing by getting in the volantor.'

'And should I at any point weary of your company?'

'You have my word that I'll let you leave.'

I decided to play along with him for the time being. Childe and I took the volantor's front pair of seats. Once ensconced, I turned around to acquaint myself with the other passenger, and then flinched as I saw him properly.

He wore a high-necked leather coat which concealed much of the lower half of his face. The upper part was shadowed under the generous rim of a Homburg, tipped down to shade his brow. Yet what remained visible was sufficient to shock me. There was only a blandly handsome silver mask; sculpted into an expression of quiet serenity. The eyes were blank silver surfaces, what I could see of his mouth a thin, slightly smiling slot.

'Doctor Trintignant,' I said.

He reached forward with a gloved hand, allowing me to shake it as one would the hand of a woman. Beneath the black velvet of the glove I felt armatures of hard metal. Metal that could crush diamond.

'The pleasure is entirely mine,' he said.

Airborne, the volantor's baroque ornamentation melted away to mirror-smoothness. Childe pushed ivory-handled control sticks forward, gaining altitude and speed. We seemed to be moving faster than the city ordinances allowed, avoiding the usual traffic corridors. I thought of the way he had followed me, researched my past and had my own volantor desert me. It would also have taken considerable resourcefulness to locate the reclusive Trintignant and persuade him to emerge from hiding.

7

Clearly Childe's influence in the city exceeded my own, even though he had been absent for so long.

'The old place hasn't changed much,' Childe said, swooping us through a dense conglomeration of golden buildings, as extravagantly tiered as the dream pagodas of a fever-racked Emperor.

'Then you've really been away? When you told me you'd faked your death, I wondered if you'd just gone into hiding.'

He answered with a trace of hesitation, 'I've been away, but not as far as you'd think. A family matter came up that was best dealt with confidentially, and I really couldn't be bothered explaining to everyone why I needed some peace and quiet on my own.'

'And faking your death was the best way to go about it?'

'Like I said, I couldn't have planned the Eighty if I'd tried. I had to bribe a lot of minor players in the project, of course, and I'll spare you the details of how we provided a corpse . . . but it all worked swimmingly, didn't it?'

'I never had any doubts that you'd died along with the rest of them.'

'I didn't like deceiving my friends. But I couldn't go to all that trouble and then ruin my plan with a few indiscretions.'

'You were friends, then?' solicited Trintignant.

'Yes, Doctor,' Childe said, glancing back at him. 'Way back when. Richard and I were rich kids – relatively rich, anyway – with not enough to do. Neither of us were interested in the stock market or the social whirl. We were only interested in games.'

'Oh. How charming. What kinds of game, might I ask?'

'We'd build simulations to test each other – extraordinarily elaborate worlds filled with subtle dangers and temptations. Mazes and labyrinths; secret passages; trapdoors; dungeons and dragons. We'd spend months inside them, driving each other crazy. Then we'd go away and make them even harder.'

'But in due course you grew apart,' the Doctor said. His synthesised voice had a curious piping quality.

'Yeah,' Childe said. 'But we never stopped being friends. It was just that Richard had spent so much time devising increasingly alien scenarios that he'd become more interested in the implied psychologies behind the tests. And I'd become interested only in the playing of the games; not their construction. Unfortunately Richard was no longer there to provide challenges for me.'

'You were always much better than me at playing them,' I said. 'In the end it got too hard to come up with something you'd find difficult. You knew the way my mind worked too well.'

'He's convinced that he's a failure,' Childe said, turning round to smile at the Doctor.

'As are we all,' Trintignant answered. 'And with some justification, it must be said. I have never been allowed to pursue my admittedly controversial interests to their logical ends. You, Mister Swift, were shunned by those who you felt should have recognised your worth in the field of speculative alien psychology. And you, Mister Childe, have never discovered a challenge worthy of your undoubted talents.'

'I didn't think you'd paid me any attention, Doctor.'

'Nor had I. I have surmised this much since our meeting.'

The volantor dropped below ground level, descending into a brightly lit commercial plaza lined with shops and boutiques. With insouciant ease, Childe skimmed us between aerial walkways and then nosed the car into a dark side-tunnel. He gunned the machine faster, our speed indicated only by the passing of red lights set into the tunnel sides. Now and then another vehicle passed us, but once the tunnel had branched and re-branched half a dozen times, no further traffic appeared. The tunnel lights were gone now and when the volantor's headlights grazed the walls they revealed ugly cracks and huge, scarred absences of cladding. These old sub-surface ducts dated back to the city's earliest days, before the domes were thrown across the crater.

Even if I had recognised the part of the city where we had entered the tunnel system, I would have been hopelessly lost by now.

'Do you think Childe has brought us together to taunt us about our lack of respective failures, Doctor?' I asked, beginning to feel uneasy again despite my earlier attempts at reassurance.

'I would consider that a distinct possibility, were Childe himself not conspicuously tainted by the same lack of success.'

'Then there must be another reason.'

'Which I'll reveal in due course,' Childe said. 'Just bear with me, will you? You two aren't the only ones I've gathered together.'

Presently we arrived somewhere.

It was a cave in the form of a near-perfect hemisphere, the great domed roof arching a clear three hundred metres from the floor. We were obviously well below Yellowstone's surface now. It was even possible that we had passed beyond the city's crater wall, so that above us lay only poisonous skies.

But the domed chamber was inhabited.

The roof was studded with an enormous number of lamps, flooding the interior with synthetic daylight. An island stood in the middle of the chamber, moated by a ring of uninviting water. A single bone-white bridge connected the mainland to the island, shaped like a great curved femur. The island was dominated by a thicket of slender, dark poplars partly concealing a pale structure situated near its middle.

Childe brought the volantor to a rest near the edge of the water and invited us to disembark.

'Where are we?' I asked, once I had stepped down.

'Query the city and find out for yourself,' Trintignant said.

The result was not what I was expecting. For a moment there

was a shocking absence inside my head, the neural equivalent of a sudden, unexpected amputation.

The Doctor's chuckle was an arpeggio played on a pipe organ. 'We have been out of range of city services from the moment we entered his conveyance.'

'You needn't worry,' Childe said. 'You are beyond city services, but only because I value the secrecy of this place. If I imagined it'd have come as a shock to you, I'd have told you already.'

'I'd have at least appreciated a warning, Roland,' I said.

'Would it have changed your mind about coming here?'

'Conceivably.'

The echo of his laughter betrayed the chamber's peculiar acoustics. 'Then are you at all surprised that I didn't tell you?'

I turned to Trintignant. 'What about you?'

'I confess my use of city services has been as limited as your own, but for rather different reasons.'

'The good Doctor needed to lie low,' Childe said. 'That meant he couldn't participate very actively in city affairs. Not if he didn't want to be tracked down and assassinated.'

I stamped my feet, beginning to feel cold. 'Good. What now?'

'It's only a short ride to the house,' Childe said, glancing towards the island.

Now a noise came steadily nearer. It was an antiquated, rumbling sound, accompanied by a odd, rhythmic sort of drumming, quite unlike any machine I had experienced. I looked towards the femoral bridge, suspecting as I did that it was exactly what it looked like: a giant, bio-engineered bone, carved with a flat roadbed. And something was approaching us over the span: a dark, complicated and unfamiliar contraption, which at first glance resembled an iron tarantula.

I felt the back of my neck prickle.

The thing reached the end of the bridge and swerved towards

11

us. Two mechanical black horses provided the motive power. They were emaciated black machines with sinewy, piston-driven limbs, venting steam and snorting from intakes. Malignant red laser-eyes swept over us. The horses were harnessed to a four-wheeled carriage slightly larger than the volantor, above which was perched a headless humanoid robot. Skeletal hands gripped iron control cables which plunged into the backs of the horses' steel necks.

'Meant to inspire confidence, is it?' I asked.

'It's an old family heirloom,' Childe said, swinging open a black door in the side of the carriage. 'My uncle Giles made automata. Unfortunately – for reasons we'll come to – he was a bit of a miserable bastard. But don't let it put you off.'

He helped us aboard, then climbed inside himself, sealed the door and knocked on the roof. I heard the mechanical horses snort; alloy hooves hammered the ground impatiently. Then we were moving, curving around and ascending the gentle arc of the bridge of bone.

'Have you been here during the entire period of your absence, Mister Childe?' Trintignant asked.

He nodded. 'Ever since that family business came up, I've allowed myself the occasional visit back to the city – just like I did today – but I've tried to keep such excursions to a minimum.'

'Didn't you have horns the last time we met?' I said.

He rubbed the smooth skin of his scalp where the horns had been. 'Had to have them removed. I couldn't very well disguise myself otherwise.'

We crossed the bridge and navigated a path between the tall trees which sheltered the island's structure. Childe's carriage pulled up to a smart stop in front of the building and I was afforded my first unobstructed view of our destination. It was not one to induce great cheer. The house's architecture was haphazard: whatever basic symmetry it might once have had was lost under a profusion of additions and modifications. The roof was a jumbled collision of angles and spires, jutting turrets and sinister oubliettes. Not all of the embellishments had been arranged at strict right angles to their neighbours, and the style and apparent age of the house varied jarringly from place to place. Since our arrival in the cave the overhead lights had dimmed, simulating the onset of dusk, but only a few windows were illuminated, clustered together in the left-hand wing. The rest of the house had a forebidding aspect, the paleness of its stone, the irregularity of its construction and the darkness of its many windows suggesting a pile of skulls.

Almost before we had disembarked from the carriage, a reception party emerged from the house. It was a troupe of servitors – humanoid household robots, of the kind anyone would have felt comfortable with in the city proper – but they had been reworked to resemble skeletal ghouls or headless knights. Their mechanisms had been sabotaged so that they limped and creaked, and they had all had their voiceboxes disabled.

'Had a lot of time on his hands, your uncle,' I said.

'You'd have loved Giles, Richard. He was a scream.'

'I'll take your word for it, I think.'

The servitors escorted us into the central part of the house, then took us through a maze of chill, dark corridors.

Finally we reached a large room walled in plush red velvet. A holoclavier sat in one corner, with a book of sheet music spread open above the projected keyboard. There was a malachite escritoire, a number of well-stocked bookcases, a single chandelier, three smaller candelabra and two fireplaces of distinctly gothic appearance, in one of which roared an actual fire. But the room's central feature was a mahogany table, around which three additional guests were gathered.

'Sorry to keep everyone waiting,' Childe said, closing a pair of sturdy wooden doors behind us. 'Now. Introductions.'

13

The others looked at us with no more than mild interest.

The only man amongst them wore an elaborately ornamented exoskeleton: a baroque support structure of struts, hinged plates, cables and servo-mechanisms. His face was a skull papered with deathly white skin, shading to black under his bladelike cheekbones. His eyes were concealed behind goggles, his hair a spray of stiff black dreadlocks.

Periodically he inhaled from a glass pipe, connected to a miniature refinery of bubbling apparatus placed before him on the table.

'Allow me to introduce Captain Forqueray,' Childe said. 'Captain – this is Richard Swift and . . . um, Doctor Trintignant.'

'Pleased to meet you,' I said, leaning across the table to shake Forqueray's hand. His grip felt like the cold clasp of a squid.

'The Captain is an Ultra; the master of the lighthugger *Apollyon*, currently in orbit around Yellowstone,' Childe added.

Trintignant refrained from approaching him.

'Shy, Doctor?' Forqueray said, his voice simultaneously deep and flawed, like a cracked bell.

'No, merely cautious. It is a matter of common knowledge that I have enemies amongst the Ultras.'

Trintignant removed his Homburg and patted his crown delicately, as if smoothing down errant hairs. Silver waves had been sculpted into his head-mask, so that he resembled a bewigged Regency fop dipped in mercury.

'You've enemies everywhere,' said Forqueray between gurgling inhalations. 'But I bear you no personal animosity for your atrocities, and I guarantee that my crew will extend you the same courtesy.'

'Very gracious of you,' Trintignant said, before shaking the Ultra's hand for the minimum time compatible with politeness. 'But why should your crew concern me?'

14

'Never mind that.' It was one of the two women speaking now. 'Who is this guy, and why does everyone hate him?'

'Allow me to introduce Hirz,' Childe said, indicating the woman who had spoken. She was small enough to have been a child, except that her face was clearly that of an adult woman. She was dressed in austere, tight-fitting black clothes which only emphasised her diminutive build. 'Hirz is – for want of a better word – a mercenary.'

'Except I prefer to think of myself as an information retrieval specialist. I specialise in clandestine infiltration for high-level corporate clients in the Glitter Band – physical espionage, some of the time. Mostly, though, I'm what used to be called a hacker. I'm also pretty damned good at my job.' Hirz paused to swig down some wine. 'But enough about me. Who's the silver dude, and what did Forqueray mean about atrocities?'

'You're seriously telling me you're unaware of Trintignant's reputation?' I said.

'Hey, listen. I get myself frozen between assignments. That means I miss a lot of shit that goes down in Chasm City. Get over it.'

I shrugged and – with one eye on the Doctor himself – told Hirz what I knew about Trintignant. I sketched in his early career as an experimental cyberneticist, how his reputation for fearless innovation had eventually brought him to Calvin Sylveste's attention.

Calvin had recruited Trintignant to his own research team, but the collaboration had not been a happy one. Trintignant's desire to find the ultimate fusion of flesh and machine had become obsessive; even – some said – perverse. After a scandal involving experimentation on unconsenting subjects, Trintignant had been forced to pursue his work alone, his methods too extreme even for Calvin.

So Trintignant had gone to ground, and continued his gruesome experiments with his only remaining subject.

Himself.

'So let's see,' said the final guest. 'Who have we got? An obsessive and thwarted cyberneticist with a taste for extreme modification. An intrusion specialist with a talent for breaking into highly protected – and dangerous – environments. A man with a starship at his disposal and the crew to operate it.'

Then she looked at Childe, and while her gaze was averted I admired the fine, faintly familiar profile of her face. Her long hair was the sheer black of interstellar space, pinned back from her face by a jewelled clasp which flickered with a constellation of embedded pastel lights. Who was she? I felt sure we had met once or maybe twice before. Perhaps we had passed each other amongst the shrines in the Monument to the Eighty, visiting the dead.

'And Childe,' she continued. 'A man once known for his love of intricate challenges, but long assumed dead.' Then she turned her piercing eyes upon me. 'And, finally, you.'

'I know you, I think—' I said, her name on the tip of my tongue.

'Of course you do.' Her look, suddenly, was contemptuous. 'I'm Celestine. You used to be married to me.'

All along, Childe had known she was here.

'Do you mind if I ask what this is about?' I said, doing my best to sound as reasonable as possible, rather than someone on the verge of losing their temper in polite company.

Celestine withdrew her hand once I had shaken it. 'Roland invited me here, Richard. Just the same way he did you, with the same veiled hints about having found something.'

'But you're . . .'

'Your ex-wife?' She nodded. 'Exactly how much do you remember, Richard? I heard the strangest rumours, you know. That you'd had me deleted from your long-term memory.'

'I had you suppressed, not deleted. There's a subtle distinction.'

She nodded knowingly. 'So I gather.'

I looked at the other guests, who were observing us. Even Forqueray was waiting, the pipe of his apparatus poised an inch from his mouth in expectation. They were waiting for me to say something; anything.

'Why exactly are you here, Celestine?'

'You don't remember, do you?'

'Remember what?'

'What it was I used to do, Richard, when we were married.'

'I confess I don't, no.'

Childe coughed. 'Your wife, Richard, was as fascinated by the alien as you were. She was one of the city's foremost specialists on the Pattern Jugglers, although she'd be entirely too modest to admit it herself.' He paused, apparently seeking Celestine's permission to continue. 'She visited them, long before you met, spending several years of her life at the study station on Spindrift. You swam with the Jugglers, didn't you, Celestine?'

'Once or twice.'

'And allowed them to reshape your mind, transforming its neural pathways into something deeply – albeit usually temporarily – alien.'

'It wasn't that big a deal,' Celestine said.

'Not if you'd been fortunate enough to have it happen to you, no. But for someone like Richard – who craved knowledge of the alien with every fibre of his existence – it would have been anything but mundane.' He turned to me. 'Isn't that true?'

'I admit I'd have done a great deal to experience communion with the Jugglers,' I said, knowing that it was pointless to deny it. 'But it just wasn't possible. My family lacked the resources to send me to one of the Juggler worlds, and the bodies that might ordinarily have funded that kind of trip – the Sylveste Institute, for instance – had turned their attentions elsewhere.'

'In which case Celestine was deeply fortunate, wouldn't you say?'

'I don't think anyone would deny that,' I said. 'To speculate about the shape of alien consciousness is one thing; but to drink it; to bathe in the full flood of it – to know it intimately, like a lover . . .' I trailed off for a moment. 'Wait a minute. Shouldn't you be on Resurgam, Celestine? There isn't time for the expedition to have gone there and come back.'

She eyed me with raptorial intent before answering, 'I never went.'

Childe leant over and refreshed my glass. 'She was turned down at the last minute, Richard. Sylveste had a grudge against anyone who'd visited the Jugglers; he suddenly decided they were all unstable and couldn't be trusted.'

I looked at Celestine wonderingly. 'Then all this time . . . ?'

'I've been here, in Chasm City. Oh, don't look so crushed, Richard. By the time I learned I'd been turned down, you'd already decided to flush me out of your past. It was better for both of us this way.'

'But the deception . . .'

Childe put one hand on my shoulder, calmingly. 'There wasn't any. She just didn't make contact again. No lies; no deception; nothing to hold a grudge about.'

I looked at him, angrily. 'Then why the hell is she here?'

'Because I happen to have use for someone with the skills that the Jugglers gave to Celestine.'

'Which included?' I said.

'Extreme mathematical prowess.'

'And why would that have been useful?'

Childe turned to the Ultra, indicating that the man should remove his bubbling apparatus.

'I'm about to show you.'

The table housed an antique holo-projection system. Childe handed out viewers which resembled lorgnette binoculars, and, like so many myopic opera buffs, we studied the apparitions which floated into existence above the polished mahogany surface.

Stars: incalculable numbers of them – hard white and blood-red gems, strewn in lacy patterns against deep velvet blue.

Childe narrated:

'The better part of two and a half centuries ago, my uncle Giles – whose somewhat pessimistic handiwork you have already seen – made a momentous decision. He embarked on what we in the family referred to as the Program, and then only in terms of extreme secrecy.'

Childe told us that the Program was an attempt at covert deep space exploration.

Giles had conceived the work, funding it directly from the family's finances. He had done this with such ingenuity that the apparent wealth of House Childe had never faltered, even as the Program entered its most expensive phase. Only a few select members of the Childe dynasty had even known of the Program's existence, and that number had dwindled as time passed.

The bulk of the money had been paid to the Ultras, who had already emerged as a powerful faction by that time.

They had built the autonomous robot space probes according to this uncle's desires, and then launched them towards a variety of target systems. The Ultras could have delivered his probes to any system within range of their lighthugger ships, but the whole point of the exercise was to restrict the knowledge of any possible discoveries to the family alone. So the envoys crossed space by themselves, at only a fraction of the speed of light, and the targets they were sent to were all poorly explored systems on the ragged edge of human space.

The probes decelerated by use of solar sails, picked the most interesting worlds to explore, and then fell into orbit around them.

Robots were sent down, equipped to survive on the surface for many decades.

Childe waved his hand across the table. Lines radiated out from one of the redder suns in the display, which I assumed was Yellowstone's star. The lines reached out towards other stars, forming a three-dimensional scarlet dandelion several dozen light-years wide.

'These machines must have been reasonably intelligent,' Celestine said. 'Especially by the standards of the time.'

Childe nodded keenly. 'Oh, they were. Cunning little blighters. Subtle and stealthy and diligent. They had to be, to operate so far from human supervision.'

'And I presume they found something?' I said.

'Yes,' Childe said testily, like a conjurer whose carefully scripted patter was being ruined by a persistent heckler. 'But not immediately. Giles didn't expect it to be immediate, of course – the envoys would take decades to reach the closest systems they'd been assigned to, and there'd still be the communicational timelag to take into consideration. So my uncle resigned himself to forty or fifty years of waiting, and that was erring on the optimistic side.' He paused and sipped from his wine. 'Too bloody optimistic, as it happened. Fifty years passed . . . then sixty . . . but nothing of any consequence was ever reported back to Yellowstone, at least not in his lifetime. The envoys did, on occasion, find something interesting – but by then other human explorers had usually stumbled on the same find. And as the decades wore on, and the envoys failed to justify their invention, my uncle grew steadily more maudlin and bitter.'

'I'd never have guessed,' Celestine said.

'He died, eventually – bitter and resentful; feeling that the universe had played some sick cosmic trick on him. He could have lived for another fifty or sixty years with the right treatments, but I think by then he knew it would be a waste of time.'

'You faked your death a century and a half ago,' I said.

'Didn't you tell me it had something to do with the family business?'

He nodded in my direction. 'That was when my uncle told me about the Program. I didn't know anything about it until then – hadn't heard even the tiniest hint of a rumour. No one in the family had. By then, of course, the project was costing us almost nothing, so there wasn't even a financial drain to be concealed.'

'And since then?'

'I vowed not to make my uncle's mistake. I resolved to sleep until the machines sent back a report, and then sleep again if the report turned out to be a false alarm.'

'Sleep?' I said.

He clicked his fingers and one entire wall of the room whisked back to reveal a sterile, machine-filled chamber.

I studied its contents.

There was a reefersleep casket of the kind Forqueray and his ilk used aboard their ships, attended by numerous complicated hunks of gleaming green support machinery. By use of such a casket, one might prolong the four hundred-odd years of a normal human lifespan by many centuries, though reefersleep was not without its risks.

'I spent a century and a half in that contraption,' he said, 'waking every fifteen or twenty years whenever a report trickled in from one of the envoys. Waking is the worst part. It feels like you're made of glass; as if the next movement you make – the next breath you take – will cause you to shatter into a billion pieces. It always passes, and you always forget it an hour later, but it's never easier the next time.' He shuddered visibly. 'In fact, sometimes I think it gets harder each time.'

'Then your equipment needs servicing,' Forqueray said dismissively. I suspected it was bluff. Ultras often wore a lock of braided hair for every crossing they had made across interstellar space and survived all the myriad misfortunes which might befall a ship. But that braid also symbolised every occasion on which they had been woken from the dead, at the end of the journey.

They felt the pain as fully as Childe did, even if they were not willing to admit it.

'How long did you spend awake each time?' I asked.

'No more than thirteen hours. That was usually sufficient to tell if the message was interesting or not. I'd allow myself one or two hours to catch up on the news; what was going on in the wider universe. But I had to be disciplined. If I'd stayed awake longer, the attraction of returning to city life would have become overwhelming. That room began to feel like a prison.'

'Why?' I asked. 'Surely the subjective time must have passed very quickly?'

'You've obviously never spent any time in reefersleep, Richard. There's no consciousness when you're frozen, granted – but the transitions to and from the cold state are like an eternity, crammed with strange dreams.'

'But you hoped the rewards would be worth it?'

Childe nodded. 'And, indeed, they may well have been. I was last woken six months ago, and I've not returned to the chamber since. Instead, I've spent that time gathering together the resources and the people for a highly unusual expedition.'

Now he made the table change its projection, zooming in on one particular star.

'I won't bore you with catalogue numbers, suffice to say that this is a system which no one around this table – with the possible exception of Forqueray – is likely to have heard of. There've never been any human colonies there, and no crewed vessel has ever passed within three light-years of it. At least, not until recently.'

The view zoomed in again, enlarging with dizzying speed.

A planet swelled up to the size of a skull, suspended above the table.

It was hued entirely in shades of grey and pale rust, cratered and gouged here and there by impacts and what must have been very ancient weathering processes. Though there was a suggestion of a wisp of atmosphere – a smoky blue halo encircling the planet – and though there were icecaps at either pole, the world looked neither habitable nor inviting.

'Cheerful-looking place, isn't it?' Childe said. 'I call it Golgotha.'

'Nice name,' Celestine said.

'But not, unfortunately, a very nice planet.' Childe made the view enlarge again, so that we were skimming the world's bleak, apparently lifeless surface. 'Pretty dismal, to be honest. It's about the same size as Yellowstone, receiving about the same amount of sunlight from its star. Doesn't have a moon. Surface gravity's close enough to one gee that you won't know the difference once you're suited up. A thin carbon dioxide atmosphere, and no sign that anything's ever evolved there. Plenty of radiation hitting the surface, but that's about your only hazard, and one we can easily deal with. Golgotha's tectonically dead, and there haven't been any large impacts on her surface for a few million years.'

'Sounds boring,' Hirz said.

'And it very probably is, but that isn't the point. You see, there's something on Golgotha.'

'What kind of something?' Celestine asked.

'That kind,' Childe said.

It came over the horizon.

It was tall and dark, its details indistinct. That first view of it was like the first glimpse of a cathedral's spire through morning fog. It tapered as it rose, constricting to a thin neck before flaring out again into a bulb-shaped finial, which in turn tapered to a needle-sharp point.

Though it was impossible to say how large the thing was, or what it was made of, it was very obviously a structure, as opposed to a peculiar biological or mineral formation. On

Grand Teton, vast numbers of tiny single-celled organisms conspired to produce the slime towers which were that world's most famous natural feature, and while those towers reached impressive heights and were often strangely shaped, they were unmistakably the products of unthinking biological processes rather than conscious design. The structure on Golgotha was too symmetric for that, and entirely too solitary. If it had been a living thing, I would have expected to see others like it, with evidence of a supporting ecology of different organisms.

Even if it were a fossil, millions of years dead, I could not believe that there would be just one on the whole planet.

No. The thing had most definitely been put there.

'A structure?' I asked Childe.

'Yes. Or a machine. It isn't easy to decide.' He smiled. 'I call it Blood Spire. Almost looks innocent, doesn't it? Until you look closer.'

We spun round the Spire, or whatever it was, viewing it from all directions. Now that we were closer, it was clear that the thing's surface was densely detailed; patterned and textured with geometrically complex forms, around which snaked intestinal tubes and branching, veinlike bulges. The effect was to undermine my earlier certainty that the thing was non-biological.

Now it looked like some sinewy fusion of animal and machine: something that might have appealed in its grotesquerie to Childe's demented uncle.

'How tall is it?' I asked.

'Two hundred and fifty metres,' Childe said.

I saw that now there were tiny glints on Golgotha's surface, almost like metallic flakes which had fallen from the side of the structure.

'What are those?' I asked.

'Why don't I show you?' Childe said.

He enlarged the view still further, until the glints resolved into distinct shapes.

They were people.

Or – more accurately – the remains of what had once been people. It was impossible to say how many there had been. All had been mutilated in some fashion: crushed or pruned or bisected; the tattered ruins of their spacesuits were still visible in one or two places. Severed parts accompanied the bodies, often several tens of metres from the rightful owner.

It was as if they had been flung away in a fit of temper.

'Who were they?' Forqueray asked.

'A crew who happened to slow down in this system to make shield repairs,' Childe said. 'Their captain was called Argyle. They chanced upon the Spire and started exploring it, believing it to contain something of immense technological value.'

'And what happened to them?'

'They went inside in small teams, sometimes alone. Inside the Spire they passed through a series of challenges, each of which was harder than the last. If they made a mistake, the Spire punished them. The punishments were initially mild, but they became steadily more brutal. The trick was to know when to admit defeat.'

I leaned forward. 'How do you know all this?'

'Because Argyle survived. Not long, admittedly, but long enough for my machine to get some sense out of him. It had been on Golgotha the whole time, you see – watching Argyle's arrival, hiding and recording them as they confronted the Spire. And it watched him crawl out of the Spire, shortly before the last of his colleagues was ejected.'

'I'm not sure I'm prepared to trust either the testimony of a machine or a dying man,' I said.

'You don't have to,' Childe answered. 'You need only consider the evidence of your eyes. Do you see those tracks in the dust? They all lead into the Spire, and there are almost none leading to the bodies.'

'Meaning what?' I said.

'Meaning that they got inside, the way Argyle claimed. Observe also the way the remains are distributed. They're not all at the same distance from the Spire. They must have been ejected from different heights, suggesting that some got closer to the summit than others. Again, it accords with Argyle's story.'

With a sinking feeling of inevitability I saw where this was heading. 'And you want us to go there and find out what it was they were so interested in. Is that it?'

He smiled. 'You know me entirely too well, Richard.'

'I thought I did. But you'd have to be quite mad to want to go anywhere near that thing.'

'Mad? Possibly. Or simply very, very curious. The question is—' He paused and leaned across the table to refill my glass, all the while maintaining eye contact. 'Which are you?'

'Neither,' I said.

But Childe could be persuasive. A month later I was frozen aboard Forqueray's ship.

two

We reached orbit around Golgotha.

Thawed from reefersleep we convened for breakfast, riding a travel pod upship to the lighthugger's meeting room.

Everyone was there, including Trintignant and Forqueray, the latter inhaling from the same impressive array of flasks, retorts and spiralling tubes he had brought with him to Yellowstone. Trintignant had not slept with the rest of us, but looked none the worse for wear. He had, Childe said, his own rather specialised plumbing requirements, incompatible with standard reefersleep systems.

'Well, how was it?' Childe asked, throwing a comradely arm around my shoulders.

'Every bit as . . . dreadful as I'd been led to expect.' My voice was slurred, sentences taking an age to form in whatever part of my brain it was that handled language. 'Still a bit fuzzy.'

'Well, we'll soon fix that. Trintignant can synthesise a medichine infusion to pep up those neural functions, can't you, Doctor?'

Trintignant looked at me with his handsome, immobile mask of a face. 'It would be no trouble at all, my dear fellow . . .'

'Thanks.' I steadied myself; my mind crawled with half-remembered images of the botched cybernetic experiments which had earned Trintignant his notoriety. The thought of him pumping tiny machines into my skull made my skin crawl. 'But I'll pass on that for now. No offence intended.'

'And absolutely none taken.' Trintignant gestured towards a vacant chair. 'Come. Sit with us and join in the discussion. The topic, rather interestingly, is the dreams some of us experienced on the way here.'

'Dreams . . . ?' I said. 'I thought it was just me. I wasn't the only one?'

'No,' Hirz said, 'you weren't the only one. I was on a moon in one of them. Earth's, I think. And I kept on trying to get inside this alien structure. Fucking thing kept killing me, but I'd always keep going back inside, like I was being brought back to life each time just for that.'

'I had the same dream,' I said, wonderingly. 'And there was another dream in which I was inside some kind of—' I halted, waiting for the words to assemble in my head. 'Some kind of underground tomb. I remember being chased down a corridor by an enormous stone ball which was going to roll over me.'

Hirz nodded. 'The dream with the hat, right?'

'My God, yes.' I grinned like a madman. 'I lost my hat, and I felt this ridiculous urge to rescue it!'

Celestine looked at me with something between icy detachment and outright hostility. 'I had that one too.'

'Me too,' Hirz said, chuckling. 'But I said fuck the hat. Sorry, but with the kind of money Childe's paying us, buying a new one ain't gonna be my biggest problem.'

An awkward moment followed, for only Hirz seemed at all comfortable about discussing the generous fees Childe had arranged as payment for the expedition. The initial sums had been large enough, but upon our return to Yellowstone we would all receive nine times as much; adjusted to match any inflation which might occur during the time – between sixty and eighty years – which Childe said the journey would span.

Generous, yes.

But I think Childe knew that some of us would have joined him even without that admittedly sweet bonus.

Celestine broke the silence, turning to Hirz. 'Did you have the one about the cubes, too?'

'Christ, yes,' the infiltration specialist said, as if suddenly remembering. 'The cubes. What about you, Richard?'

'Indeed,' I answered, flinching at the memory of that one. I had been one of a party of people trapped inside an endless series of cubic rooms, many of which contained lethal surprises. 'I was cut into pieces by a trap, actually. Diced, if I remember accurately.'

'Yeah. Not exactly on my top ten list of ways to die, either.'

Childe coughed. 'I feel I should apologise for the dreams. They were narratives I fed into your minds – Doctor Trintignant excepted – during the transition to and from reefersleep.'

'Narratives?' I said.

'I adapted them from a variety of sources, thinking they'd put us all in the right frame of mind for what lies ahead.'

'Dying nastily, you mean?' Hirz asked.

'Problem-solving, actually.' Childe served pitch-black coffee as he spoke, as if all that was ahead of us was a moderately bracing stroll. 'Of course, nothing that the dreams contained is likely to reflect anything that we'll find inside the Spire . . . but don't you feel better for having had them?'

I gave the matter some thought before responding.

'Not exactly, no,' I said.

Thirteen hours later we were on the surface, inspecting the suits Forqueray had provided for the expedition.

They were sleek white contraptions, armoured, powered and equipped with enough intelligence to fool a roomful of cyberneticians. They enveloped themselves around you, forming a seamless white surface which lent the wearer the appearance of a figurine moulded from soap. The suits quickly learned how you moved, adjusting and anticipating all the time like perfect dance partners.

Forqueray told us that each suit was capable of keeping its occupant alive almost indefinitely; that the suit would recycle bodily wastes in a near-perfect closed cycle, and could even freeze its occupant if circumstances merited such action. They could fly and would protect their user against just about any external environment, ranging from a vacuum to the crush of the deepest ocean.

'What about weapons?' Celestine asked, once we had been shown how to command the suits to do our bidding.

'Weapons?' Forqueray asked blankly.

'I've heard about these suits, Captain. They're supposed to contain enough firepower to take apart a small mountain.'

Childe coughed. 'There won't be any weapons, I'm afraid. I asked Forqueray to have them removed from the suits. No cutting tools, either. And you won't be able to achieve as much with brute force as you would with an unmodified suit. The servos won't allow it.'

'I'm not sure I understand. You're handicapping us before we go in?'

'No – far from it. I'm just abiding by the rules that the Spire sets. It doesn't allow weapons inside itself, you see – or anything else that might be used against it, like fusion torches. It senses such things and acts accordingly. It's very clever.'

I looked at him. 'Is this guesswork?'

'Of course not. Argyle already learned this much. No point making exactly the same mistakes again, is there?'

'I still don't get it,' Celestine said when we had assembled outside the shuttle, standing like so many white soap statuettes. 'Why fight the thing on its own terms at all? There are bound to be weapons on Forqueray's ship we could use from orbit; we could open it like a carcase.'

'Yes,' Childe said, 'and in the process destroy everything we came this far to learn?'

'I'm not talking about blowing it off the face of Golgotha. I'm just talking about clean, surgical dissection.'

'It won't work. The Spire is a living thing, Celestine. Or at least a machine intelligence many orders of magnitude cleverer than anything we've encountered to date. It won't tolerate violence being used against it. Argyle learned that much.

'Even if it can't defend itself against such attacks – and we don't know that – it will certainly destroy what it contains. We'll still have lost everything.'

'But still . . . no weapons?'

'Not quite,' Childe said, tapping the forehead region of his suit. 'We still have our minds, after all. That's why I assembled this team. If brute force would have been sufficient, I'd have had no need to scour Yellowstone for such fierce intellects.'

Hirz spoke from inside her own, smaller version of the armoured suit. 'You'd better not be taking the piss.'

'Forqueray?' Childe said. 'We're nearly there now. Put us down on the surface two klicks from the base of the Spire. We'll cross the remaining distance on foot.'

Forqueray obliged, bringing the triangular formation down. Our suits had been slaved to his, but now we regained independent control.

Through the suit's numerous layers of armour and padding I felt the rough texture of the ground beneath my feet. I held up a thickly gauntleted hand and felt the breeze of Golgotha's thin atmosphere caress my palm. The tactile transmission was flawless, and when I moved, the suit flowed with me so effort-lessly that I had no sense of being encumbered by it. The view was equally impressive, with the suit projecting an image directly into my visual field rather than forcing me to peer through a visor.

31

A strip along the top of my visual field showed a three-hundred-and-sixty-degree view all around me, and I could zoom in on any part of it almost without thinking. Various overlays – sonar, radar, thermal, gravimetric – could be dropped over the existing visual field with the same ease. If I looked down I could even ask the suit to edit me out of the image, so that I could view the scene from a disembodied perspective. As we walked along the suit threw traceries of light across the scenery: an etchwork of neon which would now and then coalesce around an odd-shaped rock or peculiar pattern of ground markings. After several minutes of this I had adjusted the suit's alertness threshold to what I felt was a useful level of protectivity, neither too watchful nor too complacent.

Childe and Forqueray had taken the lead on the ground. They would have been difficult to distinguish, but my suit had partially erased their suits, so that they seemed to walk unprotected save for a ghostly second skin. When they looked at me they would perceive the same consensual illusion.

Trintignant followed a little way behind, moving with the automaton-like stiffness I had now grown almost accustomed to.

Celestine followed, with me a little to her stern.

Hirz brought up the rear, small and lethal and – now that I knew her a little better – quite unlike any of the few children I had ever met.

And ahead – rising, ever rising – was the thing we had come all this way to best.

It had been visible, of course, long before we set down. The Spire was a quarter of a kilometre high, after all. But I think we had all chosen to ignore it; to map it out of our perceptions, until we were much closer. It was only now that we were allowing those mental shields to collapse; forcing our imaginations to confront the fact of the tower's existence.

Huge and silent, it daggered into the sky.

It was much as Childe had shown us, except that it seemed infinitely more massive; infinitely more present. We were still a quarter of a kilometre from the thing's base, and yet the flared top – the bulb-shaped finial – seemed to be leaning back over us, constantly on the point of falling and crushing us. The effect was exacerbated by the occasional high-altitude cloud that passed overhead, writhing in Golgotha's fast, thin jetstreams. The whole tower looked as if it were toppling. For a long moment, taking in the immensity of what stood before us – its vast age; its vast, brooding capacity for harm – the idea of trying to reach the summit felt uncomfortably close to insanity.

Then a small, rational voice reminded me that this was exactly the effect the Spire's builders would have sought.

Knowing that, it was fractionally easier to take the next step closer to the base.

'Well,' Celestine said. 'It looks like we've found Argyle.'

Childe nodded. 'Yes. Or what's left of the poor bastard.'

We had found several body parts by then, but his was the only one that was anywhere near being complete. He had lost a leg inside the Spire, but had been able to crawl to the exit before the combination of bleeding and asphyxiation killed him. It was here – dying – that he had been interviewed by Childe's envoy, which had only then emerged from its hiding place.

Perhaps he had imagined himself in the presence of a benevolent steel angel.

He was not well-preserved. There was no bacterial life on Golgotha, and nothing that could be charitably termed weather, but there were savage dust-storms, and these must have inter-mittently covered and revealed the body, scouring it in the process. Parts of his suit were missing, and his helmet had cracked open, exposing his skull. Papery sheets of skin adhered to the bone here and there, but not enough to suggest a face.

Childe and Forqueray regarded the corpse uneasily, while Trintignant knelt down and examined it in more detail. A float-cam belonging to the Ultra floated around, observing the scene with goggling arrays of tightly packed lenses.

'Whatever took his leg off did it cleanly,' the Doctor reported, pulling back the tattered layers of the man's suit fabric to expose the stump. 'Witness how the bone and muscle have been neatly severed along the same plane, like a geometric slice through a platonic solid? I would speculate that a laser was responsible for this, except that I see no sign of cauterisation. A high-pressure water-jet might have achieved the same precision of cut, or even an extremely sharp blade.'

'Fascinating, Doc,' Hirz said, kneeling down next to him. 'I'll bet it hurt like fuck, too, wouldn't you?'

'Not necessarily. The degree of pain would depend acutely on the manner in which the nerve ends were truncated. Shock does not appear to have been the primary agent in this man's demise.' Doctor Trintignant fingered the remains of a red fabric band a little distance above the end of the leg. 'Nor was the blood loss as rapid as might have been expected given the absence of cauterisation. This band was most likely a tourniquet, probably applied from his suit's medical kit. The same kit almost certainly included analgesics.'

'It wasn't enough to save him, though,' Childe said.

'No.' Trintignant stood up, the movement reminding me of an escalator. 'But you must concede that he did rather well, considering the impediments.'

For most of its height Blood Spire was no thicker than a few dozen metres, and considerably narrower just below the bulb-like upper part. But, like a slender chess piece, its lower parts swelled out considerably to form a wide base. That podium-like mass was perhaps fifty metres in diameter: a fifth of the structure's height. From a distance it appeared to rest solidly on the base: a mighty obelisk requiring the deepest of foundations to anchor it to the ground.

But it didn't.

The Spire's base failed to touch the surface of Golgotha at all, but floated above it, spaced by five or six clear metres of air. It was as if someone had constructed a building slightly above the ground, kicked away the stilts, and it had simply stayed there.

We all walked confidently towards the rim and then stopped; none of us were immediately willing to step under that overhang.

'Forqueray?' Childe said.

'Yes?'

'Let's see what that drone of yours has to say.'

Forqueray had his float-cam fly under the rim, orbiting the underside of the Spire in a lazily widening spiral. Now and then it fingered the base with a spray of laser-light, and once or twice even made contact, skittering against the flat surface. Forqueray remained impassive, glancing slightly down as he absorbed the data being sent back to his suit.

'Well?' Celestine said. 'What the hell's keeping it up?'

Forqueray took a step under the rim. 'No fields; not even a minor perturbation of Golgotha's own magnetosphere. No significant alterations in the local gravitational vector, either. And – before we assume more sophistication than is strictly necessary – there are no concealed supports.'

Celestine was silent for a few moments before answering, 'All right. What if the Spire doesn't weigh anything? There's air here; not much of it I'll grant you – but what if the Spire's mostly hollow? There might be enough buoyancy to make the thing float, like a balloon.'

'There isn't,' Forqueray said, opening a fist to catch the cam, which flew into his grasp like a trained kestrel. 'Whatever's above us is solid matter. I can't read its mass, but it's blocking

35

an appreciable cosmic-ray flux, and none of our scanning methods can see through it.'

'Forqueray's right,' Childe said. 'But I understand your reluctance to accept this, Celestine. It's perfectly normal to feel a sense of denial.'

'Denial?'

'That what we are confronting is truly alien. But I'm afraid you'll get over it, just the way I did.'

'I'll get over it when I feel like getting over it,' Celestine said, joining Forqueray under the dark ceiling.

She looked up and around, less in the manner of someone admiring a fresco than in the manner of a mouse cowering beneath a boot.

But I knew exactly what she was thinking.

In four centuries of deep space travel there had been no more than glimpses of alien sentience. We had long suspected they were out there somewhere. But that suspicion had grown less fervent as the years passed; world after world had revealed only faint, time-eroded traces of cultures that might once have been glorious but which were now utterly destroyed. The Pattern Jugglers were clearly the products of intelligence, but not necessarily intelligent themselves. And – though they had been spread from star to star in the distant past – they did not now depend on any form of technology that we recognised. The Shrouders were little better: secretive minds cocooned inside shells of restructured spacetime.

They had never been glimpsed, and their nature and intentions remained worryingly unclear.

Yet Blood Spire was different.

For all its strangeness; for all that it mocked our petty assumptions about the way matter and gravity should conduct themselves, it was recognisably a manufactured thing. And, I told myself, if it had managed to hang above Golgotha's surface until now, it was extremely unlikely to choose this moment to come crashing down.

I stepped across the threshold, followed by the others.

'Makes you wonder what kind of beings built it,' I said. 'Whether they had the same hopes and fears as us, or whether they were so far beyond us as to seem like Gods.'

'I don't give a shit who built it,' Hirz said. 'I just want to know how to get into the fucking thing. Any bright ideas, Childe?'

'There's a way,' he said.

We followed him until we stood in a small, nervous huddle under the centre of the ceiling. It had not been visible before, but directly above us was a circle of utter blackness against the mere gloom of the Spire's underside.

'That?' Hirz said.

'That's the only way in,' Childe said. 'And the only way you get out alive.'

I said, 'Roland – how exactly did Argyle and his team get inside?'

'They must have brought something to stand on. A ladder or something.'

I looked around. 'There's no sign of it now, is there?'

'No, and it doesn't matter. We don't need anything like that – not with these suits. Forqueray?'

The Ultra nodded and tossed the float-cam upwards.

It caught flight and vanished into the aperture. Nothing happened for several seconds, other than the occasional stutter of red light from the hole. Then the cam emerged, descending again into Forqueray's hand.

'There's a chamber up there,' Forqueray said. 'Flat-floored, surrounding the hole. It's twenty metres across, with a ceiling just high enough to let us stand upright. It's empty. There's what looks like a sealed door leading out of the chamber into the rest of the Spire.'

'Can we be sure there's nothing harmful in it?' I asked.

'No,' Childe said. 'But Argyle said the first room was safe. We'll just have to take his word on that one.'

'And there's room for all of us up there?'

Forqueray nodded. 'Easily.'

I suppose there should have been more ceremony to the act, but there was no sense of significance, or even foreboding, as we rose into the ceiling. It was like the first casual step onto the tame footslopes of a mountain, unweighted by any sense of the dangers that undoubtedly lay ahead.

Inside it was exactly as Forqueray had described.

The chamber was dark, but the float-cam provided some illumination and our suits' sensors were able to map out the chamber's shape and overlay this information on our visual fields.

The floor had a metalled quality to it, dented here and there, and the edge where it met the hole was rounded and worn.

I reached down to touch it, feeling a hard, dull alloy which nonetheless seemed as if it would yield given sufficient pressure. Data scrolled onto my visual readout, informing me that the floor had a temperature only one hundred and fifteen degrees above absolute zero. My palm chemosensor reported that the floor was mainly iron, laced with carbon woven into allotropic forms it could not match against any in its experience. There were microscopic traces of almost every other stable isotope in the periodic table, with the odd exception of silver. All of this was inferred, for when the chemosensor attempted to shave off a microscopic layer of the flooring for more detailed analysis, it gave a series of increasingly heated error messages before falling silent.

I tried the chemosensor against part of my own suit.

It had stopped working.

'Fix that,' I instructed my suit, authorising it to divert whatever resources it required to the task.

'Problem, Richard?' asked Childe.

'My suit's damaged. Minor, but annoying. I don't think the Spire was too thrilled about my taking a sample of it.'

'Shit. I probably should have warned you of that. Argyle's lot had the same problem. It doesn't like being cut into, either. I suspect you got off with a polite warning.'

'Generous of it,' I said.

'Be careful, all right?' Childe then told everyone else to disable their chemosensors until told otherwise. Hirz grumbled, but everyone else quietly accepted what had to be done.

In the meantime I continued my own survey of the room, counting myself lucky that my suit had not provoked a stronger reaction. The chamber's circular wall was fashioned from what looked like the same hard, dull alloy, devoid of detail except for the point where it framed what was obviously a door, raised a metre above the floor. Three blocky steps led up to it.

The door itself was one metre wide and perhaps twice that in height.

'Hey,' Hirz said. 'Feel this.'

She was kneeling down, pressing a palm against the floor.

'Careful,' I said. 'I just did that and—'

'I've turned off my chemo-whatsit, don't worry.'

'Then what are you—'

'Why don't you reach down and see for yourself?'

Slowly, we all knelt down and touched the floor. When I had felt it before it had been as cold and dead as the floor of a crypt, yet that was no longer the case. Now it was vibrating; as if somewhere not too far from here a mighty engine was shaking itself to pieces: a turbine on the point of breaking loose from its shackles. The vibration rose and fell in throbbing waves. Once every thirty seconds or so it reached a kind of crescendo, like a great slow inhalation.

'It's alive,' Hirz said.

'It wasn't like that just now.'

'I know.' Hirz turned and looked at me. 'The fucking thing just woke up, that's why. It knows we're here.'

three

I moved to the door and studied it properly for the first time.

Its proportions were reassuringly normal, requiring only that we stoop down slightly to step through. But for now the door was sealed by a smooth sheet of metal, which would presumably slide across once we had determined how to open it. The only guidance came from the door's thick metal frame, which was inscribed with faint geometric markings.

I had not noticed them before.

The markings were on either side of the door, on the uprights of the frame. Beginning from the bottom on the left-hand side, there was a dot – it was too neatly circular to be accidental – a flat-topped equilateral triangle, a pentagon and then a heptagonal figure. On the right-hand side there were three more figures with eleven, thirteen and twenty sides respectively.

'Well?' Hirz was looking over my shoulder. 'Any bright ideas?'

'Prime numbers,' I said. 'At least, that's the simplest explanation I can think of. The number of vertices of the shapes on the left-hand frame are the first four primes: one, three, five and seven.'

'And on the other frame?'

Childe answered for me. 'The eleven-sided figure is the next one in the sequence. Thirteen's one prime too high, and twenty isn't a prime at all.'

'So you're saying if we choose eleven, we win?' Hirz reached out her hand, ready to push her hand against the lowest figure on the right, which she could reach without ascending the three steps. 'I hope the rest of the tests are this simp—'

'Steady, old girl.' Childe had caught her wrist. 'Mustn't be too hasty. We shouldn't do anything until we've arrived at a consensus. Agreed?'

Hirz pulled back her hand. 'Agreed . . .'

It took only a few minutes for everyone to agree that the eleven-sided figure was the obvious choice. Celestine did not immediately accede; she looked long and hard at the right-hand frame before concurring with the original choice.

'I just want to be careful, that's all,' she said. 'We can't assume anything. They might think from right to left, so that the figures on the right form the sequence which those on the left are supposed to complete. Or they might think diagonally, or something even less obvious.'

Childe nodded. 'And the obvious choice might not always be the right one. There might be a deeper sequence – something more elegant – which we're just not seeing. That's why I wanted Celestine along. If anyone'll pick out those subtleties, it's her.'

She turned to him. 'Just don't put too much faith in whatever gifts the Jugglers might have given me, Childe.'

'I won't. Unless I have to.' Then he turned to the infiltration specialist, still standing by the frame. 'Hirz – you may go ahead.'

She reached out and touched the frame, covering the eleven-sided figure with her palm.

After a heart-stopping pause there was a clunk, and I felt the floor vibrate even more strongly than it had before. Ponderously, the door slid aside, revealing another dark chamber.

We all looked around, assessing each other.

Nothing had changed; none of us had suffered any sudden, violent injuries.

'Forqueray?' Childe said.

The Ultra knew what he meant. He tossed the float-cam through the open doorway and waited several seconds until it flew back into his grasp.

'Another metallic chamber, considerably smaller than this one. The floor is level with the door, so we'll have gained a metre or so in height. There's another raised door on the opposite side, again with markings. Other than that, I don't see anything except bare metal.'

'What about the other side of *this* door?' Childe said. 'Are there markings on it as well?'

'Nothing that the drone could make out.'

'Then let me be the guinea pig. I'll step through and we'll see what happens. I'm assuming that even if the door seals behind me, I'll still be able to open it. Argyle said the Spire didn't prevent anyone from leaving provided they hadn't attempted to access a new room.'

'Try it and see,' Hirz said. 'We'll wait on this side. If the door shuts on you, we'll give you a minute and then we'll open it ourselves.'

Childe walked up the three steps and across the threshold. He paused, looked around and then turned back to face us, looking down on us now.

Nothing had happened.

'Looks like the door stays open for now. Who wants to join me?'

'Wait,' I said. 'Before we all cross over, shouldn't we take a look at the problem? We don't want to be trapped in there if it's something we can't solve.'

Childe walked over to the far door. 'Good thinking. Forqueray, pipe my visual field through to the rest of the team, will you?'

'Done.'

We saw what Childe was seeing, his gaze tracking along the doorframe. The markings looked much like those we had just

43

solved, except that the symbols were different. Four unfamiliar shapes were inscribed on the left side of the door, spaced vertically. Each of the shapes was composed of four rectangular elements of differing sizes, butted together in varying configurations. Childe then looked at the other side of the door. There were four more shapes on the right, superficially similar to those we had already seen.

'Definitely not a geometric progression,' Childe said.

'No. Looks more like a test of conservation of symmetry through different translations,' Celestine said, her voice barely a murmur. 'The lowest three shapes on the left have just been rotated through an integer number of right angles, giving their corresponding forms on the right. But the top two shapes aren't rotationally symmetric. They're mirror images, plus a rotation.'

'So we press the top right shape, right?'

'Could be. But the left one's just as valid.'

Hirz said, 'Yeah. But only if we ignore what the last test taught us. Whoever the suckers were that made this thing, they think from left to right.'

Childe raised his hand above the right-side shape. 'I'm prepared to press it.'

'Wait.' I climbed the steps and walked over the threshold, joining Childe. 'I don't think you should be in here alone.'

He looked at me with something resembling gratitude. None of the others had stepped over yet, and I wondered if I would have done so had Childe and I not been old friends.

'Go ahead and press it,' I said. 'Even if we get it wrong, the punishment's not likely to be too severe at this stage.'

He nodded and palmed the right-side symbol.

Nothing happened.

'Maybe the left side . . . ?'

'Try it. It can't hurt. We've obviously done *something* wrong already.'

Childe moved over and palmed the other symbol on the top row.

Nothing.

I gritted my teeth. 'All right. Might as well try one of the ones we definitely know is wrong. Are you ready for that?'

He glanced at me and nodded. 'I didn't go to the hassle of bringing in Forqueray just for the free ride, you know. These suits are built to take a lot of crap.'

'Even alien crap?'

'About to find out, aren't we?'

He moved to palm one of the lower symmetry pairs.

I braced myself, unsure what to expect when we made a deliberate error, wondering if the Spire's punishment code would even apply in such a case. After all, what was clearly the correct choice had elicited no response, so what was the sense in being penalised for making the wrong one?

He palmed the shape; still nothing happened.

'Wait,' Celestine said, joining us. 'I've had an idea. Maybe it won't respond – positively or negatively – until we're all in the same room.'

'Only one way to find out,' Hirz said, joining her.

Forqueray and Trintignant followed.

When the last of them had crossed the threshold, the rear door – the one we had all come through – slid shut. There were no markings on it, but nothing that Forqueray did made it open again.

Which, I supposed, made a kind of sense. We had committed to accepting the next challenge now; the time for dignified retreats had passed. The thought was not a pleasant one. This room was smaller than the last one, and the environment was suddenly a lot more claustrophobic.

We were standing almost shoulder to shoulder.

'You know, I think the first chamber was just a warm-up,' Celestine said. 'This is where it starts getting more serious.'

'Just press the fucking thing,' Hirz said.

Childe did as he was told. As before, there was an uncomfortable pause which probably lasted only half a second, but which felt abyssally longer, as if our fates were being weighed by distant judicial machinery. Then thumps and vibrations signalled the opening of the door.

Simultaneously, the door behind us had opened again. The route out of the Spire was now clear again.

'Forqueray . . .' Childe said.

The Ultra tossed the float-cam into the darkness.

'Well?'

'This is getting a tiny bit monotonous. Another chamber, another door, another set of markings.'

'No booby-traps?'

'Nothing the drone can resolve, which I'm afraid isn't saying much.'

'I'll go in this time,' Celestine said. 'No one follow me until I've checked out the problem, understood?'

'Fine by me,' Hirz said, peering back at the escape route.

Celestine stepped into the darkness.

I decided that I was no longer enjoying the illusion of seeing everyone as if we were not wearing suits – we all looked far too vulnerable, suddenly – and ordered my own to stop editing my visual field to that extent. The transition was smooth; suits formed around us like thickening auras. Only the helmet parts remained semi-transparent, so that I could still identify who was who without cumbersome visual tags.

'It's another mathematical puzzle,' Celestine said. 'Still fairly simple. We're not really being stretched yet.'

'Yeah, well, I'll settle for not being really stretched,' Hirz said.

Childe looked unimpressed. 'Are you certain of the answer?'

'Trust me,' Celestine said. 'It's perfectly safe to enter.'

*

This time the markings looked more complicated, and at first I feared that Celestine had been over-confident.

On the left-hand side of the door – extending the height of the frame – was a vertical strip marked by many equally spaced horizontal grooves, in the manner of a ruler. But some of the cleanly cut grooves were deeper than the others. On the other side of the door was a similar ruler, but with a different arrangement of deeper grooves, not lining up with any of those on the right.

I stared at the frame for several seconds, thinking the solution would click into my mind; willing myself back into the problem-solving mode that had once seemed so natural. But the pattern of grooves refused to snap into any neat mathematical order.

I looked at Childe, seeing no greater comprehension in his face.

'Don't you see it?' Celestine said.

'Not quite,' I said.

'There are ninety-one grooves, Richard.' She spoke with the tone of a teacher who had begun to lose patience with a tardy pupil. 'Now counting from the bottom, the following grooves are deeper than the rest: the third, the sixth, the tenth, the fifteenth . . . shall I continue?'

'I think you'd better,' Childe said.

'There are seven other deep grooves, concluding with the ninety-first. You must see it now, surely. Think geometrically.'

'I am,' I said testily.

'Tell us, Celestine,' Childe said, between what was obviously gritted teeth.

She sighed. 'They're triangular numbers.'

'Fine,' Childe said. 'But I'm not sure I know what a triangular number is.'

Celestine glanced at the ceiling for a moment, as if seeking inspiration. 'Look. Think of a dot, will you?'

'I'm thinking,' Childe said.

'Now surround that dot by six neighbours, all the same distance from each other. Got that?'

'Yes.'

'Now keep on adding dots, extending out in all directions, as far as you can imagine – each dot having six neighbours.'

'With you so far.'

'You should have something resembling a Chinese chequer board. Now concentrate on a single dot again, near the middle. Draw a line from it to one of its six neighbours, and then another line to one of the two dots either side of the neighbour you just chose. Then join the two neighbouring dots. What have you a got?'

'An equilateral triangle.'

'Good. That's three taken care of. Now imagine that the triangle's sides are twice as long. How many dots are connected together now?'

Childe answered after only a slight hesitation, 'Six. I think.'

'Yes.' Celestine turned to me. 'Are you following, Richard?'

'More or less . . .' I said, trying to hold the shapes in my head.

'Then we'll continue. If we triple the size of the triangle, we link together nine dots along the sides, with an additional dot in the middle. That's ten. Continue – with a quadruple-sized triangle – and we hit fifteen.' She paused, giving us time to catch up. 'There are eight more; up to ninety-one, which has thirteen dots along each side.'

'The final groove,' I said, accepting for myself that whatever this problem was, Celestine had definitely understood it.

'But there are only seven deep grooves in that interval,' she continued. 'That means all we have to do is identify the groove on the right which corresponds to the missing triangular number.'

'All?' Hirz said.

'Look, it's simple. I *know* the answer, but you don't have to take my word for it. The triangles follow a simple sequence. If there are N dots in the lower row of the last triangle, the next one will have N plus one more. Add one to two and you've got three. Add one to two to three, and you've got six. One to two to three to four, and you've got ten. Then fifteen, then twenty-one . . .' Celestine paused. 'Look, it's senseless taking my word for it. Graph up a chequerboard display on your suits – Forqueray, can you oblige? – and start arranging dots in triangular patterns.'

We did. It took quarter of an hour, but after that time we had all – Hirz included – convinced ourselves by brute force that Celestine was right. The only missing pattern was for the fifty-five-dot case, which happened to coincide with one of the deep grooves on the right side of the door.

It was obvious, then. That *was* the one to press.

'I don't like it,' Hirz said. 'I see it now . . . but I didn't see it until it was pointed out to me. What if there's another pattern none of us are seeing?'

Celestine looked at her coldly. 'There isn't.'

'Look, there's no point arguing,' Childe said. 'Celestine saw it first, but we always knew she would. Don't feel bad about it, Hirz. You're not here for your mathematical prowess. Nor's Trintignant, nor's Forqueray.'

'Yeah, well remind me when I can do something useful,' Hirz said.

Then she pushed forward and pressed the groove on the right side of the door.

Progress was smooth and steady for the next five chambers. The problems to be solved grew harder, but after consultation the solution was never so esoteric that we could not all agree on it. As the complexity of the tasks increased, so did the area taken up by the frames, but other than that there was no change in the basic nature of the challenges. We were never forced to proceed more quickly than we chose, and the Spire always provided a clear route back to the exit every time a doorway had been traversed. The door immediately behind us would seal only once we had all entered the room where the current problem lay, which meant that we were able to assess any given problem before committing ourselves to its solution. To convince ourselves that we were indeed able to leave, we had Hirz go back the way we had come in. She was able to return to the first room unimpeded – the rear-facing doors opened and closed in sequence to allow her to pass – and then make her way back to the rest of us by using the entry codes we had already discovered.

But something she said upon her return disturbed us.

'I'm not sure if it's my imagination or not . . .'

'What?' Childe snapped.

'I think the doorways are getting narrower. And lower. There was definitely more headroom at the start than there is now. I guess we didn't notice when we took so long to move from room to room.'

'That doesn't make much sense,' Celestine said.

'As I said, maybe I imagined it.'

But we all knew she had done no such thing. The last two times I had stepped across a door's threshold my suit had bumped against the frame. I had thought nothing of it at the time – putting it down to carelessness – but that had evidently been wishful thinking.

'I wondered about the doors already,' I said. 'Doesn't it seem a little convenient that the first one we met was just the right size for us? It could have come from a human building.'

'Then why are they getting smaller?' Childe asked.

'I don't know. But I think Hirz is right. And it does worry me.'

'Me too. But it'll be a long time before it becomes a problem.' Childe turned to the Ultra. 'Forqueray – do the honours, will you?'

I turned and looked at the chamber ahead of us. The door was open now, but none of us had yet stepped across the threshold. As always, we waited for Forqueray to send his float-cam snooping ahead of us, establishing that the room contained no glaring pitfalls.

Forqueray tossed the float-cam though the open door.

We saw the usual red stutters as it swept the room in visible light. 'No surprises,' Forqueray said, in the usual slightly absent tone he adopted when reporting the cam's findings. 'Empty metallic chamber . . . only slightly smaller than the one we're standing in now. A door at the far end with a frame that extends half a metre out on either side. Complex inscriptions this time, Celestine.'

'I'll cope, don't you worry.'

Forqueray stepped a little closer to the door, one arm raised with his palm open. His expression remained calm as he waited for the drone to return to its master. We all watched, and then – as the moment elongated into seconds – began to suspect that something was wrong.

The room beyond was utterly dark; no stammering flashes now.

'The cam—' Forqueray said.

Childe's gaze snapped to the Ultra's face. 'Yes?'

'It isn't transmitting any more. I can't detect it.'

'That isn't possible.'

'I'm telling you.' The Ultra looked at us, his fear not well concealed. 'It's gone.'

Childe moved into the darkness, through the frame.

Just as I was admiring his bravery I felt the floor shudder. Out of the corner of my eye I saw a flicker of rapid motion, like an eyelid closing.

The rear door – the one that led out of the chamber in which we were standing – had just slammed shut.

Celestine fell forward. She had been standing in the gap.

'No . . .' she said, hitting the ground with a detectable thump.

'Childe!' I shouted, unnecessarily. 'Stay where you are – something just happened.'

'What?'

'The door behind us closed on Celestine. She's been injured . . .'

I was fearing the worst – that the door might have snipped off an arm or a leg as it closed – but it was, mercifully, not that serious. The door had damaged the thigh of her suit, grazing an inch of its armour away as it closed, but Celestine herself had not been injured. The damaged part was still airtight, and the suit's mobility and critical systems remained unimpaired.

Already, in fact, the self-healing mechanisms were coming into play, repairing the wound.

She sat up on the ground. 'I'm OK. The impact was hard, but I don't think I've done any permanent damage.'

'You sure?' I said, offering her a hand.

'Perfectly sure,' she said, standing up without my assistance.

'You were lucky,' Trintignant said. 'You were only partly blocking the door. Had that not been the case, I suspect your injuries would have been more interesting.'

'What happened?' Hirz asked.

'Childe must have triggered it,' Forqueray said. 'As soon as he stepped into the other room, it closed the rear door.' The Ultra stepped closer to the aperture. 'What happened to my float-cam, Childe?'

'I don't know. It just isn't here. There isn't even a trace of debris, and there's no sign of anything that could have destroyed it.'

The silence that followed was broken by Trintignant's piping tones. 'I believe this makes a queer kind of sense.'

'You do, do you?' I said.

'Yes, my dear fellow. It is my suspicion that the Spire has been tolerating the drone until now – lulling us, if you will, into a false sense of security. Yet now the Spire has decreed that we must discard that particular mental crutch. It will no longer permit us to gain any knowledge of the contents of a room until one of us steps into it. And at that moment it will prevent any of us *leaving* until we have solved that problem.'

'You mean it's changing the rules as it goes along?' Hirz asked.

The Doctor turned his exquisite silver mask towards her. 'Which rules did you have in mind, Hirz?'

'Don't fuck with me, Doc. You know what I mean.'

Trintignant touched a finger to the chin of his helmet. 'I confess I do not. Unless it is your contention that the Spire has at some point agreed to bind by a set of strictures, which I would ardently suggest is far from the case.'

'No,' I said. 'Hirz is right, in one way. There *have* been rules. It's clear that it won't tolerate us inflicting physical harm against it. And it won't allow us to enter a room until we've all stepped into the preceding one. I think those are pretty fundamental rules.'

'Then what about the drone, and the door?' asked Childe.

'It's like Trintignant said. It tolerated us playing outside the rules until now, but we shouldn't have assumed that was always going to be the case.'

Hirz nodded. 'Great. What else is it tolerating now?'

'I don't know.' I managed a thin smile. 'I suppose the only way to find out is to keep going.'

We passed through another eight rooms, taking between one and two hours to solve each.

There had been a couple of occasions when we had debated whether to continue, with Hirz usually the least keen of us, but so far the problems had not been insurmountably difficult. And we were making a kind of progress. Mostly the rooms were blank, but every now and then there was a narrow, trellised window, panelled in stained sheets of what was obviously a substance very much more resilient than glass or even diamond. Sometimes these windows opened only into gloomy interior spaces, but on one occasion we were able to look outside, able to sense some of the height we had attained. Forqueray, who had had been monitoring our journey with an inertial compass and gravitometer, confirmed that we had ascended at least fifteen vertical metres since the first chamber. That almost sounded impressive, until one considered the several hundred metres of Spire that undoubtedly lay above us. Another few hundred rooms, each posing a challenge more testing than the last?

And the doors were definitely getting smaller.

It was an effort to squeeze through now, and while the suits were able to reshape themselves to some extent, there was a limit to how compact they could become.

It had taken us sixteen hours to reach this point. At this rate it would take many days to get anywhere near the summit.

But none of us had imagined that this would be over quickly.

'Tricky,' Celestine said, after studying the latest puzzle for many minutes. 'I think I see what's going on here, but . . .'

Childe looked at her. 'You think, or you know?'

'I mean what I said. It's not easy, you know. Would you rather I let someone else take first crack at it?'

I put a hand on Celestine's arm and spoke to her privately. 'Easy. He's just anxious, that's all.'

She brushed my hand away. 'I didn't ask you to defend me, Richard.'

'I'm sorry. I didn't mean—'

'Never mind.' Celestine switched off private mode and addressed the group. 'I think these markings are shadows. Look.'

By now we had all become reasonably adept at drawing

figures using our suits' visualisation systems. These sketchy hallucinations could be painted on any surface, apparently visible to all.

Celestine, who was the best at this, drew a short red hyphen on the wall.

'See this? A one-dimensional line. Now watch.' She made the line become a square; splitting into two parallel lines joined at their ends. Then she made the square rotate until it was edge-on again, and all we could see was the line.

'We see it . . .' Childe said.

'You can think of a line as the one-dimensional shadow of a two-dimensional object, in this case a square. Understand?'

'I think we get the gist,' Trintigant said.

Celestine made the square freeze, and then slide diagonally, leaving a copy of itself to which it was joined at the corners. 'Now. We're looking at a two-dimensional figure this time; the shadow of a three-dimensional cube. See how it changes if I rotate the cube, how it elongates and contracts?'

'Yes. Got that,' Childe said, watching the two joined squares slide across each other with a hypnotically smooth motion, only one square visible as the imagined cube presented itself face-on to the wall.

'Well, I think these figures . . .' Celestine sketched a hand an inch over the intricate designs worked into the frame, 'I think what these figures represent are two-dimensional shadows of four-dimensional objects.'

'Fuck off,' Hirz said.

'Look, just concentrate, will you? This one's easy. It's a hypercube. That's the four-dimensional analogue of a cube. You just take a cube and extend it *outwards*; just the same way that you make a cube from a square.' Celestine paused, and for a moment I thought she was going to throw up her hands in despair. 'Look. Look at this.' And then she sketched something on the wall: a cube set inside a slightly larger one, to which it was joined by diagonal lines. 'That's what the three-dimensional shadow of a hypercube would look like. Now all you have to do is collapse that shadow by one more dimension, down to two, to get *this*—' and she jabbed at the beguiling design marked on the door.

'I think I see it,' Childe said, without anything resembling confidence.

Maybe I did, too – though I felt the same lack of certainty. Childe and I had certainly taunted each other with higher-dimensional puzzles in our youth, but never had so much depended on an intuitive grasp of those mind-shattering mathematical realms. 'All right,' I said. 'Supposing that *is* the shadow of a tesseract . . . what's the puzzle?'

'This,' Celestine said, pointing to the other side of the door, to what seemed like an utterly different – though no less complex – design. 'It's the same object, after a rotation.'

'The shadow changes that drastically?'

'Start getting used to it, Richard.'

'All right.' I realised she was still annoyed with me for touching her. 'What about the others?'

'They're all four-dimensional objects; relatively simple geometric forms. This one's a 4-simplex; a hypertetrahedon. It's a hyper-pyramid with five tetrahedral faces . . .' Celestine trailed off, looking at us with an odd expression on her face. 'Never mind. The point is, all the corresponding forms on the right should be the shadows of the same polytopes after a simple rotation through higher-dimensional space. But one isn't.'

'Which is?'

She pointed to one of the forms. 'This one.'

'And you're certain of that?' Hirz said. 'Because I'm sure as fuck not.'

Celestine nodded. 'Yes. I'm completely sure of it now.'

'But you can't make any of us see that this is the case?'

She shrugged. 'I guess you either see it or you don't.'

'Yeah? Well maybe we should have all taken a trip to the Pattern Jugglers. Then maybe I wouldn't be about to shit myself.'

Celestine said nothing, but merely reached out and touched the errant figure.

'There's good news and there's bad news,' Forqueray said after we had traversed another dozen or so rooms without injury.

'Give us the bad news first,' Celestine said.

Forqueray obliged, with what sounded like the tiniest degree of pleasure. 'We won't be able to get through more than two or three more doors. Not with these suits on.'

There had been no real need to tell us that. It had become crushingly obvious during the last three or four rooms that we were near the limit; that the Spire's subtly shifting internal architecture would not permit further movement within the bulky suits. It had been an effort to squeeze through the last door; only Hirz was oblivious to these difficulties.

'Then we might as well give up,' I said.

'Not exactly.' Forqueray smiled his vampiric smile. 'I said there was good news as well, didn't I?'

'Which is?' Childe said.

'You remember when we sent Hirz back to the beginning, to see if the Spire was going to allow us to leave at any point?'

'Yes,' Childe said. Hirz had not repeated the complete exercise since, but she had gone back a dozen rooms, and found that the Spire was just as co-operative as it had been before. There was no reason to think she would not have been able to make her way to the exit, had she wished.

'Something bothered me,' Forqueray said. 'When she went back, the Spire opened and closed doors in sequence to allow her to pass. I couldn't see the sense in that. Why not just open all the doors along her route?'

'I confess it troubled me as well,' Trintignant said.

'So I thought about it, and decided there must be a reason not to have all the doors open at once.'

Childe sighed. 'Which was?'

'Air,' Forqueray said.

'You're kidding, aren't you?'

The Ultra shook his head. 'When we began, we were moving in vacuum – or at least through air that was as thin as that on Golgotha's surface. That continued to be the case for the next few rooms. Then it began to change. Very slowly, I'll grant you – but my suit sensors picked up on it immediately.'

Childe pulled a face. 'And it didn't cross your mind to tell any of us about this?'

'I thought it best to wait until a pattern became apparent.' Forqueray glanced at Celestine, whose face was impassive.

'He's right,' Trintignant said. 'I too have become aware of the changing atmospheric conditions. Forqueray has also doubtless noticed that the temperature in each room has been a little warmer than the last. I have extrapolated these trends and arrived at a tentative conclusion. Within two – possibly three – rooms, we will be able to discard our suits and breathe normally.'

'Discard our suits?' Hirz looked at him as if he were insane. 'You have got to be fucking kidding.'

Childe raised a hand. 'Wait a minute. When you said air, Doctor Trintignant, you didn't say it was anything we'd be able to breathe.'

The Doctor's answer was a melodious piped refrain. 'Except it is. The ratios of the various gases are remarkably close to those we employ in our suits.'

'Which isn't possible. I don't remember providing a sample.'

Trintignant dipped his head in a nod. 'Nonetheless, it appears that one has been taken. The mix, incidentally, corresponds to precisely the atmospheric preferences of Ultras. Argyle's expedition would surely have employed a slightly different mix, so it is not simply the case that the Spire has a long memory.'

I shivered.

The thought that the Spire – this vast breathing thing through which we were scurrying like rats – had somehow reached inside the hard armour of our suits to snatch a sample of air, without our knowing, made my guts turn cold. It not only knew of our presence, but it knew – intimately – what we were.

It understood our fragility.

As if wishing to reward Forqueray for his observation, the next room contained a substantially thicker atmosphere than any of its predecessors, and was also much warmer. It was not yet capable of supporting life, but one would not have died instantly without the protection of a suit.

The challenge that the room held was by far the hardest, even by Celestine's reckoning. Once again the essence of the task lay in the figures marked on either side of the door, but now these figures were linked by various symbols and connecting loops, like the subway map of a foreign city. We had encountered some of these hieroglyphics before – they were akin to mathematical operators, like the addition and subtraction symbol – but we had never seen so many. And the problem itself was not simply a numerical exercise, but – as far as Celestine could say with any certainty – a problem about topological transformations in four dimensions.

'Please tell me you see the answer immediately,' Childe said.

'I . . .' Celestine trailed off. 'I think I do. I'm just not absolutely certain. I need to think about this for a minute.'

'Fine. Take all the time you want.'

Celestine fell into a reverie which lasted minutes, and then tens of minutes. Once or twice she would open her mouth and take a breath of air as if in readiness to speak, and on one or two other occasions she took a promising step closer to the door, but none of these things heralded the sudden, intuitive breakthrough we were all hoping for. She always returned to the same silent, standing posture. The time dragged on; first an hour and then the better part of two hours.

All this, I thought, before even Celestine had seen the answer.

It might take days if we were all expected to follow her reasoning.

Finally, however, she spoke. 'Yes. I see it.'

Childe was the first to answer. 'Is it the one you thought it was originally?'

'No.'

'Great,' Hirz said.

'Celestine . . .' I said, trying to defuse the situation. 'Do you understand why you made the wrong choice originally?'

'Yes. I think so. It was a trick answer; an apparently correct solution which contained a subtle flaw. And what looked like the clearly wrong answer turned out to be the right one.'

'Right. And you're certain of that?'

'I'm not certain of anything, Richard. I'm just saying this is what I believe the answer to be.'

I nodded. 'I think that's all any of us can honestly expect. Do you think there's any chance of the rest of us following your line of argument?'

'I don't know. How much do you understand about Kaluza-Klein spaces?'

'Not a vast amount, I have to admit.'

'That's what I feared. I could probably explain my reasoning to some of you, but there'd always be someone who didn't get it—' Celestine looked pointedly at Hirz. 'We could be in this bloody room for weeks before any of us grasp the solution. And the Spire may not tolerate that kind of delay.'

'We don't know that,' I cautioned.

'No,' Childe said. 'On the other hand, we can't afford to spend weeks solving every room. There's going to have to come a point where we put our faith in Celestine's judgement. I think that time may have come.'

60

I looked at him, remembering that his mathematical fluency had always been superior to mine. The puzzles I had set him had seldom defeated him, even if it had taken weeks for his intensely methodical mind to arrive at the solution. Conversely, he had often managed to beat me by setting a mathematical challenge of similar intricacy to the one now facing Celestine. They were not quite equals, I knew, but neither were their abilities radically different. It was just that, thanks to her experiences with the Pattern Jugglers, Celestine would always arrive at the answer with the superhuman speed of a savant.

'Are you saying I should just press it, with no consultation?' Celestine said.

Childe nodded. 'Provided everyone else agrees with me . . .'

It was not an easy decision to make, especially after having navigated so many rooms via such a ruthlessly democratic process. But we all saw the sense, even Hirz coming around to our line of thinking in the end.

'I'm telling you,' she said. 'We get through this door, I'm out of here, money or not.'

'You're giving up?' Childe asked.

'You saw what happened to those poor bastards outside. They must have thought they could keep on solving the next test.'

Childe looked sad, but said, 'I understand perfectly. But I trust you'll reassess your decision as soon as we're through?'

'Sorry, but my mind's made up. I've had enough of this shit.' Hirz turned to Celestine. 'Put us all out of our misery, will you? Make the choice.'

Celestine looked at each of us in turn. 'Are you ready for this?'

'We are,' Childe said, answering for the group. 'Go ahead.'

Celestine pressed the symbol. There was the usual yawning moment of expectation; a moment that stretched agonisingly. We all stared at the door, willing it to begin sliding open.

This time nothing happened.

'Oh God . . .' Hirz began.

Something happened then, almost before she had finished speaking, but it was over almost before we had sensed any change in the room. It was only afterwards – playing back the visual record captured by our suits – that we were able to make any sense of events.

The walls of the chamber – like every room we had passed through, in fact – had looked totally seamless. But in a flash something emerged from the wall: a rigid, sharp-ended metal rod spearing out at waist-height. It flashed through the air from wall to wall, vanishing like a javelin thrown into water. None of us had time to notice it, let alone react bodily. Even the suits – programmed to move out of the way of obvious moving hazards – were too slow. By the time they began moving, the javelin had been and gone. And if there had been only that one javelin, we might almost have missed it happening at all.

But a second emerged, a fraction of a second after the first, spearing across the room at a slightly different angle.

Forqueray happened to be standing in the way.

The javelin passed through him as if he were made of smoke; its progress was unimpeded by his presence. But it dragged behind it a comet-tail of gore, exploding out of his suit where he had been speared, just below the elbow. The pressure in the room was still considerably less than atmospheric.

Forqueray's suit reacted with impressive speed, but it was still sluggish compared to the javelin.

It assessed the damage that had been inflicted on the arm, aware of how quickly its self-repair systems could work to seal that inch-wide hole, and came to a rapid conclusion. The integrity could be restored, but not before unacceptable blood and pressure loss. Since its duty was always to keep its wearer alive, no matter what the costs, it opted to sever the arm above the wound; hyper-sharp irised blades snicked through flesh and bone in an instant.

All that took place long before any pain signals had a chance to reach his brain. The first thing Forqueray knew of his misfortune was when his arm clanged to his feet.

'I think—' he started saying. Hirz dashed over to the Ultra and did her best to support him.

Forqueray's truncated arm ended in a smooth silver iris.

'Don't talk,' Childe said.

Forqueray, who was still standing, looked at his injury with something close to fascination. 'I—'

'I said don't talk.' Childe knelt down and picked up the amputated arm, showing the evidence to Forqueray. The hole went right through it, as cleanly bored as a rifle barrel.

'I'll live,' Forqueray managed.

'Yes, you will,' Trintignant said. 'And you may also count yourself fortunate. Had the projectile pierced your body, rather than one of its extremities, I do not believe we would be having this conversation.'

'You call this fortunate?'

'A wound such as yours can be made good with only trivial intervention. We have all the equipment we need aboard the shuttle.'

Hirz looked around uneasily. 'You think the punishment's over?'

'I think we'd know if it wasn't,' I said. 'That was our first mistake, after all. We can expect things to be a little worse in future, of course.'

'Then we'd better not make any more screw-ups, had we?' Hirz was directing her words at Celestine.

I had expected an angry rebuttal. Celestine would have been perfectly correct to remind Hirz that – had the rest of us been forced to make that choice – our chances of hitting the correct answer would have been a miserable one in six.

But instead Celestine just spoke with the flat, soporific tones of one who could not quite believe she had made such an error.

'I'm sorry . . . I must have . . .'

'Made the wrong decision. Yes.' I nodded. 'And there'll undoubtedly be others. You did your best, Celestine – better than any of us could have managed.'

'It wasn't good enough.'

'No, but you narrowed the field down to two possibilities. That's a lot better than six.'

'He's right,' Childe said. 'Celestine, don't cut yourself up about this. Without you we wouldn't have got as far as we did. Now go ahead and press the other answer – the one you settled on originally – and we'll get Forqueray back to base camp.'

The Ultra glared at him. 'I'm fine, Childe. I can continue.'

'Maybe you can, but it's still time for a temporary retreat. We'll get that arm looked at properly, and then we'll come back with lightweight suits. We can't carry on much further with these, anyway – and I don't particularly fancy continuing with no armour at all.'

Celestine turned back to the frame. 'I can't promise that this is the right one, either.'

'We'll take that chance. Just hit them in sequence – best choice first – until the Spire opens a route back to the start.'

She pressed the symbol that had been her first choice, before she had analysed the problem more deeply and seen a phantom trap.

As always, Blood Spire did not oblige us with an instant judgement on the choice we had made. There was a moment when all of us tensed, expecting the javelins to come again . . . but this time we were spared further punishment.

The door opened, exposing the next chamber.

We did not step through, of course. Instead, we turned around and made our way back through the succession of rooms we had already traversed, descending all the while, almost laughing at the childish simplicity of the very earliest puzzles compared to those we had faced before the attack.

As the doors opened and closed in sequence, the air thinned out and the skin of Blood Spire became colder; less like a living thing, more like an ancient, brooding machine. But still that distant, throbbing respiratory vibration rattled the floors, lower now, and slower: the Spire letting us know it was aware of our presence and, perhaps, the tiniest bit disappointed at this turning back.

'All right, you bastard,' Childe said. 'We're retreating, but only for now. We're coming back, understand?'

'You don't have to take it personally,' I said.

'Oh, but I do,' Childe said. 'I take it very personally indeed.'

We reached the first chamber, and then dropped down through what had been the entrance hole. After that, it was just a short flight back to the waiting shuttle.

It was dark outside.

We had been in the Spire for more than nineteen hours.

four

'It'll do,' Forqueray said, tilting his new arm this way and that.

'Do?' Trintignant sounded mortally wounded. 'My dear fellow, it is a work of exquisite craftsmanship; a thing of beauty. It is unlikely that you will see its like again, unless of course I am called upon to perform a similar procedure.'

We were sitting inside the shuttle, still parked on Golgotha's surface. The ship was a squat, aerodynamically blunt cylinder which had landed tail-down and then expanded a cluster of eight bubbletents around itself: six for our personal quarters during the expedition, one commons area, and a general medical bay equipped with all the equipment Trintignant needed to do his work. Surprisingly – to me, at least, who admitted to some unfamiliarity with these things – the shuttle's fabricators had been more than able to come up with the various cybernetic components that the Doctor required, and the surgical tools at his disposal – glistening, semi-sentient things which moved to his will almost before they were summoned – were clearly state of the art by any reasonable measure.

'Yes, well, I'd have rather you'd reattached my old arm,' Forqueray said, opening and closing the sleek metal gauntlet of his replacement.

'It would have been almost insultingly trivial to do that,' Trintignant said. 'A new hand could have been cultured and regrafted in a few hours. If that did not appeal to you, I could have programmed your stump to regenerate a hand of its own accord; a perfectly simple matter of stem-cell manipulation. But what would have been the point? You would be very likely to lose it as soon as we suffer our next punishment. Now you will only be losing machinery – a far less traumatic prospect.'

'You're enjoying this,' Hirz said, 'aren't you?'

'It would be churlish to deny it,' Trintignant said. 'When you have been deprived of willing subjects as long as I have, it's only natural to take pleasure in those little opportunities for practice that fate sees fit to present.'

Hirz nodded knowingly. She had not heard of Trintignant upon our first meeting, I recalled, but she had lost no time in forming her subsequent opinion of the man. 'Except you won't just stop with a hand, will you? I checked up on you, Doc – after that meeting in Childe's house. I hacked into some of the medical records that the Stoner authorities still haven't declassified, because they're just too damned disturbing. You really went the whole hog, didn't you? Some of the things I saw in those files – your victims – they stopped me from sleeping.'

And yet still she had chosen to come with us, I thought. Evidently the allure of Childe's promised reward outweighed any reservations she might have had about sharing a room with Trintignant. But I wondered about those medical records. Certainly, the publicly released data had contained more than enough atrocities for the average nightmare. It chilled the blood to think that Trintignant's most heinous crimes had never been fully revealed.

'Is it true?' I said. 'Were there really worse things?'

'That depends,' Trintignant said. 'There were subjects upon whom I pushed my experimental techniques further than is generally realised, if that is what you mean. But did I ever approach what I considered were the true limits? No. I was always hindered.'

'Until, perhaps, now,' I said.

The rigid silver mask swivelled to face us all in turn. 'That is as maybe. But please give the following matter some consideration. I can surgically remove all your limbs now, cleanly, with the minimum of complications. The detached members could be put into cryogenic storage, replaced by prosthetic systems until we have completed the task that lies ahead of us.'

'Thanks . . .' I said, looking around at the others. 'But I think we'll pass on that one, Doctor.'

Trintigant offered his palms magnanimously. 'I am at your disposal, should you wish to reconsider.'

We spent a full day in the shuttle before returning to the Spire. I had been mortally tired, but when I finally slept, it was only to submerge myself in yet more labyrinthine dreams, much like those Childe had pumped into our heads during the reefersleep transition. I woke feeling angry and cheated, and resolved to confront him about it.

But something else snagged my attention.

There was something wrong with my wrist. Buried just beneath the skin was a hard rectangle, showing darkly through my flesh. Turning my wrist this way and that, I admired the object, acutely – and strangely – conscious of its rectilinearity. I looked around me, and felt the same visceral awareness of the other shapes which formed my surroundings. I did not know whether I was more disturbed at the presence of the alien object under my flesh, or my unnatural reaction to it.

I stumbled groggily into the common quarters of the shuttle, presenting my wrist to Childe, who was sitting there with Celestine.

She looked at me before Childe had a chance to answer. 'So you've got one too,' she said, showing me the similar shape lurking just below her own skin. The shape rhymed – there was no other word for it – with the surrounding panels and extrusions of the commons. 'Um, Richard?' she added.

'I'm feeling a little strange.'

'Blame Childe. He put them there. Didn't you, you lying rat?'

'It's easily removed,' he said, all innocence. 'It just seemed more prudent to implant the devices while you were all asleep anyway, so as not to waste any more time than necessary.'

'It's not just the thing in my wrist,' I said, 'whatever it is.'

'It's something to keep us awake,' Celestine said, her anger just barely under control. Feeling less myself than ever, I watched the way her face changed shape as she spoke, conscious of the armature of muscle and bone lying just beneath the skin.

'Awake?' I managed.

'A . . . shunt, of some kind,' she said. 'Ultras use them, I gather. It sucks fatigue poisons out of the blood, and puts other chemicals back into the blood to upset the brain's normal sleeping cycle. With one of these you can stay conscious for weeks, with almost no psychological problems.'

I forced a smile, ignoring the sense of wrongness I felt. 'It's the almost part that worries me.'

'Me too.' She glared at Childe. 'But much as I hate the little rat for doing this without my permission, I admit to seeing the sense in it.'

I felt the bump in my wrist again. 'Trintignant's work, I presume?'

'Count yourself lucky he didn't hack your arms and legs off while he was at it.'

Childe interrupted her. 'I told him to install the shunts. We can still catnap, if we have the chance. But these devices will let us stay alert when we need alertness. They're really no more sinister than that.'

'There's something else . . .' I said tentatively. I glanced at Celestine, trying to judge if she felt as oddly as I did. 'Since I've

70

been awake, I've . . . experienced things differently. I keep seeing shapes in a new light. What exactly have you done to me, Childe?'

'Again, nothing irreversible. Just a small medichine infusion—'

I tried to keep my temper. 'What sort of medichines?'

'Neural modifiers.' He raised a hand defensively, and I saw the same rectangular bulge under his skin. 'Your brain is already swarming with Demarchist implants and cellular machines, Richard, so why pretend that what I've done is anything more than a continuation of what was already there?'

'What the fuck is he talking about?' said Hirz, who had been standing at the door to the commons for the last few seconds. 'Is it to do with the weird shit I've been dealing with since waking up?'

'Very probably,' I said, relieved that at least I was not going insane. 'Let me guess – heightened mathematical and spatial awareness?'

'If that's what you call it, yeah. Seeing shapes everywhere, and thinking of them fitting together . . .'

Hirz turned to look at Childe. Small as she was, she looked easily capable of inflicting injury. 'Start talking, dickhead.'

Childe spoke with quiet calm. 'I put modifiers in your brain, via the wrist shunt. The modifiers haven't performed any radical neural restructuring, but they are suppressing and enhancing certain regions of brain function. The effect – crudely speaking – is to enhance your spatial abilities, at the expense of some less essential functions. What you are getting is a glimpse into the cognitive realms that Celestine inhabits as a matter of routine.' Celestine opened her mouth to speak, but he cut her off with a raised palm. 'No more than a glimpse, no, but I think you'll agree that – given the kinds of challenges the Spire likes to throw at us – the modifiers will give us an edge that we lacked previously.'

'You mean you've turned us all into maths geniuses, over-night?'

'Broadly speaking, yes.'

'Well, that'll come in handy,' Hirz said.

'It will?'

'Yeah. When you try and fit the pieces of your dick back together.'

She lunged for him.

'Hirz, I . . .'

'Stop,' I said, interceding. 'Childe was wrong to do this without our consent, but – given the situation we find ourselves in – the idea makes sense.'

'Whose side are you on?' Hirz said, backing away with a look of righteous fury in her eyes.

'Nobody's,' I said. 'I just want to do whatever it takes to beat the Spire.'

Hirz glared at Childe. 'All right. This time. But you try another stunt like that, and . . .'

But even then it was obvious that Hirz had come to the conclusion that I had already arrived at myself: that, given what the Spire was likely to test us with, it was better to accept these machines than ask for them to be flushed out of our systems.

There was just one troubling thought which I could not quite dismiss.

Would I have welcomed the machines so willingly before they had invaded my head, or were they partly influencing my decision?

I had no idea.

But I decided to worry about that later.

five

'Three hours,' Childe said triumphantly. 'Took us nineteen to reach this point on our last trip through. That has to mean something, doesn't it?'

'Yeah,' Hirz said snidely. 'It means it's a piece of piss when you know the answers.'

We were standing by the door where Celestine had made her mistake the last time. She had just pressed the correct topological symbol and the door had opened to admit us to the chamber beyond, one we had not so far stepped into. From now on we would be facing fresh challenges again, rather than passing through those we had already faced. The Spire, it appeared, was more interested in probing the limits of our understanding than getting us simply to solve permutations of the same basic challenge.

It wanted to break us, not stress us.

More and more I was thinking of it as a sentient thing: inquisitive and patient and – when the mood took it – immensely capable of cruelty.

'What's in there?' Forqueray said.

Hirz had gone ahead into the unexplored room.

'Well, fuck me if it isn't another puzzle.'

'Describe it, would you?'

'Weird shape shit, I think.' She was quiet for a few seconds.

'Yeah. Shapes in four dimensions again. Celestine – you wanna take a look at this? I think it's right up your street.'

'Any idea what the nature of the task is?' Celestine asked.

'Fuck, I don't know. Something to do with stretching, I think . . .'

'Topological deformations,' Celestine murmured before joining Hirz in the chamber.

For a minute or so the two of them conferred, studying the marked doorframe like a pair of discerning art critics.

On the last run through, Hirz and Celestine had shared almost no common ground: it was unnerving to see how much Hirz now grasped. The machines Childe had pumped into our skulls had improved the mathematical skills of all of us – with the possible exception of Trintignant, who I suspected had not received the therapy – but the effects had differed in nuance, degree and stability. My mathematical brilliance came in feverish, unpredictable waves, like inspiration to a laudanum-addicted poet. Forqueray had gained an astonishing fluency in arithmetic, able to count huge numbers of things simply by looking at them for a moment.

But Hirz's change had been the most dramatic of all, something even Childe was taken aback by. On the second pass through the Spire she had been intuiting the answers to many of the problems at a glance, and I was certain that she was not always remembering what the correct answer had been. Now, as we encountered the tasks that had challenged even Celestine, Hirz was still able to perceive the essence of a problem, even if it was beyond her to articulate the details in the formal language of mathematics.

And if she could not yet see her way to selecting the correct answer, she could at least see the one or two answers that were clearly wrong.

'Hirz is right,' Celestine said eventually. 'It's about topological deformations, stretching operations on solid shapes.'

74

Once again we were seeing the projected shadows of four-dimensional lattices. On the right side of the door, however, the shadows were of the same objects after they had been stretched and squeezed and generally distorted. The problem was to identify the shadow that could only be formed with a shearing, in addition to the other operations.

It took an hour, but eventually Celestine felt certain that she had selected the right answer. Hirz and I attempted to follow her arguments, but the best we could do was agree that two of the other answers would have been wrong. That, at least, was an improvement on anything we would have been capable of before the medichine infusions, but it was only moderately comforting.

Nonetheless, Celestine had selected the right answer. We moved into the next chamber.

'This is as far as we can go with these suits,' Childe said, indicating the door that lay ahead of us. 'It'll be a squeeze, even with the lighter suits – except for Hirz, of course.'

'What's the air like in here?' I asked.

'We could breathe it,' Forqueray said. 'And we'll have to, briefly. But I don't recommend that we do that for any length of time – at least not until we're forced into it.'

'Forced?' Celestine said. 'You think the doors are going to keep getting smaller?'

'I don't know. But doesn't it feel as if this place *is* forcing us to expose ourselves to it, to make ourselves maximally vulnerable? I don't think it's done with us just yet.' He paused, his suit beginning to remove itself. 'But that doesn't mean we have to humour it.'

I understood his reluctance. The Spire had hurt him, not us.

Beneath the Ultra suits which had brought us this far we had donned as much of the lightweight versions as was possible. They were skintight suits of reasonably modern design, but they were museum pieces compared to the Ultra equipment. The helmets and much of the breathing gear had been impossible to put on, so we had carried the extra parts strapped to our backs. Despite my fears, the Spire had not objected to this, but I remained acutely aware that we did not yet know all the rules under which we played.

It only took three or four minutes to get out of the bulky suits and into the new ones; most of this time was taken up running status checks. For a minute or so, with the exception of Hirz, we had all breathed Spire air.

It was astringent, blood-hot, humid, and smelt faintly of machine oil.

It was a relief when the helmets flooded with the cold, tasteless air of the suits' backpack recyclers.

'Hey.' Hirz, the only one still wearing her original suit, knelt down and touched the floor. 'Check this out.'

I followed her, pressing the flimsy fabric of my glove against the surface.

The structure's vibrations rose and fell with increased strength, as if we had excited it by removing our hard protective shells.

'It's like the fucking thing's getting a hard-on,' Hirz said.

'Let's push on,' Childe said. 'We're still armoured – just not as effectively as before – but if we keep being smart, it won't matter.'

'Yeah. But it's the being smart part that worries me. No one smart would come within pissing distance of this fucking place.'

'What does that make you, Hirz?' Celestine asked.

'Greedier than you'll ever know,' she said.

Nonetheless we made good progress for another eleven rooms. Now and then a stained-glass window allowed a view out of Golgotha's surface, which looked very far below us. By Forqueray's estimate we had gained forty-five vertical metres since entering the Spire. Although two hundred further metres lay ahead – the bulk of the climb, in fact – for the first time it began to appear possible that we might succeed. That, of course, was contingent on several assumptions. One was that the problems, while growing steadily more difficult, would not become insoluble. The other was that the doorways would not continue to narrow now that we had discarded the bulky suits.

But they did.

As always, the narrowing was imperceptible from room to room, but after five or six it could not be ignored. After ten or fifteen more rooms we would again have to scrape our way between them.

And what if the narrowing continued beyond that point?

'We won't be able to go on,' I said. 'We won't fit – even if we're naked.'

'You are entirely too defeatist,' Trintignant said.

Childe sounded reasonable. 'What would you propose, Doctor?'

'Nothing more than a few minor readjustments of the basic human body-plan. Just enough to enable us to squeeze through apertures which would be impassable with our current . . . encumbrances.'

Trintignant looked avariciously at my arms and legs.

'It wouldn't be worth it,' I said. 'I'll accept your help after I've been injured, but if you're thinking that I'd submit to anything more drastic . . . well, I'm afraid you're severely mistaken, Doctor.'

'Amen to that,' Hirz said. 'For a while back there, Swift, I really thought this place was getting to you.'

'It isn't,' I said. 'Not remotely. And in any case, we're thinking many rooms ahead here, when we might not even be able to get through the next.'

'I agree,' Childe said. 'We'll take it one at a time. Doctor Trintignant, put your wilder fantasies aside, at least for now.'

'Consider them relegated to mere daydreams,' Trintignant said.

So we pushed on.

Now that we had passed through so many doors, it was possible to see that the Spire's tasks came in waves; that there might, for instance, be a series of problems which depended on prime number theory, followed by another series which hinged on the properties of higher-dimensional solids. For several rooms in sequence we were confronted by questions related to tiling patterns – tessellations – while another sequence tested our understanding of cellular automata: odd chequerboard armies of shapes which obeyed simple rules and yet interacted in stunningly complex ways. The final challenge in each set would always be the hardest; the one where we were most likely to make a mistake. We were quite prepared to take three or four hours to pass each door, if that was the time it took to be certain – in Celestine's mind at least – that the answer was clear.

And though the shunts were leaching fatigue poisons from our blood, and though the modifiers were enabling us to think with a clarity we had never known before, a kind of exhaustion always crept over us after solving one of the harder challenges. It normally passed in a few tens of minutes, but until then we generally waited before venturing through the now open door, gathering our strength again.

In those quiet minutes we spoke amongst ourselves, discussing what had happened and what we could expect.

'It's happened again,' I said, addressing Celestine on the private channel.

Her answer came back, no more terse than I had expected. 'What?'

'For a while the rest of us could keep up with you. Even Hirz. Or, if not keep up, then at least not lose sight of you completely. But you're pulling ahead again, aren't you? Those Juggler routines are kicking in again.'

She took her time replying. 'You have Childe's medichines.'

'Yes. But all they can do is work with the basic neural

topology, suppressing and enhancing activity without altering the layout of the connections in any significant way. And the 'chines are broad-spectrum; not tuned specifically to any one of us.'

Celestine looked at the only one of us still wearing one of the original suits. 'They worked on Hirz.'

'Must have been luck. But yes, you're right. She couldn't see as far as you, though, even with the modifiers.'

Celestine tapped the shunt in her wrist, still faintly visible beneath the tight-fitting fabric of her suit. 'I took a spike of the modifiers as well.'

'I doubt that it gave you much of an edge over what you already had.'

'Maybe not.' She paused. 'Is there a point to this conversation, Richard?'

'Not really,' I said, stung by her response. 'I just . . .'

'Wanted to talk, yes.'

'And you don't?'

'You can hardly blame me if I don't, can you? This isn't exactly the place for small talk, let alone with someone who chose to have me erased from his memory.'

'Would it make any difference if I said I was sorry about that?'

I could tell from the tone of her response that my answer had not been quite the one she was expecting. 'It's easy to say you're sorry, now . . . now that it suits you to say as much. That's not how you felt at the time, is it?'

I fumbled for an answer which was not too distant from the truth. 'Would you believe me if I said I'd had you suppressed because I still loved you, and not for any other reason?'

'That's just a little too convenient, isn't it?'

'But not necessarily a lie. And can you blame me for it? We were in love, Celestine. You can't deny that. Just because things happened between us . . .' A question I had been meaning to ask her forced itself to the front of my mind. 'Why didn't you contact me again, after you were told you couldn't go to Resurgam?'

'Our relationship was over, Richard.'

'But we'd parted on reasonably amicable terms. If the Resurgam expedition hadn't come up, we might not have parted at all.'

Celestine sighed; one of exasperation. 'Well, since you asked, I *did* try and contact you.'

'You did?'

'But by the time I'd made my mind up, I learned about the way you'd had me suppressed. How do you imagine that made me feel, Richard? Like a small, disposable part of your past – something to be wadded up and flicked away when it offended you?'

'It wasn't like that at all. I never thought I'd see you again.'

She snorted. 'And maybe you wouldn't have, if it wasn't for dear old Roland Childe.'

I kept my voice level. 'He asked me along because we both used to test each other with challenges like this. I presume he needed someone with your kind of Juggler transform. Childe wouldn't have cared about our past.'

Her eyes flashed behind the visor of her helmet. 'And you don't care either, do you?'

'About Childe's motives? No. They're neither my concern nor my interest. All that bothers me now is this.'

I patted the Spire's thrumming floor.

'There's more here than meets the eye, Richard.'

'What do you mean by that?'

'Haven't you noticed how—' She looked at me for several seconds, as if on the verge of revealing something, then shook her head. 'Never mind.'

'What, for pity's sake?'

'Doesn't it strike you that Childe has been just a little too well prepared?'

'I wouldn't say there's any such thing as being too well prepared for a thing like Blood Spire, Celestine.'

'That's not what I mean.' She fingered the fabric of her skintight. 'These suits, for instance. How did he know we wouldn't be able to go all the way with the larger ones?'

I shrugged, a gesture that was now perfectly visible. 'I don't know. Maybe he learned a few things from Argyle, before he died.'

'Then what about Doctor Trintignant? That ghoul isn't remotely interested in solving the Spire. He hasn't contributed to a single problem yet. And yet he's already proved his value, hasn't he?'

'I don't follow.'

Celestine rubbed her shunt. 'These things. And the neural modifiers – Trintignant supervised their installation. And I haven't even mentioned Forqueray's arm, or the medical equipment aboard the shuttle.'

'I still don't see what you're getting at.'

'I don't know what leverage Childe's used to get his co-operation – it's got to be more than bribery or avarice – but I have a very, very nasty idea. And all of it points to something even more disturbing.'

I was wearying of this. With the challenge of the next door ahead of us, the last thing I needed was paranoiac theory-mongering.

'Which is?'

'Childe knows too much about this place.'

Another room, another wrong answer, another punishment.

It made the last look like a minor reprimand. I remembered a swift metallic flicker of machines emerging from hatches which opened in the seamless walls: not javelins now, but jointed, articulated pincers and viciously curved scissors. I remembered high-pressure jets of vivid arterial blood spraying the room like pink banners, the shards of shattered bone hammering against the walls like shrapnel. I remembered an unwanted and brutal lesson in the anatomy of the human body; the elegance with which muscle, bone and sinew were anchored to each other and the horrid ease with which they could be flensed apart – filleted – by surgically sharp metallic instruments.

I remembered screams.

I remembered indescribable pain, before the analgesics kicked in.

Afterwards, when we had time to think about what had happened, I do not think any of us thought of blaming Celestine for making another mistake. Childe's modifiers had given us a healthy respect for the difficulty of what she was doing, and – as before – her second choice had been the correct one; the one that opened a route back to the Spire's exit.

And besides . . .

Celestine had suffered as well.

It was Forqueray who had caught the worst of it, though. Perhaps the Spire, having tasted his blood once, had decided it wanted much more of it – more than could be provided by the sacrifice of a mere limb. It had quartered him: two quick opposed snips with the nightmarish scissors; a bisection follow-ed an instant later by a hideous transection.

Four pieces of Forqueray had thudded to the Spire's floor; his interior organs were laid open like a wax model in a medical school. Various machines nestled neatly amongst his innards, sliced along the same planes. What remained of him spasmed once or twice, then – with the exception of his replacement arm, which continued to twitch – he was mercifully still. A moment or two passed, and then – with whiplash speed – jointed arms seized his pieces and pulled him into the wall, leaving slick red skidmarks.

Forqueray's death would have been bad enough, but by then the Spire was already inflicting further punishment.

I saw Celestine drop to the ground, one arm pressed around the stump of another, blood spraying from the wound despite the pressure she was applying. Through her visor her face turned ghostly.

Childe's right hand was missing all the fingers. He pressed the ruined hand against his chest, grimacing, but managed to stay on his feet.

Trintignant had lost a leg. But there was no blood gushing from the wound; no evidence of severed muscle and bone. I saw only damaged mechanisms; twisted and snapped steel and plastic armatures; buzzing cables and stuttering optic fibres; interrupted feedlines oozing sickly green fluids.

Trintignant, nonetheless, fell to the floor.

I also felt myself falling, looking down to see that my right leg ended just below the knee; realising that my own blood was hosing out in a hard scarlet stream. I hit the floor – the pain of the injury having yet to reach my brain – and reached out in reflex for the stump. But only one hand presented itself; my left arm had been curtailed neatly above the wrist. In my peripheral vision I saw my detached hand, still gloved, perched on the floor like an absurd white crab.

Pain flowered in my skull.

I screamed.

'Fine.'

He stepped through the door which Hirz had just used.

'Where are you going?' I said.

'To try and talk some sense into her, that's all.'

six

'I've had enough of this shit,' Hirz said.

Childe looked up at her from his recovery couch. 'You're leaving us?'

'Damn right I am.'

'You disappoint me.'

'Fine, but I'm still shipping out.'

Childe stroked his forehead, tracing its shape with the new steel gauntlet Trintignant had attached to his arm. 'If anyone should be quitting, it isn't you, Hirz. You walked out of the Spire without a scratch. Look at the rest of us.'

'Thanks, but I've just had my dinner.'

Trintignant lifted his silver mask towards her. 'Now there is no call for that. I admit the replacements I have fashioned here possess a certain brutal *esthétique*, but in functional terms they are without equal.' As if to demonstrate his point, he flexed his own replacement leg.

It was a replacement, rather than simply the old one salvaged, repaired and reattached. Hirz – who had picked up as many pieces of us as she could manage – had never found the other part of Trintignant. Nor had an examination of the area around the Spire – where we had found the pieces of Forqueray – revealed any significant part of the Doctor. The Spire had allowed us to take back Forqueray's arm after it had been severed, but it appeared to have decided to keep all metallic things for itself.

I stood up from my own couch, testing the way my new leg supported my weight. There was no denying the excellence of Trintignant's work. The prosthesis had interfaced with my existing nervous system so perfectly that I had already accepted the leg into my body image. When I walked on it I did so with only the tiniest trace of a limp, and that would surely vanish once I had grown accustomed to the replacement.

'I could take the other one off as well,' Trintignant piped, rubbing his hands together. 'Then you would have perfect neural equilibrium . . . shall I do it?'

'You want to, don't you?'

'I admit I have always been offended by asymmetry.'

I felt my other leg; the flesh and blood one that now felt so vulnerable, so unlikely to last the course.

'You'll just have to be patient,' I said.

'Well, all things come to he who waits. And how is the arm doing?'

Like Childe, I now boasted one steel gauntlet instead of a hand. I flexed it, hearing the tiny, shrill whine of actuators. When I touched something I felt prickles of sensation; the hand was capable of registering subtle gradations of warmth or coldness. Celestine's replacement was very similar, although sleeker and somehow more feminine. At least our injuries had demanded as much, I thought; unlike Childe, who had lost only his fingers, but who had appeared to welcome more of the Doctor's gleaming handiwork than was strictly necessary.

'It'll do,' I said, remembering how much Forqueray had irritated the Doctor with the same remark.

'Don't you get it?' Hirz said. 'If Trintignant had his way, you'd be like him by now. Christ only knows where he'll stop.'

Trintignant shrugged. 'I merely repair what the Spire damages.'

'Yeah. The two of you make a great team, Doc.' She looked at him with an expression of pure loathing. 'Well, sorry, but you're not getting your hands on me.'

Trintignant appraised her. 'No great loss, when there is so little raw material with which to work.'

'Screw you, creep.'

Hirz left the room.

'Looks like she means it when she says she's quitting,' I said, breaking the silence that ensued.

Celestine nodded. 'I can't say I entirely blame her, either.'

'You don't?' Childe asked.

'No. She's right. This whole thing is in serious danger of turning into some kind of sick exercise in self-mutilation.' Celestine looked at her own steel hand, not quite masking her own revulsion. 'What will it take, Childe? What will we turn into by the time we beat this thing?'

He shrugged. 'Nothing that can't be reversed.'

'But maybe by then we won't want it reversed, will we?'

'Listen, Celestine.' Childe propped himself against a bulkhead. 'What we're doing here is trying to beat an elemental thing. Reach its summit, if you will. In that respect Blood Spire isn't very different to a mountain. It punishes us when we make mistakes, but then so do mountains. Occasionally, it kills. More often than not it leaves us only with a reminder of what it can do. Blood Spire snips off a finger or two. A mountain achieves the same effect with frostbite. Where's the difference?'

'A mountain doesn't enjoy doing it, for a start. But the Spire *does*. It's alive, Childe, living and breathing.'

'It's a machine, that's all.'

'But maybe a cleverer one than anything we've ever known before. A machine with a taste for blood, too. That's not a great combination, Childe.'

He sighed. 'Then you're giving up as well?'

'I didn't say that.'

seven

Ten hours later – buzzing with unnatural alertness; the need for sleep a distant, fading memory – we returned to Blood Spire.

'What did he say to make you come back?' I said to Hirz, between one of the challenges.

'What do you think?'

'Just a wild stab in the dark, but did he by any chance up your cut?'

'Let's just say the terms were renegotiated. Call it a perform-ance-related bonus.'

I smiled. 'Then calling you a mercenary wasn't so far off the mark, was it?'

'Sticks and stones may break my bones . . . sorry. Given the circumstances, that's not in the best possible good taste, is it?'

'Never mind.'

We were struggling out of our suits now. Several rooms earlier we had reached a point where it was impossible to squeeze through the door without first disconnecting our air-lines and removing our backpacks. We could have done without the packs, of course, but none of us wanted to breathe Spire air until it was absolutely necessary. And we would still need the packs to make our retreat, back through the unpressurised rooms. So we kept hold of them as we wriggled between rooms, fearful of letting go. We had seen the way the Spire harvested first Forqueray's drone and then Trintignant's leg, and it was likely it would do the same with our equipment if we left it unattended.

'Why are you doing it, then?' asked Hirz.

'It certainly isn't the money,' I said.

'No. I figured that part out. What, then?'

'*Because it's there.* Because Childe and I go back a long way, and I can't stand to give up on a challenge once I've accepted it.'

'Old-fashioned bullheadedness, in other words,' Celestine said.

Hirz was putting on a helmet and backpack assembly for the first time. She had just been forced to get out of her original suit and put on one of the skintights; even her small frame was now too large to pass through the constricted doors. Childe had attached some additional armour to her skintight – scablike patches of flexible woven diamond – but she must have felt more vulnerable.

I answered Celestine. 'What about you, if it isn't the same thing that keeps me coming back?'

'I want to solve the problems, that's all. For you they're just a means to an end, but for me they're the only thing of interest.'

I felt slighted, but she was right. The nature of the challenges was less important to me than discovering what was at the summit; the secret the Spire so jealously guarded.

'And you're hoping that through the problems they set us you'll eventually understand the Spire's makers?'

'Not just that. I mean, that's a significant part of it, but I also want to know what my own limitations are.'

'You mean you want to explore the gift that the Jugglers have given you?' Before she had time to answer I continued, 'I understand. And it's never been possible before, has it? You've only ever been able to test yourself against problems set by other humans. You could never map the limits of your ability; any more than a lion could test its strength against paper.'

She looked around her. 'But now I've met something that tests me.'

'And?'

Celestine smiled thinly. 'I'm not sure I like it.'

We did not speak again until we had traversed half a dozen new rooms, and then rested while the shunts mopped up the excess of tiredness which came after such efforts.

The mathematical problems had now grown so arcane that I could barely describe them, let alone grope my way towards a solution. Celestine had to do most of the thinking, therefore, but the emotional strain which we all felt was just as wearying. For an hour during the rest period I teetered on the edge of sleep, but then alertness returned like a pale, cold dawn. There was something harsh and clinical about that state of mind – it did not feel completely normal – but it enabled us to get the job done, and that was all that mattered.

We continued, passing the seventieth room – fifteen further than we had reached before. We were now at least sixty metres higher than when we had entered, and for a while it looked like we had found a tempo that suited us. It was a long time since Celestine had shown any hesitation in her answers, even if it took a couple of hours for her to reach the solution. It was as if she had found the right way of thinking, and now none of the challenges felt truly alien to her. For a while, as we passed room after room, a dangerous optimism began to creep over us.

It was a mistake.

In the seventy-first room, the Spire began to enforce a new rule. Celestine, as usual, spent at least twenty minutes studying the problem, skating her fingers over the shallowly etched markings on the frame, her lips moving silently as she mouthed possibilities.

Childe studied her with a peculiar watchfulness I had not observed before.

'Any ideas?' he said, looking over her shoulder.

'Don't crowd me, Childe. I'm thinking.'

'I know, I know. Just try and do it a little faster, that's all.'

Celestine turned away from the frame. 'Why? Are we on a schedule suddenly?'

'I'm just a little concerned about the amount of time it's taking us, that's all.' He stroked the bulge on his forearm. 'These shunts aren't perfect, and—'

'There's something else, isn't there?'

'Don't worry. Just concentrate on the problem.'

But this time the punishment began before we had begun our solution.

It was lenient, I suppose, compared to the savage dismembering that had concluded our last attempt to reach the summit. It was more of a stern admonishment to make our selection; the crack of a whip rather than the swish of a guillotine.

Something popped out of the wall and dropped to the floor.

It looked like a metal ball, about the size of a marble. For several seconds it did nothing at all. We all stared at it, knowing that something unpleasant was going to happen, but unsure what.

Then the ball trembled, and – without deforming in any way – bounced itself off the ground to knee-height.

It hit the ground and bounced again; a little higher this time.

'Celestine,' Childe said, 'I strongly suggest that you come to a decision—'

Horrified, Celestine forced her attention back to the puzzle marked on the frame. The ball continued bouncing; reaching higher each time.

'I don't like this,' Hirz said.

'I'm not exactly thrilled by it myself,' Childe told her, watching as the ball hit the ceiling and slammed back to the floor, landing to one side of the place where it had begun its bouncing.

This time its rebound was enough to make it hit the ceiling again, and on the recoil it streaked diagonally across the room, hitting one of the side walls before glancing off at a different angle. The ball slammed into Trintignant, ricocheting off his metal leg, and then connected with the walls twice – gaining speed with each collision – before hitting me in the chest. The force of it was like a hard punch, driving the air from my lungs.

I fell to the ground, emitting a groan of discomfort.

The little ball continued arcing around the room, its momentum not sapped in any appreciable way. It kept getting faster, in fact, so that its trajectory came to resemble a constantly shifting silver loom which occasionally intersected with one of us. I heard groans, and then felt a sudden pain in my leg, and the ball kept on getting faster. The sound it made was like a fusillade of gunshots, the space between each detonation growing smaller.

Childe, who had been hit himself, shouted: 'Celestine! Make your choice!'

The ball chose that moment to slam into her, making her gasp in pain. She buckled down on one knee, but in the process reached out and palmed one of the markings on the right side of the frame.

The gunshot sounds – the silver loom – even the ball itself – vanished.

Nothing happened for several more seconds, and then the door ahead of us began to open.

We inspected our injuries. There was nothing life-threatening, but we had all been bruised badly, and it was likely that a bone or two had been fractured. I was sure I had broken a rib, and Childe grimaced when he tried to put weight on his right ankle. My leg felt tender where the ball had struck me, but I could still walk, and after a few minutes the pain abated, soothed by a combination of my own medichines and the shunt's analgesics.

'Thank God we'd put the helmets back on,' I said, fingerng a deep bump in the crown. 'We'd have been pulped otherwise.'

'Would someone please tell me what just happened?' Celestine asked, inspecting her own wounds.

'I guess the Spire thought we were taking too long,' Childe said. 'It's given us as long as we like to solve the problems until now, but from now on it looks like we'll be up against the clock.'

Hirz said: 'And how long did we have?'

'After the last door opened? Forty minutes or so.'

'Forty-three, to be precise,' Trintignant said.

'I strongly suggest we start work on the next door,' Childe said. 'How long do you think we have, Doctor?'

'As an upper limit? In the region of twenty-eight minutes.'

'That's nowhere near enough time,' I said. 'We'd better retreat and come back.'

'No,' Childe said. 'Not until we're injured.'

'You're insane,' Celestine said.

But Childe ignored her. He just stepped through the door, into the next room. Behind us the exit door slammed shut.

'Not insane,' he said, turning back to us. 'Just very eager to continue.'

It was never the same thing twice.

Celestine made her selection as quickly as she could, every muscle tense with concentration, and that gave us – by Trintignant's estimation – five or six clear minutes before the Spire would demand an answer.

'We'll wait it out,' Childe said, eyeing us all to see if anyone disagreed. 'Celestine can keep checking her results. There's no sense in giving the fucking thing an answer before we have to; not when so much is at stake.'

'I'm sure of the answer,' Celestine said, pointing to the part of the frame she would eventually palm.

'Then take five minutes to clear your head. Whatever. Just don't make the choice until we're forced into it.'

'If we get through this room, Childe . . .'

'Yes?'

'I'm going back. You can't stop me.'

'You won't do it, Celestine, and you know it.'

She glared at him, but said nothing. I think what followed was the longest five minutes in my life. None of us dared speak again, unwilling to begin anything – even a word – for fear that something like the ball would return. All I heard for five minutes was our own breathing; backgrounded by the awful slow thrumming of the Spire itself.

Then something slithered out of one wall.

It hit the floor, writhing. It was an inch-thick, three-metre-long length of flexible metal.

'Back off . . .' Childe told us.

Celestine looked over her shoulder. 'You want me to press this, or not?'

'On my word. Not a moment before.'

The cable continued writhing: flexing, coiling and uncoiling like a demented eel. Childe stared at it, fascinated. The writhing grew in strength, accompanied by the slithering, hissing sounds of metal on metal.

'Childe?' Celestine asked.

'I just want to see what this thing actually—'

The cable flexed and writhed, and then propelled itself rapidly across the floor in Childe's direction. He hopped nimbly out of the way, the cable passing under his feet. The writhing had become a continuous whipcracking now, and we all pressed ourselves against the walls. The cable – having missed Childe – retreated to the middle of the room and hissed furiously. It looked much longer and thinner than it had a moment ago, as if it had elongated itself.

'Childe,' Celestine said, 'I'm making the choice in five seconds, whether you like it or not.'

'Wait, will you?'

The cable moved with blinding speed now, rearing up so that its motion was no longer confined to a few inches above the floor. Its writhing was so fast that it took on a quasi-solidity: an irregularly shaped pillar of flickering, whistling metal. I looked at Celestine, willing her to palm the frame, no matter what Childe said. I appreciated his fascination – the thing was entrancing to look at – but I suspected he was pushing curiosity slightly too far.

'Celestine . . .' I started saying.

But what happened next happened with lightning speed: a silver-grey tentacle of the blur – a thin loop of the cable – whipped out to form a double coil around Celestine's arm. It was the one Trintignant had already worked on. She looked at it in horror; the cable tightened itself and snipped the arm off. Celestine slumped to the floor, screaming.

The tentacle tugged her arm to the centre of the room, retreating back into the hissing, flickering pillar of whirling metal.

I dashed for the door, remembering the symbol she had pressed. The whirl reached a loop out to me, but I threw myself against the wall and the loop merely brushed the chest of my suit before flicking back into the mass. From the whirl, tiny pieces of flesh and bone dribbled to the ground. Then another loop flicked out and snared Hirz, wrapping around her midsection and pulling her towards the centre.

She struggled – cartwheeling her arms, her feet skidding against the floor – but it was no good. She started shouting, and then screaming.

I reached the door.

My hand hesitated over the markings. Was I remembering accurately, or had Celestine intended to press a different solution? They all looked so similar now.

Then Celestine, who was still clutching her ruined arm, nodded emphatically.

I palmed the door.

I stared at it, willing it to move. After all this, what if her choice had been wrong? The Spire seemed to draw out the moment sadistically while behind me I continued to hear the frantic hissing of the whirling cable. And something else, which I preferred not to think about.

Suddenly the noise stopped.

In my peripheral vision I saw the cable retreating back into the wall, like a snake's tongue laden with scent.

Before me, the door began to open.

Celestine's choice had been correct. I examined my state of mind and decided that I ought to be feeling relief. And perhaps, distantly, I did. At least now we would have a clear route back out of the Spire. But we would not be going forward, and I knew not all of us would be leaving.

I turned around, steeling myself against what I was about to see.

Childe and Trintignant were undamaged.

Celestine was already attending to her injury, fixing a tourniquet from her medical kit above the point where her arm ended. She had lost very little blood, and did not appear to be in very much discomfort.

'Are you all right?' I said.

'I'll make it out, Richard.' She grimaced, tugging the tourniquet tighter. 'Which is more than can be said for Hirz.'

'Where is she?'

'It got her.'

With her good hand, Celestine pointed to the place where the whirl had been only moments before. On the floor – just below the volume of air where the cable had hovered and thrashed – lay a small, neat pile of flailed human tissue.

'There's no sign of Celestine's hand,' I said. 'Or Hirz's suit.'

'It pulled her apart,' Childe said, his face drained of blood. 'Where is she?'

'It was very fast. There was just a . . . blur. It pulled her apart and then the parts disappeared into the walls. I don't think she could have felt much.'

'I hope to God she didn't.'

Doctor Trintignant stooped down and examined the pieces.

eight

Outside, in the long, steely-shadowed light of what was either dusk or dawn, we found the pieces of Hirz for which the Spire had had no use.

They were half-buried in dust, like the bluffs and arches of some ancient landscape rendered in miniature. My mind played gruesome tricks with the shapes, turning them from brutally detached pieces of human anatomy into abstract sculptures: jointed formations that caught the light in a certain way and cast their own pleasing shadows. Though some pieces of fabric remained, the Spire had retained all the metallic parts of her suit for itself. Even her skull had been cracked open and sucked dry, so that the Spire could winnow the few small precious pieces of metal she carried in her head.

And what it could not use, it had thrown away.

'We can't just leave her here,' I said. 'We've got to do something, bury her . . . at least put up some kind of marker.'

'She's already got one,' Childe said.

'What?'

'The Spire. And the sooner we get back to the shuttle, the sooner we can fix Celestine and get back to it.'

'A moment, please,' Trintignant said, fingering through another pile of human remains.

'Those aren't anything to do with Hirz,' Childe said.

Trintignant rose to his feet, slipping something into his suit's utility belt pocket in the process.

Whatever it had been was small; no larger than a marble or small stone.

'I'm going home,' Celestine said, when we were back in the safety of the shuttle. 'And before you try and talk me out of it, that's final.'

We were alone in her quarters. Childe had just given up trying to convince her to stay, but he had sent me in to see if I could be more persuasive. My heart, however, was not in it. I had seen what the Spire could do, and I was damned if I was going to be responsible for any blood other than my own.

'At least let Trintignant take care of your hand,' I said.

'I don't need steel now,' she said, stroking the glistening blue surgical sleeve which terminated her arm. 'I can manage without a hand until we're back in Chasm City. They can grow me a new one while I'm sleeping.'

The Doctor's musical voice interrupted us, Trintignant's impassive silver mask poking through into Celestine's bubble-tent partition. 'If I may be so bold . . . it may be that my services are the best you can now reasonably hope to attain.'

Celestine looked at Childe, and then at the Doctor, and then at the glistening surgical sleeve.

'What are you talking about?'

'Nothing. Only some news from home which Childe has allowed me to see.' Uninvited, Trintignant stepped fully into the room and sealed the partition behind him.

'What, Doctor?'

'Rather disturbing news, as it happens. Not long after our departure, something upsetting happened to Chasm City. A blight which afflicted everything contingent upon any micro-scopic, self-replicating system. Nanotechnology, in other words. I gather the fatalities were numbered in the millions . . .'

'You don't have to sound so bloody cheerful about it.'

Trintignant navigated to the side of the couch where Celestine was resting. 'I merely stress the point that what we consider state of the art medicine may be somewhat beyond the city's present capabilities. Of course, much may change before our return . . .'

'Then I'll just have to take that risk, won't I?' Celestine said.

'On your own head be it.' Trintignant paused and placed something small and hard on Celestine's table. Then he turned as if to leave, but stopped and spoke again. 'I am accustomed to it, you know.'

'Used to what?' I said.

'Fear and revulsion. Because of what I have become, and what I have done. But I am not an evil man. Perverse, yes. Given to peculiar desires, most certainly. But emphatically not a monster.'

'What about your victims, Doctor?'

'I have always maintained that they gave consent for the procedures I inflicted—' he corrected himself '—performed upon them.'

'That's not what the records say.'

'And who are we to argue with records?' The light played on his mask in such a fashion as to enhance the half-smile that was always there. 'Who are we, indeed.'

When Trintignant was gone, I turned to Celestine and said, 'I'm going back into the Spire. You realise that, don't you?'

'I'd guessed, but I still hope I can talk you out of it.' With her good hand, she fingered the small, hard thing Trintignant had placed on the table. It looked like a misshapen dark stone – whatever the Doctor had found amongst the dead – and for a moment I wondered why he had left it behind.

Then I said, 'I really don't think there's much point. It's

between me and Childe now. He must have known that there'd come a point when I wouldn't be able to turn away.'

'No matter what the costs?' Celestine asked.

'Nothing's without a little risk.'

She shook her head, slowly and wonderingly. 'He really got to you, didn't he.'

'No,' I said, feeling a perverse need to defend my old friend, even when I knew that what Celestine said was perfectly true. 'It wasn't Childe, in the end. It was the Spire.'

'Please, Richard. Think carefully, won't you?'

I said I would. But we both knew it was a lie.

nine

Childe and I went back.

I gazed up at it, towering over us like some brutal cenotaph. I saw it with astonishing, diamond-hard clarity. It was as if a smoky veil had been lifted from my vision, permitting thousands of new details and nuances of hue and shade to blast through. Only the tiniest, faintest hint of pixelation – seen whenever I changed my angle of view too sharply – betrayed the fact that this was not quite normal vision, but a cybernetic augmentation.

Our eyes had been removed, the sockets scrubbed and packed with far more efficient sensory devices, wired back into our visual cortices. Our eyeballs waited back at the shuttle, floating in jars like grotesque delicacies. They could be popped back in when we had conquered the Spire.

'Why not goggles?' I said when Trintignant had first explained his plans.

'Too bulky, and too liable to be snatched away. The Spire has a definite taste for metal. From now on, anything vital had better be carried as part of us – not just worn, but internalised.' The Doctor steepled his silver fingers. 'If that repulses you, I suggest you concede defeat now.'

'I'll decide what repulses me,' I said.

'What else?' Childe said. 'Without Celestine we'll need to crack those problems ourselves.'

'I will increase the density of medichines in your brains,' Trintignant said. 'They will weave a web of fullerene tubes, artificial neuronal connections supplanting your existing synaptic topology.'

'What good will that do?'

'The fullerene tubes will conduct nerve signals hundreds of times more rapidly than your existing synaptic pathways. Your neural computation rate will increase. Your subjective sense of elapsed time will slow.'

I stared at the Doctor, horrified and fascinated at the same time. 'You can do that?'

'It's actually rather trivial. The Conjoiners have being doing it since the Transenlightenment, and their methods are well documented. With them I can make time slow to a subjective crawl. The Spire may give you only twenty minutes to solve a room, but I can make it feel like several hours; even one or two days.'

I turned to Childe. 'You think that'll be enough?'

'I think it'll be a lot better than nothing, but we'll see.'

But it was better than that.

Trintignant's machines did more than just supplant our existing and clumsily slow neural pathways. They reshaped them, configuring the topology to enhance mathematical prowess, which took us onto a plateau beyond what the neural modifiers had been capable of doing. We lacked Celestine's intuitive brilliance, but we had the advantage of being able to spend longer – subjectively, at least – on a given problem.

And, for a while at least, it worked.

ten

'You're turning into a monster,' she said.

I answered, 'I'm turning into whatever it takes to beat the Spire.'

I stalked away from the shuttle, moving on slender, articulated legs like piston-driven stilts. I no longer needed armour now: Trintignant had grafted it to my skin. Tough black plaques slid over each other like the carapacial segments of a lobster.

'You even sound like Trintignant now,' Celestine said, following me. I watched her asymmetric shadow loom next to mine: she lopsided; me a thin, elongated wraith.

'I can't help that,' I said, my voice piping from the speech synthesiser that replaced my sealed-up mouth.

'You can stop. It isn't too late.'

'Not until Childe stops.'

'And then? Will even that be enough to make you give up, Richard?'

I turned to face her. Behind her faceplate I watched her try to conceal the revulsion she obviously felt.

'He won't give up,' I said.

Celestine held out her hand. At first I thought she was beckoning me, but then I saw there was something in her palm. Small, dark and hard.

'Trintignant found this outside, by the Spire. It's what he left in my room. I think he was trying to tell us something. Trying to redeem himself. Do you recognise it, Richard?'

I zoomed in on the object. Numbers flickered around it. Enhancement phased in. Surface irregularity. Topological contours. Albedo. Likely composition. I drank in the data like a drunkard.

Data was what I lived for now.

'No.'

eleven

'I can hear something.'

'Of course you can. It's the Spire, the same as it's always been.'

'No.' I was silent for several moments, wondering whether my augmented auditory system was sending false signals into my brain.

But there it was again: an occasional rumble of distant machinery, but one that was coming closer.

'I hear it now,' Childe said. 'It's coming from behind us. Along the way we've come.'

'It sounds like the doors opening and closing in sequence.'

'Yes.'

'Why would they do that?'

'Something must be coming through the rooms towards us.'

Childe thought about that for what felt like minutes, but was probably only a matter of actual seconds. Then he shook his head, dismissively. 'We have eleven minutes to get through this door, or we'll be punished. We don't have time to worry about anything extraneous.'

Reluctantly, I agreed.

I forced my attention back to the puzzle, feeling the machinery in my head pluck at the mathematical barbs of the problem. The ferocious clockwork that Trintignant had installed in my skull spun giddily. I had never understood mathematics with any great agility, but now I sensed it as a hard grid of truth underlying everything: bones shining through the thin flesh of the world.

It was almost the only thing I was now capable of thinking of at all. Everything else felt painfully abstract, whereas before the opposite had been the case. This, I knew, must be what it felt like to an idiot savant, gifted with astonishing skill in one highly specialised field of human expertise.

I had become a tool shaped so efficiently for one purpose that it could serve no other.

I had become a machine for solving the Spire.

Now that we were alone – and no longer reliant on Celestine – Childe had revealed himself as a more than adequately capable problem-solver. Several times I had found myself staring at a problem, with even my new mathematical skills momentarily unable to crack the solution, when Childe had seen the answer. Generally he was able to articulate the reasoning behind his choice, but sometimes there was nothing for it but for me to either accept his judgement or wait for my own sluggard thought processes to arrive at the same conclusion.

And I began to wonder.

Childe was brilliant now, but I sensed there was more to it than the extra layers of cognitive machinery Trintignant had installed. He was so confident now that I began to wonder if he had merely been holding back before, preferring to let the rest of us make the decisions. If that was the case, he was in some way responsible for the deaths that had already happened.

But, I reminded myself, we had all volunteered.

With three minutes to spare, the door eased open, revealing the room beyond. At the same moment the door we had come through opened as well, as it always did at this point. We could leave now, if we wished. At this time, as had been the case with every room we had passed through, Childe and I made a decision on whether to proceed further or not. There was always the danger that the next room would be the one that killed us – and every second that we spent before stepping through the doorway meant one second less available for cracking the next problem.

'Well?' I said.

His answer came back, clipped and automatic. 'Onwards.'

'We only had three minutes to spare on this one, Childe. They're getting harder now. A hell of a lot harder.'

'I'm fully aware of that.'

'Then maybe we should retreat. Gather our strength and return. We'll lose nothing by doing so.'

'You can't be sure of that. You don't know that the Spire will keep letting us make these attempts. Perhaps it's already tiring of us.'

'I still—'

But I stopped, my new, wasp-waisted body flexing easily at the approach of a footfall.

My visual system scanned the approaching object, resolving it into a figure, stepping over the threshold from the previous room. It was a human figure, but one that had, admittedly, undergone some alterations – although none that were as drastic as those that Trintignant had wrought on me. I studied the slow, painful way she made her progress. Our own movements seemed slow, but were lightning-fast by comparison.

I groped for a memory; a name; a face.

My mind, clotted with routines designed to smash mathematics, could not at first retrieve such mundane data.

Finally, however, it obliged.

'Celestine,' I said.

I did not actually speak. Instead, laser light stuttered from the mass of sensors and scanners jammed into my eyesockets. Our minds now ran too rapidly to communicate verbally, but, though she moved slowly herself, she deigned to reply.

'Yes. It's me. Are you really Richard?'

'Why do you ask?'

'Because I can hardly tell the difference between you and Childe.'

I looked at Childe, paying proper attention to his shape for what seemed the first time.

At last, after so many frustrations, Trintignant had been given free rein to do with us as he wished. He had pumped our heads full of more processing machinery, until our skulls had to be reshaped to accommodate it, becoming sleekly elongated. He cracked our ribcages open and carefully removed our lungs and hearts, putting these organs into storage. The space vacated by one lung was replaced by a closed-cycle blood oxygenating system of the kind carried in spacesuit backpacks, so that we could endure vacuum and had no need to breathe ambient air. The other lung's volume was filled by a device which circulated refrigerated fluid along a loop of tube, draining the excess heat generated by the stew of neural machines filling our heads. Nutrient systems crammed the remaining thoracic spaces; our hearts were tiny fusion-powered pumps. All other organs – stomach, intestines, genitalia – were removed, along with many bones and muscles. Our remaining limbs were detached and put into storage, replaced by skeletal prosthetics of immense strength, but which could fold and deform to enable us to squeeze through the tightest door. Our bodies were encased in exoskeletal frames to which these limbs were anchored. Finally, Trintignant gave us whiplike counterbalancing tails, and then caused our skins to envelop our metal parts, hardening here and there in lustrous grey patches of organic armour, woven from the same diamond mesh that had been used to reinforce Hirz's suit.

When he was done, we looked like diamond-hided grey-hounds.

Diamond dogs.

*

I bowed my head. 'I am Richard.'

'Then for God's sake please come back.'

'Why have you followed us?'

'To ask you. One final time.'

'You changed yourself just to come after me?'

Slowly, with the stone grace of a statue, she extended a beckoning hand. Her limbs, like ours, were mechanical, but her basic form was far less canine.

'Please.'

'You know I can't go back now. Not when I've come so far.'

Her answer was an eternity arriving. 'You don't understand, Richard. This is not what it seems.'

Childe turned his sleek, snouted face to mine.

'Ignore her,' he said.

'No,' Celestine said, who must have also been attuned to Childe's laser signals. 'Don't listen to him, Richard. He's tricked and lied to you all along. To all of us. Even to Trintignant. That's why I came back.'

'She's lying,' Childe said.

'No. I'm not. Haven't you got it yet, Richard? Childe's been here before. This isn't his first visit to the Spire.'

I convulsed my canine body in a shrug. 'Nor mine.'

'I don't mean since we arrived on Golgotha. I mean before that. Childe's been to this planet already.'

'She's lying,' Childe repeated.

'Then how did you know what to expect, in so much detail?'

'I didn't. I was just prudent.' He turned to me, so that only I could read the stammer of his lasers. 'We are wasting valuable time here, Richard.'

'Prudent?' Celestine said. 'Oh yes; you were damned prudent. Bringing along those other suits, so that when the first ones became too bulky we could still go on. And Trintignant – how did you know he'd come in so handy?'

'I saw the bodies lying around the base of the Spire,' Childe

111

answered. 'They'd been butchered by it.'

'And?'

'I decided it would be good to have someone along who had the medical aptitude to put right such injuries.'

'Yes.' Celestine nodded. 'I don't disagree with that. But that's no more than part of the truth, is it?'

I looked at Childe and Celestine in turn. 'Then what is the whole truth?'

'Those bodies aren't anything to do with Captain Argyle.'

'They're not?' I said.

'No.' Celestine's words arrived agonisingly slowly, and I began to wish that Trintignant had turned her into a diamond-skinned dog as well. 'No. Because Argyle never existed. He was a necessary fiction – a reason for Childe knowing at least something about what the Spire entailed. But the truth . . . well, why don't you tell us, Childe?'

'I don't know what you want me to say.'

Celestine smiled. 'Only that the bodies are yours.'

His tail flexed impatiently, brushing the floor. 'I won't listen to this.'

'Then don't. But Trintignant will tell you the same thing. He guessed first, not me.'

She threw something towards me.

I willed time to move more slowly. What she had thrown curved lazily through the air, following a parabola. My mind processed its course and extrapolated its trajectory with deadening precision.

I moved and opened my foreclaw to catch the falling thing.

'I don't recognise it,' I said.

'Trintignant must have thought you would.'

I looked down at the thing, trying to see it anew. I remembered the Doctor fishing amongst the bones around the Spire's base; placing something in one of his pockets. This hard, black, irregular, dully pointed thing.

What was it?

I half remembered.

'There has to be more than this,' I said.

'Of course there is,' Celestine said. 'The human remains – with the exception of what's been added since we arrived – are all from the same genetic individual. I know. Trintignant told me.'

'That isn't possible.'

'Oh, it is. With cloning, it's almost child's play.'

'This is nonsense,' Childe said.

I turned to him now, feeling the faint ghost of an emotion Trintignant had not completely excised. 'Is it really?'

'Why would I clone myself?'

'I'll answer for him,' Celestine said. 'He found this thing, but long, long before he said he did. And he visited it, and set about exploring it, using clones of himself.'

I looked at Childe, expecting him to at least proffer some shred of explanation. Instead, padding on all fours, he crossed into the next room.

The door behind Celestine slammed shut like a steel eyelid.

Childe spoke to us from the next room. 'My estimate is that we have nine or ten minutes in which to solve the next problem. I am studying it now and it strikes me as . . . challenging, to say the least. Shall we adjourn any further discussion of trivialities until we're through?'

'Childe,' I said. 'You shouldn't have done that. Celestine wasn't consulted . . .'

'I assumed she was on the team.'

Celestine stepped into the new room. 'I wasn't. At least, I didn't think I was. But it looks like I am now.'

'That's the spirit,' Childe said. And I realised then where I had seen the small, dark thing that Trintignant had retrieved from the surface of Golgotha.

I might have been mistaken.

But it looked a lot like a devil's horn.

twelve

The problem was as elegant, Byzantine, multi-layered and potentially treacherous as any we had encountered.

Simply looking at it sent my mind careering down avenues of mathematical possibility, glimpsing deep connections between what I had always assumed were theoretically distant realms of logical space. I could have stared at it for hours, in a state of ecstatic transfixion. Unfortunately, we had to solve it, not admire it. And we now had less than nine minutes.

We crowded around the door and for two or three minutes – what felt like two or three hours – nothing was said.

I broke the silence, when I sensed that I needed to think about something else for a moment.

'Was Celestine right? Did you clone yourself?'

'Of course he did,' she said. 'He was exploring hazardous territory, so he'd have been certain to bring the kind of equipment necessary to regenerate organs.'

Childe turned away from the problem. 'That isn't the same as cloning equipment.'

'Only because of artificially imposed safeguards,' Celestine answered. 'Strip those away and you can clone to your heart's content. Why regenerate a single hand or arm when you can culture a whole body?'

'What good would that do me? All I'd have done was make a mindless copy of myself.'

I said, 'Not necessarily. With memory trawls and medichines, you could go some way towards imprinting your personality and memory on any clone you chose.'

'He's right,' Celestine said. 'It's easy enough to rescript memories. Richard should know.'

Childe looked back at the problem, which was still as fiercely intractable as when we had entered.

'Six minutes left,' he said.

'Don't change the fucking subject,' Celestine said. 'I want Richard to know exactly what happened here.'

'Why?' Childe said. 'Do you honestly care what happens to him? I saw that look of revulsion when you saw what we'd done to ourselves.'

'Maybe you do revolt me,' she said, nodding. 'But I also care about someone being manipulated.'

'I haven't manipulated anyone.'

'Then tell him the truth about the clones. And the Spire, for that matter.'

Childe returned his attention to the door, evidently torn between solving the problem and silencing Celestine. Less than six minutes now remained, and though I had distracted myself, I had not come closer to grasping the solution, or even seeing a hint of how to begin.

I snapped my attention back to Childe. 'What happened with the clones? Did you send them in, one by one, hoping to find a way into the Spire for you?'

'No.' He almost laughed at my failure to grasp the truth. 'I didn't send them in ahead of me, Richard. Not at all. I sent them in *after* me.'

'Sorry, but I don't understand.'

'I went in first, and the Spire killed me. But before I did that, I trawled myself and installed those memories in a recently grown

116

clone. The clone wasn't a perfect copy of me, by any means – it had some memories, and some of my grosser personality traits, but it was under no illusions that it was anything but a recently made construct.' Childe looked back towards the problem. 'Look, this is all very interesting, but I really think—'

'The problem can wait,' Celestine said. 'I think I see a solution, in any case.'

Childe's slender body stiffened in anticipation. 'You do?'

'Just a hint of one, Childe. Keep your hackles down.'

'We don't have much time, Celestine. I'd very much like to hear your solution.'

She looked at the pattern, smiling faintly. 'I'm sure you would. I'd also like to hear what happened to the clone.'

I sensed him seethe with anger, then bring it under control. 'It – the new me – went back into the Spire and attempted to make further progress than its predecessor. Which it did, advancing several rooms beyond the point where the old me died.'

'What made it go in?' Celestine said. 'It must have known it would die in there as well.'

'It thought it had a significantly better chance of survival than the last one. It studied what had happened to the first victim and took precautions – better armour; drugs to enhance mathematical skills; some crude stabs at the medichine therapies we have been using.'

'And?' I said. 'What happened after that one died?'

'It didn't die on its first attempt. Like us, it retreated once it sensed it had gone as far as it reasonably could. Each time, it trawled itself – making a copy of its memories. These were inherited by the next clone.'

'I still don't get it,' I said. 'Why would the clone care what happened to the one after it?'

'Because . . . it never expected to die. None of them did. Call that a character trait, if you will.'

'Overweening arrogance?' Celestine offered.

'I'd prefer to think of it as a profound lack of self-doubt. Each clone imagined itself better than its predecessor; incapable of making the same errors. But they still wanted to be trawled, so that – in the unlikely event that they were killed – something would go on. So that, even if that particular clone did not solve the Spire, it would still be something with my genetic heritage that did. Part of the same lineage. Family, if you will.' His tail flicked impatiently. 'Four minutes. Celestine . . . are you ready now?'

'Almost, but not quite. How many clones were there, Childe? Before you, I mean?'

'That's a pretty personal question.'

She shrugged. 'Fine. I'll just withhold my solution.'

'Seventeen,' Childe said. 'Plus my original; the first one to go in.'

I absorbed this number; stunned at what it implied. 'Then you're . . . the nineteenth to try and solve the Spire?'

I think he would have smiled at that point, had it been anatomically possible. 'Like I said, I try and keep it in the family.'

'You've become a monster,' Celestine said, almost beneath her breath.

It was hard not to see it that way as well. He had inherited the memories from eighteen predecessors, all of whom had died within the Spire's pain-wracked chambers. It hardly mattered that he had probably never inherited the precise moment of death; the lineage was no less monstrous for that small mercy. And who was to say that some of his ancestor clones had not crawled out of the Spire, horribly mutilated, dying, but still sufficiently alive to succumb to one last trawl?

They said a trawl was all the sharper if it was performed at the moment of death, when damage to the scanned mind mattered less.

'Celestine's right,' I said. 'You've become something worse than the thing you set out to beat.'

Childe appraised me, those dense clusters of optics sweeping over me like gun barrels. 'Have you looked in a mirror lately, Richard? You're not exactly the way nature intended, you know.'

'This is just cosmetic,' I said. 'I still have my memories. I haven't allowed myself to become a—' I faltered, my brain struggling with vocabulary now that so much of it had been reassigned to the task of cracking the Spire; 'a perversion,' I finished.

'Fine.' Childe lowered his head; a posture of sadness and resignation. 'Then go back, if that's what you want. Let me stay to finish the challenge.'

'Yes,' I said. 'I think I will. Celestine? Get us through this door and I'll come back with you. We'll leave Childe to his bloody Spire.'

Celestine's sigh was one of heartfelt relief. 'Thank God, Richard. I didn't think I'd be able to convince you quite that easily.'

I nodded towards the door, suggesting that she sketch out what she thought was the likely solution. It still looked devilishly hard to me, but now that I refocused my mind on it, I thought I began to see the faintest hint of an approach, if not a full-blooded solution.

But Childe was speaking again. 'Oh, you shouldn't sound so surprised,' he said. 'I always knew he'd turn back as soon as the going got tough. That's always been his way. I shouldn't have deceived myself that he'd have changed.'

I bristled. 'That isn't true.'

'Then why turn back when we've come so far?'

'Because it isn't worth it.'

'Or is it simply that the problem's become too difficult; the challenge too great?'

'Ignore him,' Celestine said. 'He's just trying to goad you into following him. That's what this has always been about, hasn't it,

Childe? You think you can solve the Spire, where eighteen previous versions of you have failed. Where eighteen previous versions of you were butchered and flayed by the thing.' She looked around, almost as if she expected the Spire to punish her for speaking so profanely. 'And perhaps you're right, too. Perhaps you really have come closer than any of the others.'

Childe said nothing, perhaps unwilling to contradict her.

'But simply beating the Spire wouldn't be good enough,' Celestine said. 'For you'd have no witnesses. No one to see how clever you'd been.'

'That isn't it at all.'

'Then why did we all have to come here? You found Trintignant useful, I'll grant you that. And I helped you as well. But you could have done without us, ultimately. It would have been bloodier, and you might have needed to run off a few more clones . . . but I don't doubt that you could have done it.'

'The solution, Celestine.'

By my estimate we had not much more than two minutes left in which to make our selection. And yet I sensed that it was time enough. Magically, the problem had opened up before me where a moment ago it had been insoluble; like one of those optical illusions which suddenly flip from one state to another. The moment was as close to a religious experience as I cared to come.

'It's all right,' I said. 'I see it now. Have you got it?'

'Not quite. Give me a moment . . .' Childe stared at it, and I watched as the lasers from his eyes washed over the labyrinthine engravings. The red glare skittered over the wrong solution and lingered there. It flickered away and alighted on the correct answer, but only momentarily.

Childe flicked his tail. 'I think I've got it.'

'Good,' Celestine replied. 'I agree with you. Richard? Are you ready to make this unanimous?'

I thought I had misheard her, but I had not. She was saying

that Childe's answer was the right one; that the one I had been sure of was the wrong one . . .

'I thought . . .' I began. Then, desperately, stared at the problem again. Had I missed something? Childe had looked to have his doubts, but Celestine was so certain of herself. And yet what I had glimpsed had appeared beyond question. 'I don't know,' I said weakly. 'I don't know.'

'We haven't time to debate it. We've got less than a minute.'

The feeling in my belly was one of ice. Somehow, despite the layers of humanity that had been stripped from me, I could still taste terror. It was reaching me anyway; refusing to be daunted.

I felt so certain of my choice. And yet I was outnumbered.

'Richard?' Childe said again, more insistent this time.

I looked at the two of them, helplessly. 'Press it,' I said.

Childe placed his forepaw over the solution that he and Celestine had agreed on, and pressed.

I think I knew, even before the Spire responded, that the choice had not been the correct one. And yet when I looked at Celestine I saw nothing resembling shock or surprise in her expression. Instead, she looked completely calm and resigned.

And then the punishment commenced.

It was brutal, and once it would have killed us. Even with the augmentations Trintignant had given us, the damage inflicted was considerable as a scythe-tipped, triple-jointed pendulum descended from the ceiling and began swinging in viciously widening arcs. Our minds might have been able to compute the future position of a simpler pendulum, steering our bodies out of its harmful path. But the trajectory of a jointed pendulum was ferociously difficult to predict: a nightmarish demonstration of the mathematics of chaos.

But we survived, as we had survived the previous attacks. Even Celestine made it through, the flashing arc snipping off only one of her arms. I lost an arm and leg on one side, and watched – half in horror, half in fascination – as the room claimed these parts for itself; tendrils whipped out from the wall to salvage those useful conglomerations of metal and plastic. There was pain, of a sort, for Trintignant had wired those limbs into our nervous systems, so that we could feel heat and cold. But the pain abated quickly, replaced by digital numbness.

Childe got the worst of it, though.

The blade had sliced him through the middle, just below what had once been his ribcage, spilling steel and plastic guts, bone, viscera, blood and noxious lubricants onto the floor. The tendrils squirmed out and captured the twitching prize of his detached rear end, flicking tail and all.

With the hand that she still had, Celestine pressed the correct symbol. The punishment ceased and the door opened.

In the comparative calm that followed, Childe looked down at his severed trunk.

'I seem to be quite badly damaged,' he said.

But already various valves and gaskets were stemming the fluid loss; clicking shut with neat precision. Trintignant, I saw, had done very well. He had equipped Childe to survive the most extreme injuries.

'You'll live,' Celestine said, with what struck me as less than total sympathy.

'What happened?' I asked. 'Why didn't you press that one first?'

She looked at me. 'Because I knew what had to be done.'

Despite her injuries she helped us on the retreat.

I was able to stumble from room to room, balancing myself against the wall and hopping on my good leg. I had lost no great quantity of blood, for while I had suffered one or two gashes from close approaches of the pendulum, my limbs had been detached below the points where they were anchored to flesh and bone. But I still felt the shivering onset of shock, and all I wanted to do was make it out of the Spire, back to the sanctuary of the shuttle. There, I knew, Trintignant could make me whole again. Human again, for that matter. He had always promised it would be possible, and while there was much about him that I did not like, I did not think he would lie about that. It would be a matter of professional pride that his work was technically reversible.

Celestine carried Childe, tucked under her arm. What remained of him was very light, she said, and he was able to cling to her with his undamaged forepaws. I felt a spasm of horror every time I saw how little of him there was, while shuddering to think how much more intense that spasm would have been were I not already numbed by the medichines.

We had made it back through perhaps one third of the rooms when he slithered from her grip, thudding to the floor.

'What are you doing?' Celestine asked.

'What do you think?' He supported himself by his forelimbs, his severed trunk resting against the ground. The wound had begun to close, I saw, his diamond skin puckering tight to seal the damage.

Before very long he would look as if he had been made this way.

Celestine took her time before answering, 'Quite honestly, I don't know what to think.'

'I'm going back. I'm carrying on.'

Still propping myself against a wall, I said, 'You can't. You need treatment. For God's sake; you've been cut in half.'

'It doesn't matter,' Childe said. 'All I've done is lose a part of me I would have been forced to discard before very long. Eventually the doors would have been a tight squeeze even for something shaped like a dog.'

'It'll kill you,' I said.

'Or I'll beat it. It's still possible, you know.' He turned around, his rear part scraping against the floor, and then looked back over his shoulder. 'I'm going to retrace my steps back to the room where this happened. I don't think the Spire will obstruct your retreat until I step – or crawl, as it may be – into the last room we opened. But if I were you, I wouldn't take too long on the way back.' Then he looked at me, and again switched on the private frequency. 'It's not too late, Richard. You can still come back with me.'

'No,' I said. 'You're wrong. It's much too late.'

Celestine reached out to help me make my awkward way to the next door. 'Leave him, Richard. Leave him to the Spire. It's what he's always wanted, and he's had his witnesses now.'

Childe eased himself onto the lip of the door leading into the room we had just come through.

'Well?' he said.

'She's right. Whatever happens now, it's between you and the Spire. I suppose I should wish you the best of luck, except it would sound irredeemably trite.'

He shrugged; one of the few human gestures now available to him. 'I'll take whatever I can get. And I assure you that we *will* meet again, whether you like it or not.'

'I hope so,' I said, while knowing it would never be the case. 'In the meantime, I'll give your regards to Chasm City.'

'Do that, please. Just don't be too specific about where I went.'

'I promise you that. Roland?'

'Yes?'

'I think I should say goodbye now.'

Childe turned around and slithered into the darkness, propelling himself with quick, piston-like movements of his forearms.

Then Celestine took my arm and helped me towards the exit.

124

thirteen

'You were right,' I told her as we made our way back to the shuttle. 'I think I would have followed him.'

Celestine smiled. 'But I'm glad you didn't.'

'Do you mind if I ask something?'

'As long as it isn't to do with mathematics.'

'Why did you care what happened to me, and not Childe?'

'I did care about Childe,' she said firmly. 'But I didn't think any of us were going to be able to persuade him to turn back.'

'And that was the only reason?'

'No. I also thought you deserved something better than to be killed by the Spire.'

'You risked your life to get me out,' I said. 'I'm not ungrateful.'

'Not ungrateful? Is that your idea of an expression of gratitude?' But she was smiling, and I felt a faint impulse to smile as well. 'Well, at least that sounds like the old Richard.'

'There's hope for me yet, then. Trintignant can put me back the way I should be, after he's done with you.'

But when we got back to the shuttle there was no sign of Doctor Trintignant. We searched for him, but found nothing; not even a set of tracks leading away. None of the remaining suits were missing, and when we contacted the orbiting ship they had no knowledge of the Doctor's whereabouts.

Then we found him.

He had placed himself on his operating couch, beneath the loom of swift, beautiful surgical machinery. And the machines had dismantled him, separating him into his constituent components, placing some pieces of him in neatly labelled fluid-filled flasks and others in vials. Chunks of eviscerated bio-machinery floated like stinger-laden jellyfish. Implants and mechanisms glittered like small, precisely jewelled ornaments.

There was surprisingly little in the way of organic matter.

'He killed himself,' Celestine said. Then she found his hat – the Homburg – which he had placed at the head of the operating couch. Inside, tightly folded and marked in precise hand-writing, was what amounted to Trintignant's suicide note.

My dear friends, he had written.

After giving the matter no little consideration, I have decided to dispose of myself. I find the prospect of my own dismantling a more palatable one than continuing to endure revulsion for a crime I do not believe I committed. Please do not attempt to put me back together; the endeavour would, I assure you, be quite futile. I trust however that the manner of my demise – and the annotated state to which I have reduced myself – will provide some small amusement to future scholars of cybernetics.

I must confess that there is another reason why I have chosen to bring about this somewhat terminal state of affairs. Why, after all, did I not end myself on Yellowstone?

The answer, I am afraid, lies as much in vanity as anything else.

Thanks to the Spire – and to the good offices of Mister Childe – I have been given the opportunity to continue the work that was so abruptly terminated by the unpleasantness in Chasm City. And thanks to yourselves – who were so keen to learn the Spire's secrets – I have been gifted with subjects willing to submit to some of my less orthodox procedures.

You in particular, Mister Swift, have been a Godsend. I

consider the series of transformations I have wrought upon you to be my finest achievement to date. You have become my magnum opus. I fully accept that you saw the surgery merely as a means to an end, and that you would not otherwise have consented to my ministrations, but that in no way lessens the magnificence of what you have become.

And therein, I am afraid, lies the problem.

Whether you conquer the Spire or retreat from it – assuming, of course, that it does not kill you – there will surely come a time when you will desire to return to your prior form. And that would mean that I would be compelled to undo my single greatest work.

Something I would rather die than do.

I offer my apologies, such as they are, while remaining –

Your obedient servant,

T

Childe never returned. After ten days we searched the area about the Spire's base, but there were no remains that had not been there before. I supposed that there was nothing for it but to assume that he was still inside; still working his way to whatever lay at the summit.

And I wondered.

What ultimate function did the Spire serve? Was it possible that it served none but its own self-preservation? Perhaps it simply lured the curious into it, and forced them to adapt – becoming more like machines themselves – until they reached the point when they were of use to it.

At which point it harvested them.

Was it possible that the Spire was no more purposeful than a flytrap?

I had no answers. And I did not want to remain on Golgotha pondering such things. I did not trust myself not to return to the Spire. I still felt its feral pull.

So we left.

'Promise me,' Celestine said.

'What?'

'That whatever happens when we get home – whatever's become of the city – you won't go back to the Spire.'

'I won't go back,' I said. 'And I promise you that. I can even have the memory of it suppressed, so it doesn't haunt my dreams.'

'Why not,' she said. 'You've done it before, after all.'

But when we returned to Chasm City we found that Childe had not been lying. Things had changed, but not for the better. The thing that they called the Melding Plague had plunged our city back into a festering, technologically-decadent dark age. The wealth we had accrued on Childe's expedition meant nothing now, and what small influence my family had possessed before the crisis had diminished even further.

In better days, Trintignant's work could probably have been undone. It would not have been simple, but there were those who relished such a challenge, and I would probably have had to fight off several competing offers: rival cyberneticists vying for the prestige of tackling such a difficult project. Things were different. Even the crudest kinds of surgery were now difficult or impossibly expensive. Only a handful of specialists retained the means to even attempt such work, and they were free to charge whatever they liked.

Even Celestine, who had been wealthier than me, could only afford to have me repaired, not rectified. That – and the other matter – almost bankrupted us.

And yet she cared for me.

There were those who saw us and imagined that the creature with her – the thing that trotted by her like a stiff, diamond-skinned, grotesque mechanical dog – was merely a strange choice of pet. Sometimes they sensed something unusual in our relationship – the way she might whisper an aside to me, or the way I might appear to be leading her – and they would look at me, intently, before I stared into their eyes with the blinding red scrutiny of my vision.

Then they would always look away.

And for a long time – until the dreams became too much – that was how it was.

Yet now I pad into the night, Celestine unaware that I have left our apartment. Outside, dangerous gangs infiltrate the shadowed, half-flooded streets. They call this part of Chasm City the Mulch and it is the only place where we can afford to live now. Certainly we could have afforded something better – something much better – if I had not been forced to put aside money in readiness for this day. But Celestine knows nothing of that.

The Mulch is not as bad as it used to be, but it would still have struck the earlier me as a vile place in which to exist. Even now I am instinctively wary, my enhanced eyes dwelling on the various crudely fashioned blades and crossbows that the gangs flaunt. Not all of the creatures who haunt the night are technically human. There are things with gills that can barely breathe in open air. There are other things that resemble pigs, and they are the worst of all.

But I do not fear them.

I slink between shadows, my thin, doglike form confusing them. I squeeze through the gaps in collapsed buildings, effortlessly escaping the few who are foolish enough to chase me. Now and then I even stop and confront them, standing with my back arched.

My red gaze stabs through them.

I continue on my way.

Presently I reach the appointed area. At first it looks deserted – there are no gangs here – but then a figure emerges from the gloom, trudging through ankle-deep caramel-brown flood-water. The figure is thin and dark, and with each step it makes there is a small, precise whine. It comes into view and I observe that the woman – for it is a woman, I think – is wearing an exoskeleton. Her skin is the black of interstellar space, and her small, exquisitely featured head is perched above a neck which has been extended by several vertebrae. She wears copper rings around her neck, and her fingernails – which I see clicking against the thighs of her exoskeleton – are as long as stilettos.

I think she is strange, but she sees me and flinches.

'Are you . . . ?' she starts to say.

'I am Richard Swift,' I answer.

She nods almost imperceptibly – it cannot be easy, bending that neck – and introduces herself. 'I am Triumvir Verika Abebi, of the lighthugger *Poseidon*. I sincerely hope you are not wasting my time.'

'I can pay you, don't you worry.'

She looks at me with something between pity and awe. 'You haven't even told me what it is you want.'

'That's easy,' I say. 'I want you to take me somewhere.'

Turquoise Days

'Set sail in those Turquoise Days'

Echo and the Bunnymen

one

Naqi Okpik waited until her sister was safely asleep before she stepped onto the railed balcony that circled the gondola.

It was the most perfectly warm and still summer night in months. Even the breeze caused by the airship's motion was warmer than usual, as soft against her cheek as the breath of an attentive lover. Above, yet hidden by the black curve of the vacuum-bag, the two moons were nearly at their fullest. Microscopic creatures sparkled a hundred metres under the airship, great schools of them daubing galaxies against the profound black of the sea. Spirals, flukes and arms of luminescence wheeled and coiled as if in thrall to secret music.

Naqi looked to the rear, where the airship's ceramic-jacketed sensor pod carved a twinkling furrow. Pinks and rubies and furious greens sparkled in the wake. Occasionally they darted from point to point with the nervous motion of kingfishers. As ever, she was alert to anything unusual in movements of the messenger sprites, anything that might merit a note in the latest circular, or even a full-blown article in one of the major journals of Juggler studies. But there was nothing odd happening tonight, no yet-to-be catalogued forms or behaviour patterns, nothing that might indicate more significant Pattern Juggler activity.

She walked around the airship's balcony until she had reached the stern, where the submersible sensor pod was tethered by a long fibre-optic dragline. Naqi pulled a long hinged stick from her pocket, flicked it open in the manner of a courtesan's fan and then waved it close to the winch assembly. The default watercoloured lilies and sea serpents melted away, replaced by tables of numbers, sinuous graphs and trembling histograms. A glance established that there was nothing surprising here either, but the data would still form a useful calibration set for other experiments.

As she closed the fan – delicately, for it was worth almost as much as the airship itself – Naqi reminded herself that it was a day since she had gathered the last batch of incoming messages. Rot had taken out the connection between the antenna and the gondola during the last expedition, and since then collecting the messages had become a chore, to be taken in turns or traded for less tedious tasks.

Naqi gripped a handrail and swung out behind the airship. Here the vacuum-bag overhung the gondola by only a metre, and a grilled ladder allowed her to climb around the overhang and scramble onto the flat top of the bag. She moved gingerly, bare feet against rusting rungs, doing her best not to disturb Mina. The airship rocked and creaked a little as she found her balance on the top and then was again silent and still. The churning of its motors was so quiet that Naqi had long ago filtered the sound from her experience.

All was calm, beautifully so.

In the moonlight the antenna was a single dark flower rising from the broad back of the bladder. Naqi started moving along the railed catwalk that led to it, steadying herself as she went but feeling much less vertigo than would have been the case in daylight.

Then she froze, certain that she was being watched.

Just within Naqi's peripheral vision appeared a messenger sprite. It had flown to the height of the airship and was now shadowing it from a distance of ten or twelve metres. Naqi gasped, delighted and unnerved at the same time. Apart from dead specimens this was the first time Naqi had ever seen a sprite this close. The organism had the approximate size and morphology of a terrestrial hummingbird, yet it glowed like a lantern. Naqi recognised it immediately as a long-range packet carrier. Its belly would be stuffed with data coded into tightly packed wads of RNA, locked within microscopic protein capsomeres. The packet carrier's head was a smooth teardrop, patterned with luminous pastel markings, but lacking any other detail save for two black eyes positioned above the midline. Inside the head was a cluster of neurones, which encoded the positions of the brightest circumpolar stars. Other than that, sprites had only the most rudimentary kind of intelligence. They existed to shift information between nodal points in the ocean when the usual chemical signalling pathways were deemed too slow or imprecise. The sprite would die when it reached its destination, consumed by microscopic organisms that would unravel and process the information stored in the capsomeres.

And yet Naqi had the acute impression that it was watching her: not just the airship, but *her*, with a kind of watchful curiosity that made the hairs on the back of her neck bristle. And then – just at the point when the feeling of scrutiny had become unsettling – the sprite whipped sharply away from the airship. Naqi watched it descend back towards the ocean and then coast above the surface, bobbing now and then like a skipping stone. She remained still for several more minutes, convinced that something of significance had happened, though aware too of how subjective the experience had been; how unimpressive it would seem if she tried to explain it to Mina tomorrow. Anyway, Mina was the one with the special bond with the ocean, wasn't she? Mina was the one who scratched her arms at night; Mina was the one who had too high a conformal index to be allowed into the swimmer corps. It was always Mina.

It was never Naqi.

The antenna's metre-wide dish was anchored to a squat plinth inset with weatherproofed controls and readouts. It was century-old *Pelican* technology, like the airship and the fan. Many of the controls and displays were dead, but the unit was still able to lock onto the functioning satellites. Naqi flicked open the fan and copied the latest feeds into the fan's remaining memory. Then she knelt down next to the plinth, propped the fan on her knees and sifted through the messages and news summaries of the last day. A handful of reports had arrived from friends in Prachuap-Pangnirtung and Umingmaktok snowflake cities, another from an old boyfriend in the swimmer corps station on Narathiwat atoll. He had sent her a list of jokes that were already in wide circulation. She scrolled down the list, grimacing more than grinning, before finally managing a half-hearted chuckle at one that had previously escaped her. Then there were a dozen digests from various special interest groups related to the Jugglers, along with a request from a journal editor that she critique a paper. Naqi skimmed the paper's abstract and thought that she was probably capable of reviewing it.

She checked through the remaining messages. There was a note from Dr Sivaraksa saying that her formal application to work on the Moat project had been received and was now under consideration. There had been no official interview, but Naqi had met Sivaraksa a few weeks earlier when both of them happened to be in Umingmaktok. Sivaraksa had been in an encouraging mood during the meeting, though Naqi couldn't say whether that was because she'd given a good impression or because Sivaraksa had just had his tapeworm swapped for a nice new one. But Sivaraksa's message said she could expect to hear the result in a day or two. Naqi wondered idly how she would break the news to Mina if she was offered the job. Mina was critical of the whole idea of the Moat and would probably take a dim view of her sister having anything to do with it.

Scrolling down further, she read another message from a scientist in Qaanaaq requesting access to some calibration data she had obtained earlier in the summer. Then there were four or five automatic weather advisories, drafts of two papers she was contributing to, and an invitation to attend the amicable divorce of Kugluktuk and Gjoa, scheduled to take place in three weeks' time. Following that there was a summary of the latest worldwide news – an unusually bulky file – and then there was nothing. No further messages had arrived for eight hours.

There was nothing particularly unusual about that – the ailing network was always going down – but for the second time that night the back of Naqi's neck tingled. Something *must* have happened, she thought.

She opened the news summary and started reading. Five minutes later she was waking Mina.

'I don't think I want to believe it,' Mina Okpik said.

Naqi scanned the heavens, dredging childhood knowledge of the stars. With some minor adjustment to allow for parallax, the old constellations were still more or less valid when seen from Turquoise.

'That's it, I think.'

'What?' Mina said, still sleepy.

Naqi waved her hand at a vague area of the sky, pinned between Scorpius and Hercules. 'Ophiuchus. If our eyes were sensitive enough, we'd be able to see it now: a little prick of blue light.'

'I've had enough of little pricks for one lifetime,' Mina said, tucking her arms around her knees. Her hair was the same pure black as Naqi's, but trimmed into a severe, spiked crop which made her look younger or older depending on the light. She wore black shorts and a shirt that left her arms bare. Luminous tattoos in emerald and indigo spiralled around the piebald marks of random fungal invasion that covered her arms, thighs, neck and cheeks. The fullness of the moons caused the fungal patterns to glow a little themselves, shimmering with the same emerald and indigo hues. Naqi had no tattoos and scarcely any fungal patterns of her own; she couldn't help but feel slightly envious of her sister's adornments.

Mina continued, 'But seriously, you don't think it might be a mistake?'

'I don't think so, no. See what it says there? They detected it weeks ago, but they kept quiet until now so that they could make more measurements.'

'I'm surprised there wasn't a rumour.'

Naqi nodded. 'They kept the lid on it pretty well. Which doesn't mean there isn't going to be a lot of trouble.'

'Mm. And they think this blackout is going to help?'

'My guess is official traffic's still getting through. They just don't want the rest of us clogging up the network with endless speculation.'

'Can't blame us for that, can we? I mean, everyone's going to be guessing, aren't they?'

'Maybe they'll announce themselves before very long,' Naqi said doubtfully.

While they had been speaking the airship had passed into a zone of the sea largely devoid of bioluminescent surface life. Such zones were almost as common as the nodal regions where the network was thickest, like the gaping voids between clusters of galaxies. The wake of the sensor pod was almost impossible to pick out, and the darkness around them was absolute, relieved only by the occasional mindless errand of a solitary messenger sprite.

Mina said: 'And if they don't?'

'Then I guess we're all in a lot more trouble than we'd like.'

For the first time in a century a ship was approaching Turquoise, commencing its deceleration from interstellar cruise speed. The flare of the lighthugger's exhaust was pointed straight at the Turquoise system. Measurement of the Doppler shift of the flame showed that the vessel was still two years out, but that was hardly any time at all on Turquoise. The ship had yet to announce itself, but even if it turned out to have nothing but benign intentions – a short trade stopover, perhaps – the effect on Turquoise society would be incalculable. Everyone knew of the troubles that had followed the arrival of *Pelican in Impiety*. When the Ultras moved into orbit there had been much unrest below. Spies had undermined lucrative trade deals. Cities had jockeyed for prestige, competing for technological tidbits. There had been hasty marriages and equally hasty separations. A century later, old enmities smouldered just beneath the surface of cordial intercity politics.

It wouldn't be any better this time.

'Look,' Mina said, 'it doesn't have to be all that bad. They might not even want to talk to us. Didn't a ship pass through the system about seventy years ago without so much as a by-your-leave?'

Naqi agreed; it was mentioned in a sidebar to one of the main articles. 'They had engine trouble, or something. But the experts say there's no sign of anything like that this time.'

'So they've come to trade. What have we got to offer them that we didn't have last time?'

'Not much, I suppose.'

Mina nodded knowingly. 'A few works of art that probably won't travel very well. Ten-hour-long nose-flute symphonies, anyone?' She pulled a face. 'That's supposedly my culture, and even I can't stand it. What else? A handful of discoveries about the Jugglers, which have more than likely been replicated else-where a dozen times. Technology, medicine? Forget it.'

'They must think we have something worth coming here for,' Naqi said. 'Whatever it is, we'll just have to wait and see, won't we? It's only two years.'

'I expect you think that's quite a long time,' Mina said.

'Actually—'

Mina froze.

'Look!'

Something whipped past in the night, far below, then a handful of them, then a dozen, and then a whole bright squadron. Messenger sprites, Naqi realised – but she had never seen so many of them moving at once, and on what was so evidently the same errand. Against the darkness of the ocean the lights were mesmerising: curling and weaving, swapping positions and occasionally veering far from the main pack before arcing back towards the swarm. Once again one of the sprites climbed to the altitude of the airship, loitering for a few moments on fanning wings before whipping off to rejoin the others. The swarm receded, becoming a tight ball of fireflies, and then only a pale globular smudge. Naqi watched until she was certain that the last sprite had vanished into the night.

'Wow,' Mina said quietly.

'Have you ever seen anything like that?'

'Never.'

'Bit funny that it should happen tonight, wouldn't you say?'

'Don't be silly,' Mina said. 'The Jugglers can't possibly know about the ship.'

'We don't know that for sure. Most people heard about this ship hours ago. That's more than enough time for someone to have swum.'

Mina conceded her younger sister's point. 'Still, information flow isn't usually that clear-cut. The Jugglers store patterns, but they seldom show any sign of comprehending actual content. We're dealing with a mindless biological archiving system, a museum without a curator.'

'That's one view.'

Mina shrugged. 'I'd love to be proved otherwise.'

'Well, do you think we should try following them? I know we

can't track sprites over any distance, but we might be able to keep up for a few hours before we drain the batteries.'

'We wouldn't learn much.'

'We won't know until we've tried,' Naqi said, gritting her teeth. 'Come on – it's got to be worth a go, hasn't it? I reckon that swarm moved a bit slower than a single sprite. We'd at least have enough for a report, wouldn't we?'

Mina shook her head. 'All we'd have is a single observation with a little bit of speculation thrown in. You know we can't publish that sort of thing. And anyway, assuming that sprite swarm did have something to do with the ship, there are going to be hundreds of similar sightings tonight.'

'I just thought it might take our minds off the news.'

'Perhaps it would. But it would also make us unforgivably late for our target.' Mina dropped the tone of her voice, making an obvious effort to sound reasonable. 'Look, I understand your curiosity. I feel it as well. But the chances are it was either a statistical fluke or part of a global event everyone else will have had a much better chance to study. Either way we can't contribute anything useful, so we might as well just forget about it.' She rubbed at the marks on her forearm, tracing the Paisley-patterned barbs and whorls of glowing colouration. 'And I'm tired, and we have several busy days ahead of us. I think we just need to put this one down to experience, all right?'

'Fine,' Naqi said.

'I'm sorry, but I just know we'd be wasting our time.'

'I said fine.' Naqi stood up and steadied herself on the railing that traversed the length of the airship's back.

'Where are you going?'

'To sleep. Like you said, we've got a busy day coming up. We'd be fools to waste time chasing a fluke, wouldn't we?'

An hour after dawn they crossed out of the dead zone. The sea below began to thicken with floating life, becoming soupy and torpid. A kilometre or so further in and the soup showed ominous signs of structure: a blue-green stew of ropy strands and wide, kelplike plates. They suggested the floating, half-digested entrails of embattled sea monsters.

Within another kilometre the floating life had become a dense vegetative raft, stinking of brine and rotting cabbage. Within another kilometre of that the raft had thickened to the point where the underlying sea was only intermittently visible. The air above the raft was humid, hot and pungent with microscopic irritants. The raft itself was possessed of a curiously beguiling motion, bobbing and writhing and gyring according to the ebb and flow of weirdly localised current systems. It was as if many invisible spoons were stirring a great bowl of spinach. Even the shadow of the airship, pushed far ahead of it by the low sun, had some influence on the movement of the material. The Pattern Juggler biomass scurried and squirmed to evade the track of the shadow, and the peculiar purposefulness of the motion reminded Naqi of an octopus she had seen in the terrestrial habitats aquarium on Umingmaktok, squeezing its way through impossibly small gaps in the glass prison of its tank.

Presently they arrived at the precise centre of the circular raft. It spread away from them in all directions, hemmed by a distant ribbon of sparkling sea. It felt as if the airship had come to rest above an island, as fixed and ancient as any geological feature. The island even had a sort of geography: humps and ridges and depressions sculpted into the cloying texture of layered biomass. But there were few islands on Turquoise, especially at this latitude, and the Juggler node was only a few days old. Satellites had detected its growth a week earlier, and Mina and Naqi had been sent to investigate. They were under strict instructions simply to hover above the island and deploy a handful of tethered sensors. If the node showed any signs of being unusual, a more experienced team would be sent out from Umingmaktok by high-speed dirigible. Most nodes dispersed within twenty to thirty days, so there was always a need for some urgency. They might even send trained swimmers, eager to dive into the sea and open their minds to alien communion. Ready – as they called it – to *ken* the ocean.

But first things first: chances were this node would turn out to be interesting rather than exceptional.

'Morning,' Mina said when Naqi approached her. Mina was swabbing the sensor pod she had reeled in earlier, collecting the green mucus that had adhered to its ceramic teardrop. All human artefacts eventually succumbed to biological attack from the ocean, although ceramics were the most resilient.

'You're cheerful,' Naqi said, trying to make the statement sound matter-of-fact rather than judgmental.

'Aren't you? It's not everyone gets a chance to study a node up this close. Make the most of it, sis. The news we got last night doesn't change what we have to do today.'

Naqi scraped the back of her hand across her nose. Now that the airship was above the node she was breathing vast numbers of aerial organisms into her lungs with each breath. The smell was redolent of ammonia and decomposing vegetation. It required an intense effort of will not to keep rubbing her eyes rawer than they already were. 'Do you see anything unusual?'

'Bit early to say.'

'So that's a "no", then.'

'You can't learn much without probes, Naqi.' Mina dipped a swab into a collection bag, squeezing tight the plastic seal. Then she dropped the bag into a bucket between her feet. 'Oh, wait. I saw another of those swarms, after you'd gone to sleep.'

'I thought you were the one complaining about being tired.'

Mina dug out a fresh swab and rubbed vigorously at a deep olive smear on the side of the sensor. 'I picked up my messages, that's all. Tried again this morning, but the blackout still hasn't been lifted. I picked up a few short-wave radio signals from the closest cities, but they were just transmitting a recorded message from the Snowflake Council: stay tuned and don't panic.'

'So let's hope we don't find anything significant here,' Naqi said, 'because we won't be able to report it if we do.'

'They're bound to lift the blackout soon. In the meantime I think we have enough measurements to keep us busy. Did you find that spiral sweep programme in the airship's avionics box?'

'I haven't looked for it,' Naqi said, certain that Mina had never mentioned such a thing before. 'But I'm sure I can programme something from scratch in a few minutes.'

'Well, let's not waste any more time than necessary. Here.' Smiling, she offered Naqi the swab, its tip laden with green slime. 'You take over this and I'll go and dig out the programme.'

Naqi took the swab after a moment's delay.

'Of course. Prioritise tasks according to ability, right?'

'That's not what I meant,' Mina said soothingly. 'Look, let's not argue, shall we? We were best friends until last night. I just thought it would be quicker . . .' She trailed off and shrugged. 'You know what I mean. I know you blame me for not letting us follow the sprites, but we had no choice but to come here. Understand that, will you? Under any other circumstances—'

'I understand,' Naqi said, realising as she did how sullen and childlike she sounded; how much she was playing the petulant younger sister. The worst of it was that she knew Mina was right. At dawn it all looked much clearer.

'Do you? Really?'

Naqi nodded, feeling the perverse euphoria that came with an admission of defeat. 'Yes. Really. We'd have been wrong to chase them.'

Mina sighed. 'I was tempted, you know. I just didn't want you to see how tempted I was, or else you'd have found a way to convince me.'

'I'm that persuasive?'

144

'Don't underestimate yourself, sis. I know I never would.' Mina paused and took back the swab. 'I'll finish this. Can you handle the sweep programme?'

Naqi smiled. She felt better now. The tension between them would still take a little while to dissipate, but at least things were easier now. Mina was right about something else: they were best friends, not just sisters.

'I'll handle it,' Naqi said.

Naqi stepped through the hermetic curtain into the air-conditioned cool of the gondola. She closed the door, rubbed her eyes and then sat down at the navigator's station. The airship had flown itself automatically from Umingmaktok, adjusting its course to take cunning advantage of jet streams and weather fronts. Now it was in hovering mode: once or twice a minute the electrically driven motors purred, stabilising the craft against gusts of wind generated by the microclimate above the Juggler node. Naqi called up the current avionics programme, a menu of options appearing on a flat screen. The options quivered; Naqi thumped the screen with the back of her hand until the display behaved itself. Then she scrolled down through the other flight sequences, but there was no preprogramme spiral loaded into the current avionics suite. Naqi rummaged around in the background files, but there was nothing to help her there either. She was about to start hacking something together – at a push it would take her half an hour to assemble a routine – when she remembered that she had once backed up some earlier avionics files onto the fan. She had no idea if they were still there, or even if there was anything useful amongst the cache, but it was probably worth taking the time to find out. The fan lay closed on a bench; Mina must have left it there after she had verified that the blackout was still in force.

Naqi grabbed the fan and spread it open across her lap. To her surprise, it was still active: instead of the usual watercolour patterns the display showed the messages she had been scrolling through earlier.

She looked closer and frowned. These were not her messages at all. She was looking at the messages Mina had copied onto the fan during the night. Naqi felt an immediate prickle of guilt: she should snap the fan shut, or at the very least close her sister's mail and move into her own area of the fan. But she did neither of those things. Telling herself that it was only what anyone else would have done, she accessed the final message in the list and examined its incoming time-stamp. To within a few minutes, it had arrived at the same time as the final message Naqi had received.

Mina had been telling the truth when she said that the blackout was continuing.

Naqi glanced up. Through the window of the gondola she could see the back of her sister's head, bobbing up and down as she checked winches along the side.

Naqi looked at the body of the message. It was nothing remarkable, just an automated circular from one of the Juggler special-interest groups. Something about neurotransmitter chemistry.

She exited the circular, getting back to the list of incoming messages. She told herself that she had done nothing shameful so far. If she closed Mina's mail now, she would have nothing to feel really guilty about.

But a name she recognised jumped out at her from the list of messages: Dr Jotah Sivaraksa, manager of the Moat project. The man she had met in Umingmaktok, glowing with renewed vitality after his yearly worm change. What could Mina possibly want with Sivaraksa?

She opened the message, read it.

It was exactly what she had feared, and yet not dared to believe.

Sivaraksa was responding to Mina's request to work on the

Moat. The tone of the message was conversational, in stark contrast to the businesslike response Naqi had received. Sivaraksa informed her sister that her request had been appraised favourably, and that while there were still one or two other candidates to be considered, Mina had so far emerged as the most convincing applicant. Even if this turned out not to be the case, Sivaraksa continued – and that was not very likely – Mina's name would be at the top of the list when further vacancies became available. In short, she was more or less guaranteed a chance to work on the Moat within the year.

Naqi read the message again, just in case there was some highly subtle detail that threw the entire thing into a different, more benign light.

Then she snapped shut the fan with a sense of profound fury. She placed it back where it was, exactly as it had been.

Mina pushed her head through the hermetic curtain.

'How's it coming along?'

'Fine,' Naqi said. Her voice sounded drained of emotion even to herself. She felt stunned and mute. Mina would call her a hypocrite were she to object to her sister having applied for exactly the same job she had . . . but there was more to it than that. Naqi had never been as openly critical of the Moat project as her sister. By contrast, Mina had never missed a chance to denounce both the project and the personalities behind it.

Now that was real hypocrisy.

'Got that routine cobbled together?'

'Coming along,' Naqi said.

'Something the matter?'

'No,' Naqi forced a smile, 'no. Just working through the details. Have it ready in a few minutes.'

'Good. Can't wait to start the sweep. We're going to get some beautiful data, sis. And I think this is going to be a significant node. Maybe the largest this season. Aren't you glad it came our way?'

'Thrilled,' Naqi said, before returning to her work.

Thirty specialised probes hung on telemetric cables from the underside of the gondola, dangling like the venom-tipped stingers of some grotesque aerial jellyfish. The probes sniffed the air metres above the Juggler biomass, or skimmed the fuzzy green surface of the formation. Weighted plumb lines penetrated to the sea beneath the raft, sipping the organism-infested depths dozens of metres under the node. Radar mapped larger structures embedded within the node – dense kernels of compacted biomass, or huge cavities and tubes of inscrutable function – while sonar graphed the topology of the many sinewy organic cables which plunged into darkness, umbilicals anchoring the node to the seabed. Smaller nodes drew most of their energy from sunlight and the breakdown of sugars and fats in the sea's other floating micro-organisms but the larger formations, which had a vastly higher information-processing burden, needed to tap belching aquatic fissures, active rifts in the ocean bed kilometres under the waves. Cold water was pumped down each umbilical by peristaltic compression waves, heated by being circulated in the superheated thermal environment of the underwater volcanoes, and then pumped back to the surface.

In all this sensing activity, remarkably little physical harm was done to the extended organism itself. The biomass sensed the approach of the probes and rearranged itself so that they passed through with little obstruction, even those scything lines that reached into the water. Energy was obviously being consumed to avoid the organism sustaining damage, and by implication the measurements must therefore have had some effect on the node's information-processing efficiency. The effect was likely to be small, however, and since the node was already subject to constant changes in its architecture – some probably intentional, and some probably forced on it by other factors in its environment – there appeared to be little point in worrying about the harm caused by the human investigators. Ultimately, so much was still guesswork. Although the swimmer teams had learned a great deal about the Pattern Jugglers' encoded information, almost everything else about them – how and why they stored the neural patterns, and to what extent the patterns were subject to subsequent postprocessing – remained unknown. And those were merely the immediate questions. Beyond that were the real mysteries, which everyone wanted to solve, but right now they were simply beyond the scope of possible academic study. What they would learn today could not be expected to shed any light on those profundities. A single data point – even a single clutch of measurements – could not usually prove or disprove anything, but it might later turn out to play a vital role in a chain of argument, even if it was only in the biasing of some statistical distribution closer to one hypothesis than another. Science, as Naqi had long since realised, was as much a swarming, social process as it was something driven by ecstatic moments of personal discovery.

It was something she was proud to be part of.

The spiral sweep continued uneventfully, the airship chugging around in a gently widening circle. Morning shifted to early afternoon, and then the sun began to climb down towards the horizon, bleeding pale orange into the sky through soft-edged cracks in the cloud cover. For hours Naqi and Mina studied the incoming results, the ever-sharper scans of the node appearing on screens throughout the gondola. They discussed the results cordially enough, but Naqi could not stop thinking about Mina's betrayal. She took a spiteful pleasure in testing the extent to which her sister would lie, deliberately forcing the conversation around to Dr Sivaraksa and the project he steered.

'I hope I don't end up like one of those deadwood bureaucrats,' Naqi said, when they were discussing the way their careers might evolve. 'You know, like Sivaraksa.' She observed Mina

149

pointedly, yet giving nothing away. 'I read some of his old papers; he used to be pretty good once. But now look at him.'

'It's easy to say that,' Mina said, 'but I bet he doesn't like being away from the front line any more than we would. But someone has to manage these big projects. Wouldn't you rather it was someone who'd at least *been* a scientist?'

'You sound like you're defending him. Next you'll be telling me you think the Moat is a good idea.'

'I'm not defending Sivaraksa,' Mina said. 'I'm just saying—' She eyed her sister with a sudden glimmer of suspicion. Had she guessed that Naqi knew? 'Never mind. Sivaraksa can fight his own battles. We've got work to do.'

'Anyone would think you were changing the subject,' Naqi said. But Mina was already on her way out of the gondola to check the equipment again.

At dusk the airship arrived at the perimeter of the node, completed one orbit, then began to track inwards again. As it passed over the parts of the node previously mapped, time-dependent changes were highlighted on the displays: arcs and bands of red superimposed against the lime and turquoise false-colour of the mapped structures. Most of the alterations were minor: a chamber opening here or closing there, or a small alteration in the network topology to ease a bottleneck between the lumpy subnodes dotted around the floating island. Other changes were more mysterious in function, but conformed to other studies. They were studied at enhanced resolution, the data prioritised and logged.

It looked as if the node was large, but in no way unusual.

Then night came, as swiftly as it always did at those latitudes. Mina and Naqi took turns, one sleeping for two- or three-hour stretches while the other kept an eye on the readouts. During a lull Naqi climbed up onto the top of the airship and tried the antenna again, and for a moment was gladdened when she saw that a new message had arrived. But the message itself turned out to be a statement from the Snowflake Council stating that the blackout on civilian messages would continue for at least another two days, until the current 'crisis' was over. There were allusions to civil disturbances in two cities, with curfews being imposed, and imperatives to ignore all unofficial news sources concerning the nature of the approaching ship.

Naqi wasn't surprised that there was trouble, though the extent of it took her aback. Her instincts were to believe the government line. The problem, from the government's point of view at least, was that nothing was yet known for certain about the nature of the ship, and so by being truthful they ended up sounding like they were keeping something back. They would have been far better off making up a plausible lie, which could be gently moulded towards accuracy as time passed.

Mina rose after midnight to begin her shift. Naqi went to sleep and dreamed fitfully, seeing in her mind's eye red smears and bars hovering against amorphous green. She had been staring at the readouts too intently, for too many hours.

Mina woke her excitedly before dawn.

'Now I'm the one with the news,' she said.

'What?'

'Come and see for yourself.'

Naqi rose from her hammock, neither rested nor enthusiastic. In the dim light of the cabin Mina's fungal patterns shone with peculiar intensity: abstract detached shapes that only implied her presence.

Naqi followed the shapes onto the balcony.

'What,' she said again, not even bothering to make it sound like a question.

'There's been a development,' Mina said.

Naqi rubbed the sleep from her eyes. 'With the node?'

'Look. Down below. Right under us.'

Naqi pressed her stomach hard against the railing and leaned over as far as she dared. She had felt no real vertigo until they had lowered the sensor lines, and then suddenly there had been a physical connection between the airship and the ground. Was it her imagination, or had the airship lowered itself to about half its previous altitude, reeling in the lines at the same time?

The midnight light was all spectral shades of milky grey. The creased and crumpled landscape of the node reached away into mid-grey gloom, merging with the slate of the overlying cloud deck. Naqi saw nothing remarkable, other than the surprising closeness of the surface.

'I mean *really* look down,' Mina said.

Naqi pushed herself against the railing more than she had dared before, until she was standing on the very tips of her toes. Only then did she see it: directly below them was a peculiar circle of darkness, almost as if the airship was casting a distinct shadow beneath itself. It was a circular zone of exposed seawater, like a lagoon enclosed by the greater mass of the node. Steep banks of Juggler biomass, its heart a deep charcoal grey, rimmed the lagoon. Naqi studied it quietly. Her sister would judge her on any remark she made.

'How did you see it?' she asked eventually.

'See it?'

'It can't be more than twenty metres wide. A dot like that would have hardly shown up on the topographic map.'

'Naqi, you don't understand. I didn't steer us over the hole. It appeared below us, as we were moving. Listen to the motors. We're *still* moving. The hole's shadowing us. It follows us precisely.'

'Must be reacting to the sensors,' Naqi said.

'I've hauled them in. We're not trailing anything within thirty metres of the surface. The node's reacting to us, Naqi – to the presence of the airship. The Jugglers know we're here, and they're sending us a signal.'

'Maybe they are. But it isn't our job to interpret that signal.

We're just here to make measurements, not to interact with the Jugglers.'

'So whose job is it?' Mina asked.

'Do I have to spell it out? Specialists from Umingmaktok.'

'They won't get here in time. You know how long nodes last. By the time the blackout's lifted, by the time the swimmer corps hotshots get here, we'll be sitting over a green smudge and not much more. This is a significant find, Naqi. It's the largest node this season and it's making a deliberate and clear attempt to invite swimmers.'

Naqi stepped back from the railing. 'Don't even think about it.'

'I've been thinking about it all night. This isn't just a large node, Naqi. Something's happening – that's why there's been so much sprite activity. If we don't swim here, we might miss something unique.'

'And if we do swim, we'll be violating every rule in the book. We're not trained, Mina. Even if we learned something – even if the Jugglers deigned to communicate with us – we'd be ostracised from the entire scientific community.'

'That would depend on what we learned, wouldn't it?'

'Don't do this, Mina. It isn't worth it.'

'We won't know if it's worth it or not until we try, will we?' Mina extended a hand. 'Look. You're right in one sense. Chances are pretty good nothing will happen. Normally you have to offer them a gift – a puzzle, or something rich in information. We haven't got anything like that. What'll probably happen is we'll hit the water and there won't be any kind of biochemical interaction. In which case, it doesn't matter. We don't have to tell anyone. And if we do learn something, but it isn't significant – well, we don't have to tell anyone about that either. Only if we learn something major. Something so big that they'll have to forget about a minor violation of protocol.'

'A minor violation—?' Naqi began, almost laughing at Mina's audacity.

'The point is, sis, we have a win-win situation here. And it's been handed to us on a plate.'

'You could also argue that we've been handed a major chance to fuck up spectacularly.'

'You read it whichever way you like. I know what I see.'

'It's too dangerous, Mina. People have died . . .' Naqi looked at Mina's fungal patterns, enhanced and emphasised by her tattoos. 'You flagged high for conformality. Doesn't that worry you slightly?'

'Conformality's just a fairy tale they use to scare children into behaving,' said Mina. ' "Eat all your greens or the sea will swallow you up forever." I take it about as seriously as I take the Thule kraken, or the drowning of Arviat.'

'The Thule kraken is a joke, and Arviat never existed in the first place. But the last time I checked, conformality was an accepted phenomenon.'

'It's an accepted research topic. There's a distinction.'

'Don't split hairs—' Naqi began.

Mina gave every indication of not having heard Naqi speak. Her voice was distant, as if she were speaking to herself. It had a lilting, singsong quality. 'Too late to even think about it now. But it isn't long until dawn. I think it'll still be there at dawn.'

She pushed past Naqi.

'Where are you going now?'

'To catch some sleep. I need to be fresh for this. So do you.'

They hit the lagoon with two gentle, anticlimactic splashes. Naqi was underwater for a moment before she bobbed to the surface, holding her breath. At first she had to make a conscious effort to start breathing again: the air immediately above the water was so saturated with microscopic organisms that choking was a real possibility. Mina, surfacing next to her, drew in gulps with wild enthusiasm, as if willing the tiny creatures to invade her lungs. She shrieked delight at the sudden cold. When they had both gained equilibrium, treading with their shoulders above water, Naqi was finally able to take stock. She saw everything through a stinging haze of tears. The gondola hovered above them, poised beneath the larger mass of the vacuum bladder. The life-raft that it had deployed was sparkling-new, rated for one hundred hours against moderate biological attack. But that was for mid-ocean, where the density of Juggler organisms would be much less than in the middle of a major node. Here, the hull might only endure a few tens of hours before it was consumed.

Once again, Naqi wondered if she should withdraw. There was still time. No real damage had yet been done. She could be back in the boat and back aboard the airship in a minute or so. Mina might not follow her, but she did not have to be complicit in her sister's actions. But Naqi knew she would not be able to turn back. She could not show weakness now that she had come this far.

'Nothing's happening . . .' she said.

'We've only been in the water a minute,' Mina said.

The two of them wore black wetsuits. The suits themselves could become buoyant if necessary – the right sequence of tactile commands and dozens of tiny bladders would inflate around the chest and shoulder area – but it was easy enough to tread water. In any case, if the Jugglers initiated contact, the suits would probably be eaten away in minutes. The swimmers who had made repeated contact often swam naked or near-naked, but neither Naqi nor Mina were yet prepared for that level of abject surrender to the ocean's assault. After another minute the water no longer felt as cold. Through gaps in the cloud cover the sun was harsh on Naqi's cheek. It etched furiously bright lines in the bottle-green surface of the lagoon, lines that coiled and shifted into fleeting calligraphic shapes as if conveying secret messages. The calm water lapped gently against their upper bodies. The walls of the lagoon were metre-high masses of fuzzy vegetation, like the steep banks of a river. Now and then Naqi felt something brush gently against her feet, like a passing frond or strand of seaweed. The first few times she flinched at the contact, but after a while it became strangely soothing. Occasionally something stroked one hand or the other, then moved playfully away. When she lifted her hands from the sea, mats of gossamer green draped from her fingers like the tattered remains of expensive gloves. The green material slithered free and slipped back into the sea. It tickled between her fingers.

'Nothing's happened yet,' Naqi said, more quietly this time.

'You're wrong. The shoreline's moved closer.'

Naqi looked at it. 'It's a trick of perspective.'

'I assure you it isn't.'

Naqi looked back at the raft. They had drifted five or six metres from it. It might as well have been a mile, for all the sense of security that the raft now offered. Mina was right: the lagoon was closing in on them, gently, slowly. If the lagoon had been twenty metres wide when they had entered, it must now be a third smaller. There was still time to escape before the hazy green walls squeezed in on them, but only if they moved now, back to the raft, back into the safety of the gondola.

'Mina . . . I want to go. We're not ready for this.'

'We don't need to be ready. It's going to happen.'

'We're not trained!'

'Call it learning on the job, in that case.' Mina was still trying to sound outrageously calm, but it wasn't working. Naqi heard it in her voice: she was either terribly frightened or terribly excited.

'You're more scared than I am,' she said.

'I am scared,' said Mina, 'scared we'll screw this up. Scared we'll blow this opportunity. Understand? I'm *that* kind of scared.'

Either Naqi was treading water less calmly, or the water itself had become visibly more agitated in the last few moments. The green walls were perhaps ten metres apart, and were no longer quite the sheer vertical structures they had appeared before. They had taken on form and design, growing and complexifying by the second. It was akin to watching a distant city emerge from fog, the revealing of bewildering, plunging layers of mesmeric detail, more than the eye or the mind could process.

'It doesn't look as if they're expecting a gift this time,' Mina said.

Veined tubes and pipes coiled and writhed around each other in constant, sinuous motion, making Naqi think of some hugely magnified circuitry formed from plant parts. It was restless, living circuitry that never quite settled into one configuration. Now and then chequerboard designs appeared, or intricately interlocking runes. Sharply geometric patterns flickered from point to point, echoed, amplified and subtly iterated at each move. Distinct three-dimensional shapes assumed brief solidity, carved from greenery as if by the deft hand of a topiarist. Naqi glimpsed unsettling anatomies: the warped memories of alien bodies that had once entered the ocean, a million, or a billion years ago. Here was a three-jointed limb, there the shieldlike curve of an exoskeletal plaque. The head of something that was almost equine melted into a goggling mass of faceted eyes. Fleetingly, a human form danced from the chaos. But only once. Alien swimmers vastly outnumbered human swimmers.

Here were the Pattern Jugglers, Naqi knew. The first explorers had mistaken these remembered forms for indications of actual sentience, thinking that the oceanic mass was a kind of community of intelligences. It was an easy mistake to have made, but it was some way from the truth. These animate shapes were enticements, like the gaudy covers of books. The minds themselves were captured only as frozen traces. The only living intelligence within the ocean lay in its own curatorial system.

To believe anything else was heresy.

The dance of bodies became too rapid to follow. Pastel-coloured lights glowed from deep within the green structure, flickering and stuttering. Naqi thought of lanterns burning in the depths of a forest. Now the edge of the lagoon had become irregular, extending peninsulas towards the centre of the dwindling circle of water, while narrow bays and inlets fissured back into the larger mass of the node. The peninsulas sprouted grasping tendrils, thigh-thick at the trunk but narrowing to the dimensions of plant fronds, and then narrowing further, bifurcating into lacy, fernlike hazes of awesome complexity. They diffracted light like the wings of dragonflies. They were closing over the lagoon, forming a shimmering canopy. Now and then a sprite – or something smaller but equally bright – arced from one bank of the lagoon to another. Brighter things moved through the water like questing fish. Microscopic organisms were detaching from the larger fronds and tendrils, swarming in purposeful clouds. They batted against her skin, against her eyelids. Every breath that she took made her cough. The taste of the Pattern Jugglers was sour and medicinal. They were in her, invading her body.

She panicked. It was as if a tiny switch had flipped in her mind. Suddenly all other concerns melted away. She had to get out of the lagoon immediately, no matter what Mina would think of her.

Thrashing more than swimming, Naqi tried to push herself towards the raft, but as soon as the panic reaction had kicked in, she had felt something else slide over her. It was not so much paralysis as an immense sense of inertia. Moving, even breathing, became problematic. The boat was impossibly distant. She was no longer capable of treading water. She felt heavy, and when she looked down she saw that a green haze had enveloped the parts of her body that she could see above water. The organisms were adhering to the fabric of her wetsuit.

158

'Mina—' she called, 'Mina!'

But Mina only looked at her. Naqi sensed that her sister was experiencing the same sort of paralysis. Mina's movements had become languid; instead of panic, what Naqi saw on her face was profound resignation and acceptance. It was dangerously close to serenity.

Mina wasn't frightened at all.

The patterns on her neck were flaring vividly. Her eyes were closed. Already the organisms had begun to attack the fabric of her suit, stripping it away from her flesh. Naqi could feel the same thing happening to her own suit. There was no pain, for the organisms stopped short of attacking her skin. With a mighty effort she hoisted her forearm from the water, studying the juxtaposition of pale flesh and dissolving black fabric. Her fingers were as stiff as iron.

But – and Naqi clung to this fact – the ocean recognised the sanctity of organisms, or at least, thinking organisms. Strange things might happen to people who swam with the Jugglers, things that might be difficult to distinguish from death or near-death. But people always emerged afterwards, changed perhaps, but essentially whole. No matter what happened now, they would survive. The Jugglers always returned those who swam with them, and even when they did effect changes, they were seldom permanent.

Except, of course, for those who didn't return.

No, Naqi told herself. What they were doing was foolish, and might perhaps destroy their careers, but they would survive. Mina had flagged high on the conformality index when she had applied to join the swimmer corps, but that didn't mean she was necessarily at risk. Conformality merely implied a rare connection with the ocean. It verged on the glamorous.

Now Mina was going under. She had stopped moving entirely. Her eyes were blankly ecstatic.

Naqi wanted to resist that same impulse to submit, but all the strength had flowed away from her. She felt herself begin the same descent. The water closed over her mouth, then her eyes, and in a moment she was under. She felt herself a toppled statue sliding towards the seabed. Her fear reached a crescendo, and then passed it. She was not drowning. The froth of green organisms had forced itself down her throat, down her nasal passage. She felt no fright. There was nothing except a profound feeling that this was what she had been born to do.

Naqi knew what was happening, what was *going* to happen. She had studied enough reports on swimmer missions. The tiny organisms were infiltrating her entire body, creeping into her lungs and bloodstream. They were keeping her alive, while at the same time flooding her with chemical bliss. Droves of the same tiny creatures were seeking routes to her brain, inching along the optic nerve, the aural nerve, or crossing the blood-brain barrier itself. They were laying tiny threads behind them, fibres that extended back into the larger mass of organisms suspended in the water around her. In turn, these organisms would establish data-carrying channels back into the primary mass of the node . . . And the node itself was connected to other nodes, both chemically and via the packet-carrying sprites. The green threads bound Naqi to the entire ocean. It might take hours for a signal to reach her mind from halfway around Turquoise, but it didn't matter. She was beginning to think in Juggler time, her own thought processes seeming pointlessly quick, like the motion of bees.

She sensed herself becoming vaster.

She was no longer just a pale, hard-edged thing labelled *Naqi*, suspended in the lagoon like a dying starfish. Her sense of self was rushing out towards the horizon in all directions, encompassing first the node and then the empty oceanic waters around it. She couldn't say precisely how this information was reaching her. It wasn't through visual imagery, but more an intensely detailed spatial awareness. It was as if spatial awareness had suddenly become her most vital sense.

She supposed this was what swimmers meant when they spoke of *kenning*.

She *kenned* the presence of other nodes over the horizon, their chemical signals flooding her mind, each unique, each bewilderingly rich in information. It was like hearing the roar of a hundred crowds. And at the same time she *kenned* the ocean depths, the cold fathoms of water beneath the node, the life-giving warmth of the crustal vents. Closer, too, she *kenned* Mina. They were two neighbouring galaxies in a sea of strangeness. Mina's own thoughts were bleeding into the sea, into Naqi's mind, and in them Naqi felt the reflected echo of her own thoughts, picked up by Mina . . .

It was glorious.

For a moment their minds orbited each other, *kenning* each other on a level of intimacy neither had dreamed possible.

Mina . . . Can you feel me?

I'm here, Naqi. Isn't this wonderful?

The fear was gone, utterly. In its place was a marvellous feeling of immanence. They had made the right decision, Naqi knew. She had been right to follow Mina. Mina was deliciously happy, basking in the same hopeful sense of security and promise.

And then they began to sense other minds.

Nothing had changed, but it was suddenly clear that the roaring signals from the other nodes were composed of count-less individual voices, countless individual streams of chemical information. Each stream was the recording of a mind that had entered the ocean at some point. The oldest minds – those that had entered in the deep past – were the faintest, but they were also the most numerous. They had begun to sound alike, the shapes of their stored personalities blurring into each other, no matter how different – how alien – they had been to start with. The minds that had been captured more recently were sharper and more variegated, like oddly shaped pebbles on a beach. Naqi *kenned* brutal alienness, baroque architectures of mind shaped by outlandish chains of evolutionary contingency. The only thing any of them had in common was that they had all reached a certain threshold of tool-using intelligence, and had all – for whatever reason – been driven into interstellar space, where they had encountered the Pattern Jugglers. But that was like saying the minds of sharks and leopards were alike because they had both evolved to hunt. The differences between the minds were so cosmically vast that Naqi felt her own mental processes struggling to accommodate them.

Even that was becoming easier. Subtly – slowly enough that from moment to moment she was not aware of it – the organisms in her skull were retuning her neural connections, allowing more and more of her own consciousness to seep out into the extended processing-loom of the sea.

Now she sensed the most recent arrivals.

They were all human minds, each a glittering gem of distinctness. Naqi *kenned* a great gulf in time between the earliest human mind and the last recognisably alien one. She had no idea if it was a million years or a billion, but it felt immense. At the same time she grasped that the ocean had been desperate for an injection of variety, but while these human minds were welcome, they were not exotic enough, just barely sufficient to break the tedium.

The minds were snapshots, frozen in the conception of a single thought. It was like an orchestra of instruments, all sustaining a single, unique note. Perhaps there was a grindingly slow evolution in those minds – she felt the merest subliminal hint of change – but if that were the case, it would take centuries to complete a thought . . . thousands of years to complete the simplest internalised statement. The newest minds might not even have recognised that they had been swallowed by the sea.

And now Naqi could perceive a single mind flaring louder than the others.

It was recent, and human, and there was something about it that struck her as discordant. The mind was damaged, as if it had been captured imperfectly. It was disfigured, giving off squalls of hurt. It had suffered dreadfully. It was reaching out to her, craving love and affection; it searched for something to cling to in the abyssal loneliness it now knew.

Images ghosted through her mind. Something was burning. Flames licked through the interstitial gaps in a great black structure. She couldn't tell if it was a building or a vast, pyramidal bonfire.

She heard screams, and then something hysterical, which she at first took for more screaming, until she realised that it was something far, far worse. It was laughter, and as the flames roared higher, consuming the mass, smothering the screams, the laughter only intensified.

She thought it might be the laughter of a child.

Perhaps it was her imagination, but this mind appeared more fluid than the others. Its thoughts were still slow – far slower than Naqi's – but the mind appeared to have usurped more than its share of processing resources. It was stealing computational cycles from neighbouring minds, freezing them into absolute stasis while it completed a single sluggish thought.

The mind worried Naqi. Pain and fury was boiling off it.

Mina *kenned* it too. Naqi tasted Mina's thoughts and knew that her sister was equally disturbed by the mind's presence. Then she felt the mind's attention shift, drawn to the two inquisitive minds that had just entered the sea. It became aware of both of them, quietly watchful. A moment or two passed, and then the mind slipped away, back to wherever it had come from.

What was that . . .?

She felt her sister's reply. *I don't know. A human mind. A conformal, I think. Someone who was swallowed by the sea. But it's gone now.*

No, it hasn't. It's still there. Just hiding.

Millions of minds have entered the sea, Naqi. Thousands of conformals, perhaps, if you think of all the aliens that came before us. There are bound to be one or two bad apples.

That wasn't just a bad apple. It was like touching ice. And it sensed us. It reacted to us. Didn't it?

She sensed Mina's hesitation.

We can't be sure. Our own perceptions of events aren't necessarily reliable. I can't even be certain we're having this conversation. I might be talking to myself . . .

Mina . . . Don't talk like that. I don't feel safe.

Me neither. But I'm not going to let one frightening thing unnecessarily affect me.

Something happened then. It was a loosening, a feeling that the ocean's grip on Naqi had just relented to a significant degree. Mina, and the roaring background of other minds, fell away to something much more distant. It was as if Naqi had just stepped out of a babbling party into a quiet adjacent room, and was even now moving further and further away from the door.

Her body tingled. She no longer felt the same deadening paralysis. Pearl-grey light flickered above. Without being sure whether she was doing it herself, she rose towards the surface. She was aware that she was moving away from Mina, but for now all that mattered was to escape the sea. She wanted to be as far from that discordant mind as possible.

Her head rammed through a crust of green into air. At the same moment the Juggler organisms fled her body in a convulsive rush. She thrashed stiff limbs and took in deep, panicked breaths. The transition was horrible, but it was over in a few seconds. She looked around, expecting to see the sheer walls of the lagoon, but all she saw in one direction was open water. Naqi felt panic rising again. Then she kicked herself around and saw a wavy line of bottle-green that had to be the perimeter of the node, perhaps half a kilometre away from her present

164

position. The airship was a distant silvery teardrop that appeared to be perched on the surface of the node itself.

In her fear she did not immediately think of Mina. All she wanted to do was reach the safety of the airship, to be aloft. Then she saw the raft, bobbing only one or two hundred metres away. Somehow it had been transplanted to the open waters as well. It looked distant but reachable. She started swimming, fear giving her strength and sense of purpose. In truth, she was well within the true boundary of the node: the water was still thick with suspended micro-organisms, so that it was more like swimming through cold green soup. It made each stroke harder, but she did not have to expend much effort to stay afloat.

Did she trust the Pattern Jugglers not to harm her? Perhaps. After all, she had not encountered *their* minds at all – if they even *had* minds. They were merely the archiving system. Blaming them for that one poisoned mind was like blaming a library for one hateful book.

But still, it had unnerved her profoundly. She wondered why none of the other swimmers had ever communicated their encounters with such a mind. After all, she remembered it well enough now, and she was nearly out of the ocean. She might forget shortly – there were bound to be subsequent neurological effects – but under other circumstances there would have been nothing to prevent her relating her experiences to a witness or inviolable recording system.

She kept swimming, and began to wonder why Mina hadn't emerged from the waters as well. Mina had been just as terrified. But Mina had also been more curious, and more willing to ignore her fears. Naqi had grasped the opportunity to leave the ocean once the the Jugglers released their grip on her. But what if Mina had elected to remain?

What if Mina was still down there, still in communion with the Jugglers?

Naqi reached the raft and hauled herself aboard, being careful

165

not to capsize it. She saw that the raft was still largely intact. It had been moved, but not damaged, and although the ceramic sheathing was showing signs of attack, peppered here and there with scabbed green accretions, it was certainly good for another few hours. The rot-hardened control systems were alive, and still in telemetric connection with the distant airship.

Naqi had crawled from the sea naked. Now she felt cold and vulnerable. She pulled an aluminised quilt from the raft's supply box and wrapped it around herself. It did not stop her from shivering, did not make her feel any less nauseous, but at least it afforded some measure of symbolic barrier against the sea.

She looked around again, but there was still no sign of Mina.

Naqi folded aside the weatherproof control cover and tapped commands into the matrix of waterproofed keys. She waited for the response from the airship. The moment stretched. But there it was: a minute shift in the dull gleam on the silver back of the vacuum bladder. The airship was turning, pivoting like a great slow weather vane. It was moving, responding to the raft's homing command.

But where was Mina?

Now something moved in the water next to her, coiling in weak, enervated spasms. Naqi looked at it with horrified recognition. She reached over, still shivering, and with appalled gentleness fished the writhing thing from the sea. It lay in her fingers like a baby sea serpent. It was white and segmented, half a metre long. She knew exactly what it was.

It was Mina's worm. It meant Mina had died.

two

Two years later Naqi watched a spark fall from the heavens.

Along with many hundreds of spectators, she was standing on the railed edge of one of Umingmaktok's elegant cantilevered arms. It was afternoon. Every visible surface of the city had been scoured of rot and given a fresh coat of crimson or emerald paint. Amber bunting had been hung along the metal stay-lines that supported the tapering arms protruding from the city's towering commercial core. Most of the berthing slots around the perimeter were occupied by passenger or cargo craft, while many smaller vessels were holding station in the immediate airspace around Umingmaktok. The effect, which Naqi had seen on her approach to the city a day earlier, had been to turn the snowflake into a glittering, delicately ornamented vision. By night they had fireworks displays. By day, as now, conjurors and confidence tricksters wound their way through the crowds. Nose-flute musicians and drum dancers performed impromptu atop improvised podia. Kick-boxers were being cheered on as they moved from one informal ring to another, pursued by whistle-blowing proctors. Hastily erected booths were marked with red and yellow pennants, selling refreshments, souvenirs or tattoo-work, while pretty costumed girls who wore backpacks equipped with tall flagstaffs sold drinks or ices. The children had balloons and rattles marked with the emblems of both

Umingmaktok and the Snowflake Council, and many of them had had their faces painted to resemble stylised space travellers. Puppet theatres had been set up here and there, running through exactly the same small repertoire of stories that Naqi remembered from her childhood. The children were enthralled nonetheless; mouths agape at each miniature epic, whether it was a roughly accurate account of the world's settlement – with the colony ship being stripped to the bone for every gram of metal it held – or something altogether more fantastic, like the drowning of Arviat. It didn't matter to the children that one was based in fact and the other was pure mythology. To them the idea that every city they called home had been cannibalised from the belly of a four-kilometre-long ship was no more or less plausible than the idea that the living sea might occasionally snatch cities beneath the waves when they displeased it. At that age everything was both magical and mundane, and she supposed that the children were no more nor less excited by the prospect of the coming visitors than they were by the promised fireworks display, or the possibility of further treats if they were well-behaved. Other than the children, there were animals: caged monkeys and birds, and the occasional expensive pet being shown off for the day. One or two servitors stalked through the crowd, and occasionally a golden float-cam would bob through the air, loitering over a scene of interest like a single detached eyeball. Turquoise had not seen this level of celebration since the last acrimonious divorce, and the networks were milking it remorselessly, over-analysing even the tiniest scrap of information.

This was, in truth, exactly the kind of thing Naqi would normally have gone to the other side of the planet to avoid. But something had drawn her this time, and made her wangle the trip out from the Moat at an otherwise critical time in the project. She could only suppose that it was a need to close a particular chapter in her life, one that had begun the night before Mina's death. The detection of the Ultra ship – they now knew that it was named *Voice of Evening* – had been the event that triggered the blackout, and the blackout had been Mina's justification for the two of them attempting to swim with the Jugglers. Indirectly, therefore, the Ultras were 'responsible' for whatever had happened to Mina. That was unfair, of course, but Naqi nonetheless felt the need to be here now, if only to witness the visitors' emergence with her own eyes and see if they really were the monsters of her imagination. She had come to Umingmaktok with a stoic determination that she would not be swept up by the hysteria of the celebrations. Yet now that she had made the trip, now that she was amidst the crowd, drunk on the chemical buzz of human excitement, with a nice fresh worm hooked onto her gut wall, she found herself in the perverse position of actually enjoying the atmosphere.

And now everyone had noticed the falling spark.

The crowd turned their heads into the sky, ignoring the musicians, conjurors and confidence tricksters. The backpacked girls stopped and looked aloft along with the others, shielding their eyes against the midday glare. The spark was the shuttle of *Voice of Evening*, now parked in orbit around Turquoise.

Everyone had seen Captain Moreau's ship by now, either with their own eyes as a moving star, or via the images captured by the orbiting cameras or ground-based telescopes. The ship was dark and sleek, outrageously elegant. Now and then its Conjoiner drives flickered on just enough to trim its orbit, those flashes like brief teasing windows into daylight for the hemisphere below.

A ship like that could do awful things to a world, and everyone knew it.

But if Captain Moreau and his crew meant ill for Turquoise, they'd had ample opportunity to do harm already. They had been silent at two years out, but at one year out the *Voice of Evening* had transmitted the usual approach signals, requesting permission to stopover for three or four months. It was a formality – no one argued with Ultras – but it was also a gladdening sign that they intended to play by the usual rules.

Over the next year there had been a steady stream of communications between the ship and the Snowflake Council. The official word was that the messages had been designed to establish a framework for negotiation and person-to-person trade. The Ultras would need to update their linguistics software to avoid being confused by the subtleties of the Turquoise dialects, which, although based on Canasian, contained confusing elements of Inuit and Thai, relics of the peculiar social mix of the original settlement coalition.

The falling shuttle had slowed to merely supersonic speed now, shedding its plume of ionised air. Dropping speed with each loop, it executed a lazily contracting spiral above Umingmaktok. Naqi had rented cheap binoculars from one of the vendors. The lenses were scuffed, shimmering with the pink of fungal bloom. She visually locked onto the shuttle, its roughly delta shape wobbling in and out of sharpness. Only when it was two or three thousand metres above Umingmaktok could she see it clearly. It was very elegant, a pure brilliant white like something carved from cloud. Beneath the manta-like hull complex machines – fans and control surfaces – moved too rapidly to be seen as anything other than blurs of subliminal motion. She watched as the ship reduced speed until it hovered at the same altitude as the snowflake city. Above the roar of the crowd – an ecstatic, flag-waving mass – all Naqi heard was a shrill hum, almost too far into ultrasound to detect.

The ship approached slowly. It had been given instructions for docking with the arm adjacent to the one where Naqi and the other spectators gathered. Now that it was close it was apparent that the shuttle was larger than any of the dirigible craft normally moored to the city's arms; by Naqi's estimate it was at least half as wide as the city's central core. But it slid into its designated mooring point with exquisite delicacy. Bright red symbols flashed onto the otherwise blank white hull, signifying airlocks, cargo ports and umbilical sockets. Gangways were swung out from the arm to align with the doors and ports. Dockers, supervised by proctors and city officials, scrambled along the precarious connecting ways and attempted to fix magnetic berthing stays onto the shuttle's hull. The magnetics slid off the hull. They tried adhesive grips next, and these were no more successful. After that, the dockers shrugged their shoulders and made exasperated gestures in the direction of the shuttle.

The roar of the crowd had died down a little by now.

Naqi felt the anticipation as well. She watched as an entourage of VIPs moved to the berthing position, led by a smooth, faintly cherubic individual that Naqi recognised as Tak Thonburi, the mayor of Umingmaktok and presiding chair of the Snowflake Council. Tak Thonburi was happily overweight and had a permanent cowlick of black hair, like an inverted question mark tattooed upon his forehead. His cheeks and brow were mottled with pale green. Next to him was the altogether leaner frame of Jotah Sivaraksa. It was no surprise that Dr Sivaraksa should be here today, for the Moat project was one of the most significant activities of the entire Snowflake Council. His iron-grey eyes flashed this way and that as if constantly triangulating the positions of enemies and allies alike. The group was accompanied by armed, ceremonially dressed proctors and a triad of martial servitors. Their articulation points and sensor apertures were lathered in protective sterile grease, to guard against rot.

Though they tried to hide it, Naqi could tell that the VIPs were nervous. They moved a touch too confidently, making their trepidation all the more evident.

The red door symbol at the end of the gangway pulsed brighter and a section of the hull puckered open. Naqi squinted, but even through the binoculars it was difficult to make out anything other than red-lit gloom. Tak Thonburi and his officials stiffened. A sketchy figure emerged from the shuttle, lingered on the threshold and then stepped with immense slowness into full sunlight.

The crowd's reaction – and to some extent Naqi's own – was double-edged. There was a moment of relief that the messages from orbit had not been outright lies. Then there was an equally brief tang of shock at the actual appearance of Captain Moreau. The man was at least a third taller than anyone Naqi had ever seen in her life, yet commensurately thinner, his seemingly brittle frame contained within a jade-coloured mechanical exo-skeleton of ornate design. The skeleton lent his movements something of the lethargic quality of a stick insect.

Tak Thonburi was the first to speak. His amplified voice boomed out across the six arms of Umingmaktok, echoing off the curved surfaces of the multiple vacuum-bladders that held the city aloft. Float-cams jostled for the best camera angle, swarming around him like pollen-crazed bees.

'Captain Moreau . . . Let me introduce myself. I am Tak Thonburi, mayor of Umingmaktok Snowflake City and incumbent chairman of the Snowflake Council of All Turquoise. It is my pleasure to welcome you, your crew and passengers to Umingmaktok, and to Turquoise itself. You have my word that we will do all in our power to make your visit as pleasant as possible.'

The Ultra moved closer to the official. The door to the shuttle remained open behind him. Naqi's binocs picked out red hologram serpents on the jade limbs of the skeleton.

The Ultra's own voice boomed at least as loud, but emanated from the shuttle rather than Umingmaktok's public address system. 'People of greenish-blue . . .' The captain hesitated, then tapped one of the stalks projecting from his helmet. 'People of Turquoise . . . Chairman Thonburi . . . Thank you for your welcome, and for your kind permission to assume orbit. We have accepted it with gratitude. You have my word . . . as captain of the lighthugger *Voice of Evening* . . . that we will abide by the strict terms of your generous offer of hospitality.' His mouth continued to move even during the pauses, Naqi noticed: the translation system was lagging. 'You have my additional guarantee that no harm will be done to your world, and Turquoise law will be presumed to apply to the occupants . . . of all bodies and vessels in your atmosphere. All traffic between my ship and your world will be subject to the authorisation of the Snowflake Council, and any member of the council will – under the . . . auspices of the council – be permitted to visit *Voice of Evening* at any time, subject to the availability of a . . . suitable conveyance.'

The captain paused and looked at Tak Thonburi expectantly. The mayor wiped a nervous hand across his brow, smoothing his kiss-curl into obedience. 'Thank you . . . Captain.' Tak Thonburi's eyes flashed to the other members of the reception party. 'Your terms are of course more than acceptable. You have my word that we will do all in our power to assist you and your crew, and that we will do our utmost to ensure that the forthcoming negotiations of trade proceed in an equable manner . . . and in such a way that both parties will be satisfied upon their conclusion.'

The captain did not respond immediately, allowing an uncomfortable pause to draw itself out. Naqi wondered if it was really the fault of the software, or whether Moreau was just playing on Tak Thonburi's evident nervousness.

'Of course,' the Ultra said, finally. 'Of course. My sentiments entirely . . . Chairman Thonburi. Perhaps now wouldn't be a bad time to introduce my guests?'

On his cue three new figures emerged from *Voice of Evening*'s shuttle. Unlike the Ultra, they could almost have passed for ordinary citizens of Turquoise. There were two men and one woman, all of approximately normal height and build, each with

173

long hair, tied back in elaborate clasps. Their clothes were brightly coloured, fashioned from many separate fabrics of yellow, orange, red and russet, and various permutations of the same warm sunset shades. The clothes billowed around them, rippling in the light afternoon breeze. All three members of the party wore silver jewellery, far more than was customary on Turquoise. They wore it on their fingers, in their hair, hanging from their ears.

The woman was the first to speak, her voice booming out from the shuttle's PA system.

'Thank you, Captain Moreau. Thank you also, Chairman Thonburi. We are delighted to be here. I am Amesha Crane, and I speak for the Vahishta Foundation. Vahishta's a modest scientific organisation with its origins in the cometary prefectures of the Haven Demarchy. Lately we have been expanding our realm of interest to encompass other solar systems, such as this one.' Crane gestured at the two men who had accompanied her from the shuttle. 'My associates are Simon Matsubara and Rafael Weir. There are another seventeen of us aboard the shuttle. Captain Moreau carried us here as paying passengers aboard *Voice of Evening,* and as such Vahishta gladly accepts all the terms already agreed upon.'

Tak Thonburi looked even less sure of himself. 'Of course. We welcome your . . . interest. A scientific organisation, did you say?'

'One with a special interest in the study of the Jugglers,' Amesha Crane answered. She was the most strikingly attractive member of the trio, with fine cheekbones and a wide, sensual mouth that looked to be always on the point of smiling or laughing. Naqi felt that the woman was sharing something with her, something private and amusing. Doubtless everyone in the crowd felt the same vague sense of complicity.

Crane continued, 'We have no Pattern Jugglers in our own system, but that hasn't stopped us from focusing our research

174

on them, collating the data available from the worlds where Juggler studies are ongoing. We've been doing this for decades, sifting inference and theory, guesswork and intuition. Haven't we, Simon?'

The man nodded. He had sallow skin and a fixed, quizzical expression.

'No two Juggler worlds are precisely alike,' Simon Matsubara said, his voice as clear and confident as the woman's. 'And no two Juggler worlds have been studied by precisely the same mix of human socio-political factions. That means that we have a great many variables to take into consideration. Despite that, we believe we have identified similarities that may have been over-looked by the individual research teams. They may even be very important similarities, with repercussions for wider humanity. But in the absence of our own Jugglers, it is difficult to test our theories. That's where Turquoise comes in.'

The other man – Naqi recalled his name was Rafael Weir – began to speak. 'Turquoise has been largely isolated from the rest of human space for the better part of two centuries.'

'We're aware of this,' said Jotah Sivaraksa. It was the first time any member of the entourage other than Tak Thonburi had spoken. To Naqi he sounded irritated, though he was doing his best to hide it.

'You don't share your findings with the other Juggler worlds,' said Amesha Crane. 'Nor – to the best of our knowledge – do you intercept their cultural transmissions. The consequence is that your research on the Jugglers has been untainted by any outside considerations – the latest fashionable theory, the latest ground-breaking technique. You prefer to work in scholarly isolation.'

'We're an isolationist world in other respects,' Tak Thonburi said. 'Believe it or not, it actually rather suits us.'

'Quite,' Crane said, with a hint of sharpness. 'But the point remains. Your Jugglers are an uncontaminated resource. When a swimmer enters the ocean, their own memories and person-

175

ality may be absorbed into the Juggler sea. The prejudices and preconceptions that swimmer carries inevitably enter the ocean in some shape or form – diluted, confused, but nonetheless present in some form. And when the next swimmer enters the sea, and opens their mind to communion, what they perceive – what they *ken*, in your own terminology – is irrevocably tainted by the preconceptions introduced by the previous swimmer. They may experience something that confirms their deepest suspicion about the nature of the Jugglers – but they can't be sure that they aren't simply picking up the mental echoes of the last swimmer, or the swimmer before that.'

Jotah Sivaraksa nodded. 'What you say is undoubtedly true. But we've had just as many cycles of fashionable theory as anyone else. Even within Umingmaktok there are a dozen different research teams, each with their own views.'

'We accept that,' Crane said, with an audible sigh. 'But the degree of contamination is slight compared to other worlds. Vahishta lacks the resources for a trip to a previously unvisited Juggler world, so the next best thing is to visit one that has suffered the smallest degree of human cultural pollution. Turquoise fits the bill.'

Tak Thonburi held the moment before responding, playing to the crowd again. Naqi rather admired the way he did it.

'Good. I'm very . . . pleased . . . to hear it. And might I ask just what it is about our ocean that we can offer you?'

'Nothing except the ocean itself,' said Amesha Crane. 'We simply wish to join you in its study. If you will allow it, members of the Vahishta Foundation will collaborate with native Turquoise scientists and study teams. They will shadow them and offer interpretation or advice when requested. Nothing more than that.'

'That's all?'

Crane smiled. 'That's all. It's not as if we're asking the world, is it?'

Naqi remained in Umingmaktok for three days after the arrival, visiting friends and taking care of business for the Moat. The newcomers had departed, taking their shuttle to one of the other snowflake cities – Prachuap or the recently married Qaanaaq-Pangnirtung, perhaps – where a smaller but no less worthy group of city dignitaries would welcome Captain Moreau and his passengers.

In Umingmaktok the booths and bunting were packed away and normal business resumed. Litter abounded. Worm dealers did brisk business, as they always did during times of mild gloom. There were far fewer transport craft moored to the arms, and no sign at all of the intense media presence of a few days before. Tourists had gone back to their home cities and the children were safely back in school. Between meetings Naqi sat in the midday shade of half-empty restaurants and bars, observing the same puzzled disappointment in every face she encountered. Deep down she felt it herself. For two years they had been free to imprint every possible fantasy on the approaching ship. Even if the newcomers had arrived with less than benign intent, there would still have been something interesting to talk about: the possibility, however remote, that one's own life might be about to become drastically more exciting.

But now none of that was going to happen. Undoubtedly Naqi would be involved with the visitors at some point, allowing them to visit the Moat or one of the outlying research zones she managed, but there would be nothing life-changing.

She thought back to that night with Mina, when they had heard the news. Everything had changed then. Mina had died, and Naqi had found herself taking her sister's role in the Moat. She had risen to the challenge and promotions had followed with gratifying swiftness, until she was in effective charge of the Moat's entire scientific programme. But that sense of closure she had yearned for was still absent. The men she had slept with –

men who were almost always swimmers – had never provided it, and by turns they had each lost patience with her, realising that they were less important to her as people than what they represented, as connections to the sea. It had been months since her last romance, and once Naqi had recognised the way her own subconscious was drawing her back to the sea, she had drawn away from contact with swimmers. She had been drifting since then, daring to hope that the newcomers would allow her some measure of tranquillity.

But the newcomers had not supplied it.

She supposed she would have to find it elsewhere.

On the fourth day Naqi returned to the Moat on a high-speed dirigible. She arrived near sunset, dropping down from high altitude to see the structure winking back at her, a foreshortened ellipse of grey-white ceramic lying against the sea like some vast discarded bracelet. From horizon to horizon there were several Juggler nodes visible, webbed together by the faintest of filaments – to Naqi they looked like motes of ink spreading into blotting paper – but there were also smaller dabs of green within the Moat itself.

The structure was twenty kilometres wide and now it was nearly finished. Only a narrow channel remained where the two ends of the bracelet did not quite meet: a hundred-metre-wide sheer-sided aperture flanked on either side by tall, ramshackle towers of accommodation modules, equipment sheds and construction cranes. To the north, strings of heavy cargo dirigibles ferried processed ore and ceramic cladding from Narathiwat atoll, lowering it down to the construction teams on the Moat.

They had been working here for nearly twenty years. The hundred metres of the Moat that projected above the water was only one tenth of the full structure – a kilometre-high ring resting on the seabed. In a matter of months the gap – little more than a notch in the top of the Moat – would be sealed, closed off by immense hermetically tight sea-doors. The process would be necessarily slow and delicate, for what was being attempted here was not simply the closing-off of part of the sea. The Moat was an attempt to isolate a part of the living ocean, sealing off a community of Pattern Juggler organisms within its impervious ceramic walls.

The high-speed dirigible swung low over the aperture. The thick green waters streaming through the cut had the phlegmatic consistency of congealing blood. Thick, ropy tendrils permitted information transfer between the external sea and the cluster of small nodes within the Moat. Swimmers were constantly present, either inside or outside the Moat, *kenning* the state of the sea and establishing that the usual Juggler processes continued unabated.

The dirigible docked with one of the two flanking towers.

Naqi stepped out, back into the hectic corridors and office spaces of the project building. It felt distinctly odd to be back on absolutely firm ground. Although one was seldom aware of it, Umingmaktok was never quite still: no snowflake city or airship ever was. But she would get used to it; in a few hours she would be immersed in her work, having to think of a dozen different things at once, finessing solution pathways, balancing budgets against quality, dealing with personality clashes and minor turf wars, and perhaps – if she was very lucky – managing an hour or two of pure research. Aside from the science, none of it was particularly challenging, but it kept her mind off other things. And after a few days of that, the arrival of the visitors would begin to feel like a bizarre, irrelevant interlude in an otherwise monotonous dream. She supposed that two years ago she would have been grateful for that. Life could indeed continue much as she had always imagined it would.

But when she arrived at her office there was a message from Dr Sivaraksa. He needed to speak to her urgently.

*

Dr Jotah Sivaraksa's office on the Moat was a good deal less spacious than his quarters in Umingmaktok, but the view was superb. His accommodation was perched halfway up one of the towers that flanked the cut through the Moat, buttressed out from the main mass of prefabricated modules like a partially opened desk drawer. Dr Sivaraksa was writing notes when she arrived. For a few moments Naqi lingered at the sloping window, watching the construction activity hundreds of metres below. Railed machines and helmeted workers toiled on the flat upper surface of the Moat, moving raw materials and equipment to the assembly sites. Above, the sky was a perfect cobalt-blue, marred now and then by the passing green-stained hull of a cargo dirigible. The sea beyond the Moat had the dimpled texture of expensive leather.

Dr Sivaraksa cleared his throat and, when Naqi turned, he gestured at the vacant seat on the opposite side of his desk.

'Life treating you well?'

'Can't complain, sir.'

'And work?'

'No particular problems that I'm aware of.'

'Good. Good.' Sivaraksa made a quick, cursive annotation in the notebook he had opened on his desk, then slid it beneath the smoky-grey cube of a paperweight. 'How long has it been now?'

'Since what, sir?'

'Since your sister . . . Since Mina . . .' He seemed unable to complete the sentence, substituting a spiralling gesture made with his index finger. His finely boned hands were marbled with veins of olive green.

Naqi eased into her seat. 'Two years, sir.'

'And you're . . . over it?'

'I wouldn't exactly say I'm over it, no. But life goes on, like they say. Actually I was hoping . . .' Naqi had been about to tell him how she had imagined the arrival of the visitors would close that chapter. But she doubted she would be able to convey her feelings in a way Dr Sivaraksa would understand. 'Well, I was hoping I'd have put it all behind me by now.'

'I knew another conformal, you know. Fellow from Gjoa. Made it into the élite swimmer corps before anyone had the foggiest idea . . .'

'It's never been proven that Mina was conformal, sir.'

'No, but the signs were there, weren't they? To one degree or another we're all subject to symbiotic invasion by the ocean's micro-organisms. But conformals show an unusual degree of susceptibility. On one hand it's as if their own bodies actively invite the invasion, shutting down the usual inflammatory or foreign cell rejection mechanisms. On the other, the ocean seems to tailor its messengers for maximum effectiveness, as if the Jugglers have selected a specific target they wish to absorb. Mina had very strong fungal patterns, did she not?'

'I've seen worse,' Naqi said, which was not entirely a lie.

'But not, I suspect, in anyone who ever attempted to commune. I understand you had ambitions to join the swimmer corps yourself?'

'Before all that happened.'

'I understand. And now?'

Naqi had never told anyone that she had joined Mina in the swimming incident. The truth was that even if she had not been present at the time of Mina's death, her encounter with the rogue mind would have put her off entering the ocean for life.

'It isn't for me. That's all.'

Jotah Sivaraksa nodded gravely. 'A wise choice. Aptitude or not, you'd have almost certainly been filtered out of the swimmer corps. A direct genetic connection to a conformal – even an unproven conformal – would be too much of a risk.'

'That's what I assumed, sir.'

'Does it trouble you, Naqi?'

181

She was wearying of this. She had work to do: deadlines to meet that Sivaraksa himself had imposed.

'Does what trouble me?'

He nodded at the sea. Now that the play of light had shifted minutely, it looked less like dimpled leather than a sheet of beaten bronze. 'The thought that Mina might still be out there . . . in some sense.'

'It might trouble me if I were a swimmer, sir. Other than that . . . No. I can't say that it does. My sister died. That's all that mattered.'

'Swimmers have occasionally reported encountering minds – essences – of the lost, Naqi. The impressions are often acute. The conformed leave their mark on the ocean at a deeper, more permanent level than the impressions left behind by mere swimmers. One senses that there must be a purpose to this.'

'That wouldn't be for me to speculate, sir.'

'No.' He glanced down at the compad and then tapped his forefinger against his upper lip. 'No. Of course not. Well, to the matter at hand—'

She interrupted him. 'You swam once, sir?'

'Yes. Yes, I did.' The moment stretched. She was about to say something – anything – when Sivaraksa continued, 'I had to stop for medical reasons. Otherwise I suppose I'd have been in the swimmer corps for a good deal longer, at least until my hands started turning green.'

'What was it like?'

'Astonishing. Beyond anything I'd expected.'

'Did they change you?'

At that he smiled. 'I never thought that they did, until now. After my last swim I went through all the usual neurological and psychological tests. They found no anomalies; no indications that the Jugglers had imprinted any hints of alien personality or rewired my mind to think in an alien way.'

Sivaraksa reached across the desk and held up the smoky cube

182

that Naqi had taken for a paperweight. 'This came down from *Voice of Evening*. Examine it.'

Naqi peered into the milky-grey depths of the cube. Now that she saw it closely she realised that there were things embedded within the translucent matrix. There were chains of unfamiliar symbols, intersecting at right angles. They resembled the complex white scaffolding of a building.

'What is it?'

'Mathematics. Actually, a mathematical argument – a proof, if you like. Conventional mathematical notation – no matter how arcane – has evolved so that it can be written down on a two-dimensional surface, like paper or a readout. This is a three-dimensional syntax, liberated from that constraint. Its enormously richer, enormously more elegant.' The cube tumbled in Sivaraksa's hand. He was smiling. 'No one could make head or tail of it. Yet when I looked at it for the first time I nearly dropped it in shock. It made perfect sense to me. Not only did I understand the theorem, but I also understood the point of it. It's a joke, Naqi. A pun. This mathematics is rich enough to embody humour. And understanding *that* is the gift they left me. It was sitting in my mind for twenty-eight years, like an egg waiting to hatch.'

Abruptly, Sivaraksa placed the cube back on the table.

'Something's come up,' he said.

From somewhere came the distant, prolonged thunder of a dirigible discharging its cargo of processed ore. It must have been one of the last consignments.

'Something, sir?'

'They've asked to see the Moat.'

'They?'

'Crane and her Vahishta mob. They've requested an oversight of all major scientific centres on Turquoise, and naturally enough we're on the list. They'll be visiting us, spending a couple of days seeing what we've achieved.'

'I'm not too surprised that they've asked to visit, sir.'

'No, but I was hoping we'd have a few months' grace. We don't. They'll be here in a week.'

'That's not necessarily a problem for us, is it?'

'It mustn't become one,' Sivaraksa said. 'I'm putting you in charge of the visit, Naqi. You'll be the interface between Crane's group and the Moat. That's quite a responsibility, you understand. A mistake – the tiniest gaffe – could undermine our standing with the Snowflake Council.' He nodded at the compad. 'Our budgetary position is precarious. Frankly, I'm in Tak Thonburi's lap. We can't afford any embarrassments.'

'No sir.'

She certainly did understand. The job was a poisoned chalice, or at the very least, a chalice with the strong potential to become poisoned. If she succeeded – if the visit went smoothly, with no hitches – Sivaraksa could still take much of the credit for it. If it went wrong, on the other hand, the fault would be categorically hers.

'One more thing.' Sivaraksa reached under his desk and produced a brochure that he slid across to her. The brochure was marked with a prominent silver snowflake motif. It was sealed with red foil. 'Open it; you have clearance.'

'What is it, sir?'

'A security report on our new friends. One of them has been behaving a bit oddly. You'll need to keep an eye on him.'

For inscrutable reasons of their own, the liaison committee had decided she would be introduced to Amesha Crane and her associates a day before the official visit, when the party was still in Sukhothai-Sanikiluaq. The journey there took the better part of two days, even allowing for the legs she took by high-speed dirigible or the ageing, unreliable trans-atoll railway line between Narathiwat and Cape Dorset. She arrived at Sukhothai-Sanikiluaq in a velvety purple twilight, catching the tail end of a fireworks display. The two snowflake cities had only been married three weeks, so the arrival of the off-worlders was an excellent pretext for prolonging the celebrations. Naqi watched the fireworks from a civic landing stage perched halfway up Sukhothai's core, starbursts and cataracts of scarlet, indigo and intense emerald green brightening the sky above the vacuum-bladders. The colours reminded her of the organisms that she and Mina had seen in the wake of their airship. The recollection left her suddenly sad and drained, convinced that she had made a terrible mistake by accepting this assignment.

'Naqi?'

It was Tak Thonburi, coming out to meet her on the balcony. They had already exchanged messages during the journey. He was dressed in full civic finery and appeared more than a little drunk.

'Chairman Thonburi.'

'Good of you come to here, Naqi.' She watched his eyes map her contours with scientific rigour, lingering here and there around regions of particular interest. 'Enjoying the show?'

'You certainly seem to be, sir.'

'Yes, yes. Always had a thing about fireworks.' He pressed a drink into her hand and together they watched the display come to its mildly disappointing conclusion. There was a lull then, but Naqi noticed that the spectators on the other balconies were reluctant to leave, as if waiting for something. Presently a stunning display of three-dimensional images appeared, generated by powerful projection apparatus in the *Voice of Evening*'s shuttle. Above Sukhothai-Sanikiluaq, Chinese dragons as large as mountains fought epic battles. Sea monsters convulsed and writhed in the night. Celestial citadels burned. Hosts of purple-winged fiery angels fell from the heavens in tightly knit squadrons, clutching arcane instruments of music or punishment.

A marbled giant rose from the sea, as if woken from some aeons-long slumber.

It was very, very impressive.

'Bastards,' Thonburi muttered.

'Sir?'

'Bastards,' he said, louder this time. 'We know they're better than us. But do they have to keep reminding us?'

He ushered her into the reception chamber where the Vahishta visitors were being entertained. The return indoors had a magical sharpening effect on his senses. Naqi suspected that the ability to turn drunkenness on and off like a switch must be one of the most hallowed of diplomatic skills.

He leaned towards her, confidentially. 'Did Jotah mention any—'

'Security considerations, Chairman? Yes, I think I got the message.'

'It's probably nothing, only—'

'I understand. Better safe than sorry.'

He winked, touching a finger against the side of his nose. 'Precisely.'

The interior was bright after the balcony. Twenty Vahishta delegates were standing in a huddle near the middle of the room. The captain was absent – little had been seen of Moreau since the shuttle's arrival in Umingmaktok – but the delegates were talking to a clutch of local bigwigs, none of whom Naqi recognised. Thonburi steered her into the fray, oblivious to the conversations that were taking place.

'Ladies and gentleman . . . I would like to introduce Naqi Okpik. Naqi oversees the scientific programme on the Moat. She'll be your host for the visit to our project.'

'Ah, Naqi.' Amesha Crane leaned over and shook her hand. 'A pleasure. I just read your papers on information propagation methods in class-three nodes. Erudite.'

'They were collaborative works,' Naqi said. 'I really can't take too much credit.'

'Ah, but you can. All of you can. You achieved those findings with the minimum of resources, and you made very creative use of some extremely simplistic numerical methods.'

'We muddle through,' Naqi said.

Crane nodded enthusiastically. 'It must give you a great sense of satisfaction.'

Tak Thonburi said, 'It's a philosophy, that's all. We conduct our science in isolation, and we enjoy only limited communication with other colonies. As a social model it has its disadvantages, but it means we aren't forever jealous of what they're achieving on some other world that happens to be a few decades ahead of us because of an accident of history or location. We think that the benefits outweigh the costs.'

'Well, it seems to work,' Crane said. 'You have a remarkably stable society here, Chairman. Verging on the utopian, some might say.'

Tak Thonburi caressed his cowlick. 'We can't complain.'

'Nor can we,' said the man Naqi recognised as quizzical-faced Simon Matsubara. 'If you hadn't enforced this isolation, your own Juggler research would have been as hopelessly compromised as everywhere else.'

'But the isolation isn't absolute, is it?'

The voice was quiet, but commanding.

Naqi followed the voice to the speaker. It was Rafael Weir, the man who had been identified as a possible security risk. Of the three who had emerged from Moreau's shuttle, he was the least remarkable looking, possessing the kind of amorphous face that would allow him to blend in with almost any crowd. Had her attention not been drawn to him, he would have been the last one she noticed. He was not unattractive, but there was nothing particularly striking or charismatic about his looks. According to the security dossier, he had made a number of efforts to break away from the main party of the delegation while they had been visiting research stations. They could have been accidents – one or two other party members had become separated at other times – but it was beginning to look a little too deliberate.

'No,' Tak Thonburi answered. 'We're not absolute isolationists, or we'd never have given permission for *Voice of Evening* to assume orbit around Turquoise. But we don't solicit passing traffic either. Our welcome is as warm as anyone's, we hope, but we don't encourage visitors.'

'Are we the first to visit since your settlement?' Weir asked.

'The first starship?' Tak Thonburi shook his head. 'No. But it's been a number of years since the last one.'

'Which was?'

'The *Pelican in Impiety*, a century ago.'

'An amusing coincidence, then,' Weir said.

Tak Thonburi narrowed his eyes. 'Coincidence?'

'The *Pelican*'s next port of call was Haven, if I'm not mistaken. "It was *en route* from Zion, but it made a trade stopover around Turquoise."' He smiled. 'And we have come from Haven, so history already binds our two worlds, albeit tenuously.'

Thonburi's eyes narrowed. He was trying to read Weir and evidently failing. 'We don't talk about the *Pelican* too much. There were technical benefits – vacuum-bladder production methods, information technologies . . . but there was also a fair bit of unpleasantness. The wounds haven't entirely healed.'

'Let's hope this visit will be remembered more fondly,' Weir said.

Amesha Crane nodded, fingering one of the items of silver jewellery in her hair. 'Agreed. All the indications are favourable, at the very least. We've arrived at a most auspicious time.' She turned to Naqi. 'I find the Moat project fascinating, and I'm sure I speak for the entire Vahishta delegation. I may as well tell you that no one else has attempted anything remotely like it. Tell me, scientist to scientist, do you honestly think it will work?'

'We won't know until we try,' Naqi said. Any other answer would have been politically hazardous: too much optimism and the politicians would have started asking just why the expensive project was needed in the first place. Too much pessimism and they would ask exactly the same question.

'Fascinating, all the same.' Crane's expression was knowing, as if she understood Naqi's predicament perfectly. 'I understand that you're very close to running the first experiment?'

'Given that it's taken us twenty years to get this far, yes, we're close. But we're still looking at three to four months, maybe longer. It's not something we want to rush.'

'That's a great pity,' Crane said, turning now to Thonburi. 'In three to four months we might be on our way. Still, it would have been something to see, wouldn't it?'

Thonburi leaned towards Naqi. The alcohol on his breath was a fog of cheap vinegar. 'I suppose there wouldn't be any chance of accelerating the schedule, would there?'

'Out of the question, I'm afraid,' Naqi said

'That's just too bad,' said Amesha Crane. Still toying with her jewellery, she turned to the others. 'But we mustn't let a little detail like that spoil our visit, must we?'

They returned to the Moat using the *Voice of Evening*'s shuttle. There was another civic reception to be endured upon arrival, but it was a much smaller affair than the one in Sukhothai-Sanikiluaq. Dr Jotah Sivaraksa was there, of course, and once Naqi had dealt with the business of introducing the party to him she was able to relax for the first time in many hours, melting into the corner of the room and watching the interaction between visitors and locals with a welcome sense of detachment. Naqi was tired and had difficulty keeping her eyes open. She saw everything through a sleepy blur, the delegates surrounding Sivaraksa like pillars of fire, the fabric of their costumes rippling with the slightest movement, reds and russets and chrome yellows dancing like sparks or sheets of flame. Naqi left as soon as she felt it was polite to do so, and when she reached her bed she fell immediately into troubled sleep, dreaming of squadrons of purple-winged angels falling from the skies and of the great giant rising from the depths, clawing the seaweed and kelp of ages from his eyes.

In the morning she awoke without really feeling refreshed. Anaemic light pierced the slats on her window. She was not due to meet the delegates again for another three or four hours, so there was time to turn over and try and catch some proper sleep. But she knew from experience that it would be futile.

She got up. To her surprise, there was a new message on her console from Jotah Sivaraksa. What, she wondered, did he have to say to her that he could not have said at the reception, or later this morning?

She opened the message and read.

'Sivaraksa,' she said to herself. 'Are you insane? It can't be done.'

The message informed her that there had been a change of plan. The first closure of the sea-doors would be attempted in two days, while the delegates were still on the Moat.

It was pure madness. They were months away from that. Yes, the doors could be closed – the basic machinery for doing that was in place – and yes, the doors would be hermetically tight for at least one hundred hours after closure. But nothing else was ready. The sensitive monitoring equipment, the failsafe sub-systems, the backups . . . None of that would be in place and operational for many weeks. Then there was supposed to be at least six weeks of testing, slowly building up to the event itself . . .

To do it in two days made no sense at all, except to a politician. At best all they would learn was whether or not the Jugglers had remained inside the Moat when the door was closed. They would learn nothing about how the data flow was terminated, or how the internal connections between the nodes adapted to the loss of contact with the wider ocean.

Naqi swore and hit the console. She wanted to blame Sivaraksa, but she knew that was unfair. Sivaraksa had to keep the politicians happy, or the whole project would be endangered. He was just doing what he had to do, and he almost certainly liked it even less than she did.

Naqi pulled on shorts and a T-shirt and found some coffee in one of the adjoining mess rooms. The Moat was deserted, quiet except for the womblike throb of generators and air-circulation systems. A week ago it would have been as noisy now as at any other time of day, for the construction had continued around the clock. But the heavy work was finished; the last ore dirigible had arrived while Naqi was away. All that remained was the relatively light work of completing the Moat's support subsystems. Despite what Sivaraksa had said in his message there was really very little additional work needed to close the doors. Even two days of frantic activity would make no difference to the usefulness of the stunt.

When she'd calmed down, she returned to her room and called Sivaraksa. It was still far too early, but seeing that the bastard had already ruined her day she saw no reason not to reciprocate.

'Naqi.' His silver hair was a sleep-matted mess on the screen. 'I take it you got my message?'

'You didn't think I'd take it lying down, did you?'

'I don't like it any more than you do. But I see the political necessity.'

'Do you? This isn't like switching a light on and off, Jotah.' His eyes widened at the familiarity, but she pressed on regardless. 'If we screw up the first time, there might never be a second chance. The Jugglers have to play along. Without them all you've got here is a very expensive mid-ocean refuelling point. Does that make political sense to you?'

He pushed green fingers through the mess of his hair. 'Have some breakfast, get some fresh air, then come to my office. We'll talk about it then.'

'I've had breakfast, thanks very much.'

'Then get the fresh air. You'll feel better for it.' Sivaraksa rubbed his eyes. 'You're not very happy about this, are you?'

'It's bloody madness. And the worst thing is that you know it.'

'And my hands are tied. Ten years from now, Naqi, you'll be sitting in my place having to make similar decisions. And ten to one there'll be some idealistic young scientist telling you what a hopeless piece of deadwood you are.' He managed a weary smile. 'Mark my words, because I want you to remember this conversation when it happens.'

'There's nothing I can do to stop this, is there?'

'I'll be in my office in—' Sivaraksa looked aside at a clock, 'thirty minutes. We can talk about it properly then.'

'There's nothing to talk about.'

But even as she said that she knew she sounded petulant and inflexible. Sivaraksa was right: it was impossible to manage a project as complex and expensive as the Moat without a degree of compromise.

Naqi decided that Sivaraksa's advice – at least the part about getting some fresh air – was worth heeding. She descended a helical staircase until she reached the upper surface of the Moat's ring-shaped wall. The concrete was cold beneath her bare feet and a pleasantly cool breeze caressed her legs and arms. The sky had brightened on one horizon. Machines and supplies were arranged neatly on the upper surface ready for use, although further construction would be halted until the delegates completed their visit. Stepping nimbly over the tracks, conduits and cables that crisscrossed each other on the upper surface, Naqi walked to the side. A high railing, painted in high-visibility rot-resistant sealer, fenced the inner part of the Moat.

She touched it to make sure it was dry, then leaned over. The distant side of the Moat was a colourless thread, twenty kilometres away, like a very low wall of sea mist.

What could be done in two days? Nothing. Or at least nothing compared to what had always been planned. But if the new schedule was a *fait accompli* – and that was the message she was getting from Sivaraksa – then it was her responsibility to find a way to squeeze some scientific return from the event. She looked down at the cut, and at the many spindly gantries and catwalks that spanned the aperture or hung some way towards the centre of the Moat. Perhaps if she arranged for some standard-issue probes to be prepared today, the type dropped from dirigibles . . .

Naqi's eyes darted around, surveying fixtures and telemetry conduits.

It would be hard work to get them in place in time, and even harder to get them patched into some kind of real-time acquisition system . . . But it *was* doable, just barely. The data quality would be laughable compared to the supersensitive instruments that were going to be installed over the next few months . . . But crude was a lot better than nothing at all.

She laughed, aloud. An hour ago she would have stuck pins into herself rather than collaborate in this kind of fiasco.

Naqi walked along the railing until she reached a pair of pillar-mounted binoculars. They were smeared with rot-protection. She wiped the lens and eyepieces clean with the rag that was tied to the pedestal, then swung the binoculars in a slow arc, panning across the dark circle of water trapped within the Moat. Only vague patches of what Naqi would have called open water were visible. The rest was either a verdant porridge of Juggler organisms, or fully grown masses of organised floating matter, linked together by trunks and veins of the same green biomass. The latest estimate was that there were three small nodes within the ring. The smell was atrocious, but that was an excellent sign as well: it correlated strongly with the density of organisms in the nodes. She had experienced that smell many times, but it never failed to slam her back to that morning when Mina had died.

As much as the Pattern Jugglers 'knew' anything, they were surely aware of what was planned here. They had drunk the minds of the swimmers who had already entered the sea near or within the Moat, and not one of those swimmers was ignorant of the project's ultimate purpose. It was possible that that knowledge simply couldn't be parsed into a form the aliens would understand, but Naqi considered that unlikely: the closure of the Moat would be about as stark a concept as one could imagine. If nothing else, geometry was the one thing the Jugglers did understand. And yet the aliens chose to remain within the closing Moat, hinting that they would tolerate the final closure that would seal them off from the rest of the ocean.

Perhaps they were not impressed. Perhaps they knew that the event would not rob them of every channel of communication, but only the chemical medium of the ocean. Sprites and other airborne organisms would still be able to cross the barrier. It was impossible to tell. The only way to know was to complete the experiment – to close the massive sea-doors – and see what happened.

She leaned back, taking her eyes from the binoculars.

Now Naqi saw something unexpected. It was a glint of hard white light, scudding across the water within the Moat.

Naqi squinted, but still she could not make out the object. She swung the binoculars hard around, got her eyes behind them and then zigzagged until something flashed through the field of view. She backed up and locked onto it.

It was a boat, and there was someone in it.

She keyed in the image zoom/stabilise function and the craft swelled to clarity across a clear kilometre of sea. The craft was a ceramic-hulled vessel of the type that the swimmer teams used, five or six metres long from bow to stern. The person sat behind a curved spray shield, their hands on the handlebars of the control pillar. An inboard thruster propelled the boat without ever touching water.

The figure was difficult to make out, but the billowing orange clothes left no room for doubt. It was one of the Vahishta delegates. And Naqi fully expected it to be Rafael Weir.

He was headed towards the closest node.

For an agonising few moments she did not know what to do. He was going to attempt to swim, she thought, just like she and Mina had done. And he would be no better prepared for the experience. She had to stop him, somehow. He would reach the node in only a few minutes.

Naqi sprinted back to the tower, breathless when she arrived. She reached a communications post and tried to find the right channel for the boat. But either she was doing it wrong or Weir had sabotaged the radio. What next? Technically, there was a security presence on the Moat, especially given the official visit. But what did the security goons know about chasing boats? All their training was aimed at dealing with internal crises, and none of them were competent to go anywhere near an active node.

She called them anyway, alerting them to what had happened. Then she called Sivaraksa, telling him the same news. 'I think it's Weir,' she said. 'I'm going to try and stop him.'

'Naqi . . .' he said warningly.

'This is my responsibility, Jotah. Let me handle it.'

Naqi ran back outside again. The closest elevator down to sea level was out of service; the next one was a kilometre further around the ring. She didn't have that much time. Instead she jogged along the line of railings until she reached a break that admitted entry to a staircase that descended the steep inner wall of the Moat. The steps and handrails had been helpfully greased with antirot, which made her descent that more treacherous.

There were five hundred steps down to sea level but she took them two or three at a time, sliding down the handrails until she reached the grilled platforms where the stairways reversed direction. All the while she watched the tiny white speck of the boat, seemingly immobile now that it was so far away, but undoubtedly narrowing the distance to the node with each minute. As she worked her way down she had plenty of time to think about what was going through the delegate's head. She was sure now that it was Weir. It did not really surprise her that he wanted to swim: it was what everyone who studied the Jugglers yearned for. But why make this unofficial attempt now when a little gentle persuasion would have made it possible anyway? Given Tak Thonburi's eagerness to please the delegates, it would not have been beyond the bounds of possibility for a swimming expedition to be organised . . . The corps would have protested, but just like Naqi they would have been given a forceful lesson in the refined art of political compromise.

But evidently Weir hadn't been prepared to wait. It all made sense, at any rate: the times when he had dodged away from the party before must have all been abortive attempts to reach the Jugglers. But only now had he been able to seize his opportunity.

Naqi reached the water level, where jetties floated on ceramic-sheathed pontoons. Most of the boats were suspended out of the water on cradles, to save their hulls from unnecessary degradation. Fortunately, there was an emergency rescue boat already afloat. Its formerly white hull had the flaking, pea-green scab patterning of advanced rot, but it still had a dozen or so hours of seaworthiness in it. Naqi jumped aboard, released the boat from its moorings and fired up the thruster. In a moment she was racing away from the jetty, away from the vast, stained edifice of the Moat itself. She steered a course through the least viscous stretches of water, avoiding conspicuous rafts of green matter.

She peered ahead through the boat's spray-drenched shield. It had been easy to keep track of Weir's boat when she had been a hundred metres higher, but now she kept losing him behind swells or miniature islands of Juggler matter. After a minute or so she gave up trying to follow the boat, and instead diverted her concentration to finding the quickest route to the node.

She flipped on the radio. 'Jotah? This is Naqi. I'm in the water, closing on Weir.'

There was a pause, a crackle, then: 'What's the status?'

She had to shout over the abrasive *thump, thump, thump* of the boat, even though the thruster was nearly silent.

'I'll reach the node in four or five minutes. Can't see Weir, but I don't think it matters.'

'We can see him. He's still headed for the node.'

'Good. Can you spare some more boats, in case he decides to make a run for another node?'

'They'll be leaving in a minute or so. I'm waking everyone I can.'

'What about the other delegates?'

Sivaraksa did not answer her immediately. 'Most are still asleep. I have Amesha Crane and Simon Matsubara in my office, however.'

'Let me speak to them.'

'Just a moment,' he said, after the same brief hesitation.

'Crane here,' said the woman.

'I think I'm chasing Weir. Can you confirm that?'

'He isn't accounted for,' she told Naqi. 'But it'll be a few minutes until we can be certain it's him.'

'I'm not expecting a surprise. Weir already had a question mark over him, Amesha. We were waiting for him to try something.'

'Were you?' Perhaps it was her imagination, but Crane sounded genuinely surprised. 'Why? What had he done?'

'You don't know?'

'No . . .' Crane trailed off.

'He was one of us,' Matsubara said. 'A good . . . delegate. We had no reason to distrust him.'

Perhaps Naqi was imagining this as well, but it almost sounded as if Matsubara had intended to say 'disciple' rather than 'delegate'.

Crane came back on the radio. 'Please do your best to apprehend him, Naqi. This is a source of great embarrassment to us. He mustn't do any harm.'

Naqi gunned the boat harder, no longer bothering to avoid the smaller patches of organic matter. 'No,' she said. 'He mustn't.'

three

Something changed ahead.

'Naqi?' It was Jotah Sivaraksa's voice.

'What?'

'Weir's slowed his boat. From our vantage point it looks as if he's reached the perimeter of the node. He seems to be circumnavigating it.'

'I can't see him yet. He must be picking the best spot to dive in.'

'But it won't work, will it?' Sivaraksa asked. 'There has to be an element of cooperation with the Jugglers. They have to invite the swimmer to enter the sea, or nothing happens.'

'Maybe he doesn't realise that,' Naqi said, under her breath. It was of no concern to her how closely Weir was adhering to the usual method of initiating Juggler communion. Even if the Jugglers did not cooperate – even if all Weir did was flounder in thick green water – there was no telling the hidden harm that might be done. She had already grudgingly accepted the acceleration of the closure operation. There was no way she was going to tolerate another upset, another unwanted perturbation of the experimental system. Not on her watch.

'He's stopped,' Sivaraksa said excitedly. 'Can you see him yet?'

Naqi stood up in her seat, even though she felt perilously

unbalanced. 'Wait. Yes, I think so. I'll be there in a minute or so.'

'What are you going to do?' Crane asked. 'I hesitate to say it, but Weir may not respond to rational argument at this point. Simply requesting that he leave the water won't necessarily work. Um, do you have a weapon?'

'Yes,' Naqi said. 'I'm sitting in it.'

She did not allow herself to relax, but at least now she felt that the situation was slipping back into her control. She would kill Weir rather than have him contaminate the node.

His boat was visible now only as a smudge of white, inter-mittently popping up between folds and hummocks of shifting green. Her imagination sketched in the details. Weir would be preparing to swim, stripping off until he was naked, or nearly so. Perhaps he would feel some kind of erotic charge as he prepared for immersion. She did not doubt that he would be apprehensive, and perhaps he would hesitate on the threshold of the act, teetering on the edge of the boat before committing himself to the water. But a fanatic desire had driven him this far and she doubted that it would fail him.

'Naqi—'

'Jotah?'

'Naqi, he's moving again. He didn't enter the water. He didn't even look like he had any intention of swimming.'

'He saw I was coming. I take it he's heading for the next closest node?'

'Perhaps . . .' But Jotah Sivaraksa sounded far from certain.

She saw the boat again. It was moving fast – much faster than it had appeared before – but that was only because she was now seeing lateral motion.

The next node was a distant island framed by the background of the Moat's encircling rim. If he headed that way she would be hard behind him all the way there as well. No matter his desire to swim, he must realise that she could thwart his every attempt.

Naqi looked back. The twin towers framing the cut were smothered in a haze of sea mist, their geometric details smeared into a vague suggestion of haphazard complexity. They suggested teetering, stratified sea-stacks, million-year-old towers of weathered and eroded rock guarding the narrow passage to the open ocean. Beneath them, winking in and out of clarity, she saw three or four other boats making their way into the Moat. The ponderous teardrop of a passenger dirigible was nosing away from the side of one of the towers, the low dawn sun throwing golden highlights along the fluted lines of its gondola. Naqi made out the sleek deltoid of the *Voice of Evening*'s shuttle, but it was still parked where it had landed.

She looked back to the node where Weir had hesitated.

Something was happening.

The node had become vastly more active than a minute earlier. It resembled a green, steep-sided volcanic island that was undergoing some catastrophic seismic calamity. The entire mass of the node was trembling, rocking and throbbing with an eerie regularity. Concentric swells of disturbed water raced away from it, sickening troughs that made the speeding boat pitch and slide. Naqi slowed her boat, some instinct telling her that it was now largely futile to pursue Weir. Then she turned around so that she faced the node properly and, cautiously, edged closer, ignoring the nausea she felt as the boat ducked and dived from crest to trough.

The node, like all nodes, had always shown a rich surface topology: fused hummocks and tendrils; fabulous domes and minarets and helter-skelters of organised biomass, linked and entangled by a telegraphic system of draping aerial tendrils. In any instant it resembled a human city – or, more properly, a fairy-tale human city – that had been efficiently smothered in green moss. The bright moving motes of sprites dodged through the interstices, the portholes and arches of the urban mass. The metropolitan structure only hinted at the node's Byzantine interior architecture, and much of that could only be glimpsed or implied.

But this node was like a city going insane. It was accelerating, running through cycles of urban renewal and redesign with indecent haste. Structures were evolving before Naqi's eyes. She had seen change this rapid just before Mina was taken, but normally those kinds of changes happened too slowly to be seen at all, like the daily movement of shadows.

The throbbing had decreased, but the flickering change was now throwing out a steady, warm, malodorous breeze. And when she stopped the boat – she dared come no closer now – Naqi heard the node. It was like the whisper of a billion forest leaves presaging a summer storm.

Whatever was happening here, it was about to become catastrophic.

Some fundamental organisation had been lost. The changes were happening too quickly, with too little central coordination. Tendrils thrashed like whips, unable to connect to anything. They flailed against each other. Structures were forming and collapsing. The node was fracturing, so that there were three, four, perhaps five distinct cores of flickering growth. As soon as she had the measure of it, the process shifted it all. Meagre light flickered within the epileptic mass. Sprites swarmed in confused flight patterns, orbiting mindlessly between foci. The sound of the node had become a distant shriek.

'It's dying . . .' Naqi breathed.

Weir had done something to it. What, she couldn't guess. But this could not be a coincidence.

The shrieking died down.

The breeze ceased.

The node had stopped its convulsions. She looked at it, hoping against hope that perhaps it had overcome whatever destabilising influence Weir had introduced. The structures were still misshapen, there was still an impression of incoherence, but the city was inert. The cycling motion of the sprites slowed, and a few of them dropped down into the mass, as if to roost.

A calm had descended.

Then Naqi heard another sound. It was lower than anything she had heard before – almost subsonic. It sounded less like thunder than like a very distant, very heated conversation.

It was coming from the approximate centre of the node.

She watched as a smooth green mound rose from the centre, resembling a flattened hemisphere. It grew larger by the second, assimilating the malformed structures with quiet indifference. They disappeared into the surface of the mound as if into a wall of fog, but they did not emerge again. The mound only increased its size, rumbling towards Naqi. The entire mass of the node was changing into a single undifferentiated mass.

'Jotah . . .' she said.

'We see it, Naqi. We see it but we don't understand it.'

'Weir must have used some kind of . . . weapon against it,' she said.

'We don't know that he's harmed it . . . He might just have precipitated a change to a state we haven't documented.'

'That still makes it a weapon in my book. I'm scared, Jotah.'

'You think I'm not?'

Around her the sea was changing. She had forgotten about the submerged tendrils that connected the nodes. They were as thick as hawsers, and now they were writhing and thrashing just beneath the surface of the water. Green-tinged spume lifted into the air. It was as if unseen aquatic monsters were wrestling, locked in some dire, to-the-death contest.

'Naqi . . . We're seeing changes in the closest of the two remaining nodes.'

'No,' she said, as if denying it would make any difference.

'I'm sorry . . .'

'Where is Weir?'

'We've lost him. There's too much surface disturbance.'

She realised then what had to be done. The thought arrived in her head with a crashing urgency.

'Jotah . . . You have to close the sea-doors. Now. Immediately. Before whatever Weir's unleashed has a chance to reach open ocean. That also happens to be Weir's only escape route.'

Sivaraksa, to his credit, did not argue. 'Yes. You're right. I'll start closure. But it will take quite a few minutes . . .'

'I know, Jotah!'

She cursed herself for not having thought of this sooner, and cursed Sivaraksa for the same error. But she could hardly blame either of them. Closure had never been something to take lightly. A few hours ago it had been an event months in the future – an experiment to test the willingness of the Jugglers to cooperate with human plans. Now it had turned into an emergency amputation, something to be done with brutal haste.

She peered at the gap between the towers. At the very least it would take several minutes for Sivaraksa to initiate closure. It was not simply a matter of pressing a button on his desk, but of rousing two or three specialist technicians, who would have to be immediately convinced that this was not some elaborate hoax. And then the machinery would have to work. The mechanisms that forced the sea-doors together had been tested numerous times . . . But the machinery had never been driven to its limit; the doors had never moved more than a few metres together. Now they would have to work perfectly, closing with watchmaker precision.

And when had anything on Turquoise ever worked the first time?

There. The tiniest, least perceptible narrowing of the gap. It was all happening with agonising slowness.

She looked back to what remained of the node. The mound

had consumed all the biomass available to it and had now ceased its growth. It was as if a child had sculpted in clay some fantastically intricate model of a city, which a callous adult had then squashed into a single blank mass, erasing all trace of its former complexity. The closest of the remaining nodes was showing something of the same transformation, Naqi saw: it was running through the frantic cycle that had presaged the emergence of the mound. She guessed now that the cycle had been the node's attempt to nullify whatever Weir had used against it, like a computer trying to reallocate resources to compensate for some crippling viral attack.

She could do nothing for the Jugglers now.

Naqi turned the boat around and headed back towards the cut. The sea-doors had narrowed the gap by perhaps a quarter.

The changes taking place within the Moat had turned the water turbulent, even at the jetty. She hitched the boat to a mooring point and then took the elevator up the side of the wall, preferring to sprint the distance along the top rather than face the climb. By the time she reached the cut the doors were three-quarters of the way to closure and, to Naqi's immense relief, the machinery had yet to falter.

She approached the tower. She had expected to see more people out on the top of the Moat, even if she knew that Sivaraksa would still be in his control centre. But no one was around. This was just beginning to register as a distinct wrongness when Sivaraksa emerged into daylight, stumbling from the door at the foot of the tower.

For an instant she was on the point of calling his name. Then she realised that he was stumbling because he had been injured – his fingers were scarlet with blood – and that he was trying to get away from someone or something.

Naqi dropped to the ground behind a stack of construction

slabs. Through gaps between the slabs she observed Sivaraksa. He was swatting at something, like a man being chased by a persistent wasp. Something tiny and silver harried him. More than one thing, in fact: a small swarm of them, streaming out the open door. Sivaraksa fell to his knees with a moan, brushing ineffectually at his tormentors. His face was turning red, smeared with his own blood. He slumped on one side.

Naqi remained frozen with fear.

A person stepped from the open door.

The figure was garbed in shades of fire. It was Amesha Crane. For an absurd moment Naqi assumed that the woman was about to spring to Sivaraksa's assistance. It was something about her demeanour. Naqi found it hard to believe that someone so apparently serene could commit such a violent act.

But Crane did not step closer to Sivaraksa. She merely extended her arms before her, with her fingers outspread. She sustained the oddly theatrical gesture, the muscles in her neck standing proud and rigid.

The silver things departed Sivaraksa.

They swarmed through the air, slowing as they neared Crane. Then, with a startling degree of orchestrated obedience, they slid onto her fingers, locked themselves around her wrists, clasped onto the lobes of her ears.

Her jewellery had attacked Sivaraksa.

Crane glanced at the man one last time, spun on her heels and then retreated back into the tower.

Naqi waited until she was certain the woman was not coming back, then started to emerge from behind the pile of slabs. But Sivaraksa saw her. He said nothing, but his agonised eyes widened enough for Naqi to get the warning. She remained where she was, her heart hammering.

Nothing happened for another minute.

Then something moved above, changing the play of light across the surface of the Moat. The *Voice of Evening*'s shuttle was detaching from the tower, a flicker of white machinery beneath the manta curve of its hull.

The shuttle loitered above the cut, as if observing the final moment of closure. Naqi heard the huge doors grind shut. Then the shuttle banked and headed into the circular sea, no more than two hundred metres above the waves. Some distance out it halted and executed a sharp right-angled turn. Then it resumed its flight, moving concentrically around the inner wall.

Sivaraksa closed his eyes. She thought he might have died, but then he opened them again and made the tiniest of nods. Naqi left her place of hiding. She crossed the open ground to Sivaraksa in a low, crablike stoop.

She knelt down by him, cradling his head in one hand and holding his own hand with the other. 'Jotah . . . What happened?'

He managed to answer her. 'They turned on us. The nineteen other delegates. As soon as—' He paused, summoning strength. 'As soon as Weir made his move.'

'I don't understand.'

'Join the club,' he said, managing a smile.

'I need to get you inside,' she said.

'Won't help. Everyone else is dead. Or will be by now. They murdered us all.'

'No.'

'Kept me alive until the end. Wanted me to give the orders.' He coughed. Blood spattered her hand.

'I can still get you—'

'Naqi. Save yourself. Get help.'

She realised that he was about to die.

'The shuttle?'

'Looking for Weir. I think.'

'They want Weir back?'

'No. Heard them talking. They want Weir dead. They have to be sure.'

Naqi frowned. She understood none of this, or at least her understanding was only now beginning to crystallise. She had labelled Weir as the villain because he had harmed her beloved Pattern Jugglers. But Crane and her entourage had murdered people, dozens, if what Sivaraksa said was correct. They appeared to want Weir dead as well. So what did that make Weir, now?

'Jotah . . . I have to find Weir. I have to find out why he did this.' She looked back towards the centre of the Moat. The shuttle was continuing its search. 'Did your security people get a trace on him again?'

Sivaraksa was near the end. She thought he was never going to answer her. 'Yes,' he said finally. 'Yes, they found him again.'

'And? Any idea where he is? I might still be able to reach him before the shuttle does.'

'Wrong place.'

She leaned closer. 'Jotah?'

'Wrong place. Amesha's looking in the wrong place. Weir got through the cut. He's in the open ocean.'

'I'm going after him. Perhaps I can stop him . . .'

'Try,' Sivaraksa said. 'But I'm not sure what difference it will make. I have a feeling, Naqi. A very bad feeling. Things are ending. It was good, wasn't it? While it lasted?'

'I haven't given up just yet,' Naqi said.

He found one last nugget of strength. 'I knew you wouldn't. Right to trust you. One thing, Naqi. One thing that might make a difference . . . if it comes to the worst, that is—'

'Jotah?'

'Tak Thonburi told me this . . . the most top secret, known only to the Snowflake Council. Arviat, Naqi—'

For a moment she thought she had misheard him, or that he was sliding into delirium. 'Arviat? The city that sinned against the sea?'

'It was real,' Sivaraksa said.

*

There were a number of lifeboats and emergency service craft stored at the top of near-vertical slipways, a hundred metres above the external sea. She took a small but fast emergency craft with a sealed cockpit, her stomach knotting as the vessel commenced its slide towards the ocean. The boat submerged before resurfacing, boosted up to speed and then deployed ceramic hydrofoils to minimise the contact between the hull and the water. Naqi had no precise heading to follow, but she believed Weir would have followed a reasonably straight line away from the cut, aiming to get as far away from the Moat as possible before the other delegates realised their mistake. It would require only a small deviation from that course to take him to the nearest external node, which was as likely a destination as any.

When she was twenty kilometres from the Moat, Naqi allowed herself a moment to look back. The structure was a thin white line etched on the horizon, the towers and the now-sealed cut faintly visible as interruptions in the line's smoothness. Quills of dark smoke climbed from a dozen spots along the length of the structure. It was too far for Naqi to be certain that she saw flames licking from the towers, but she considered it likely.

The closest external node appeared over the horizon fifteen minutes later. It was nowhere as impressive as the one that had taken Mina, but it was still a larger, more complex structure than any of the nodes that had formed within the Moat – a major urban megalopolis, perhaps, rather than a moderately sized city. Against the skyline Naqi saw spires and rotundas and coronets of green, bridged by a tracery of elevated tendrils. Sprites were rapidly moving silhouettes. There was motion, but it was largely confined to the flying creatures. The node was not yet showing the frenzied changes she had witnessed within the Moat.

Had Weir gone somewhere else?

She pressed onwards, slowing the boat slightly now that the water was thickening with micro-organisms and it was necessary to steer around the occasional larger floating structure. The boat's sonar picked out dozens of submerged tendrils converging on the node, suspended just below the surface. The tendrils reached away in all directions, to the limits of the boat's sonar range. Most would have reached over the horizon, to nodes many hundreds of kilometres away. But it was a topological certainty that some of them had been connected to the nodes inside the Moat. Evidently, Weir's contagion had never escaped through the cut. Naqi doubted that the doors had closed in time to impede whatever chemical signals were transmitting the fatal message. It was more likely that some latent Juggler self-protection mechanism had cut in, the dying nodes sending emergency termination-of-connection signals that forced the tendrils to sever without human assistance.

Naqi had just decided that she had guessed wrongly about Weir's plan when she saw a rectilinear furrow gouged right through one of the largest subsidiary structures. The wound was healing itself as she watched – it would be gone in a matter of minutes – but enough remained for her to tell that Weir's boat must have cleaved through the mass very recently. It made sense. Weir had already demonstrated that he had no interest in preserving the Pattern Jugglers.

With renewed determination, Naqi gunned the boat forward. She no longer worried about inflicting local damage on the floating masses. There was a great deal more at stake than the well-being of a single node.

She felt a warmth on the back of her neck.

At the same instant the sky, sea and floating structures ahead of her pulsed with a cruel brightness. Her own shadow stretched forward ominously. The brightness faded over the next few seconds, and then she dared to look back, half-knowing what she would see.

A mass of hot, roiling gas was climbing into the air from the centre of the node. It tugged a column of matter beneath it, like the knotted and gnarled spinal column of a horribly swollen brain. Against the mushroom cloud she saw the tiny moving speck of the delegates' shuttle.

A minute later the sound of the explosion reached her, but although it was easily the loudest thing she had ever heard, it was not as deafening as she had expected. The boat lurched; the sea fumed, and then was still again. She assumed that the Moat's wall had absorbed much of the energy of the blast.

Suddenly fearful that there might be another explosion, Naqi turned back towards the node. At the same instant she saw Weir's boat, racing perhaps three hundred metres ahead of her. He was beginning to curve and slow as he neared the impassable perimeter of the node. Naqi knew that she did not have time to delay.

That was when Weir saw her. His boat sped up again, arcing hard away. Naqi steered immediately, certain that her boat was faster and that it was now only a matter of time before she had him. A minute later Weir's boat disappeared around the curve of the node's perimeter. She might have stood a chance of getting an echo from his hull, but this close to the node all sonar returns were too garbled to be of any use. Naqi steered anyway, hoping that Weir would make the tactical mistake of striking for another node. In open water he stood no chance at all, but perhaps he understood that as well.

She had circumnavigated a third of the node's perimeter when she caught up with him again. He had not tried to run for it. Instead he had brought the boat to a halt within the comparative shelter of an inlet on the perimeter. He was standing up at the rear of the boat, with something small and dark in his hand.

Naqi slowed her boat as she approached him. She had popped back the canopy before it occurred to her that Weir might be equipped with the same weapons as Crane.

She stood up herself. 'Weir?'

He smiled. 'I'm sorry to have caused so much trouble. But I don't think it could have happened any other way.'

She let this pass. 'That thing in your hand?'

'Yes?'

'It's a weapon, isn't it?'

She could see it clearly now. It was merely a glass bauble, little larger than a child's marble. There was something opaque inside it, but she could not tell if it contained fluid or dark crystals.

'I doubt that a denial would be very plausible at this point.' He nodded, and she sensed the lifting, partially at least, of some appalling burden. 'Yes, it's a weapon. A Juggler killer.'

'Until today, I'd have said no such thing was possible.'

'I doubt that it was very easy to synthesise. Countless biological entities have entered their oceans, and none of them have ever brought anything with them that the Jugglers couldn't assimilate in a harmless fashion. Doubtless some of those entities tried to inflict deliberate harm, if only out of morbid curiosity. None of them succeeded. Of course, you can kill Jugglers by brute force—' He looked towards the Moat, where the mushroom cloud was dissipating. 'But that isn't the point. Not subtle. But this is. It exploits a logical flaw in the Jugglers' own informational processing algorithms. It's insidious. And no, humans most certainly didn't invent it. We're clever, but we're not *that* clever.'

Naqi strove to keep him talking. 'Who made it, Weir?'

'The Ultras sold it to us in a presynthesised form. I've heard rumours that it was found inside the topmost chamber of a heavily fortified alien structure . . . Another that it was synthesised by a rival group of Jugglers. Who knows? Who cares, even? It does what we ask of it. That's all that matters.'

'Please don't use it, Rafael.'

'I have to. It's what I came here to do.'

'But I thought you all loved the Jugglers.'

His fingers caressed the glass globe. It looked terribly fragile. 'We?'

'Crane . . . Her delegates.'

'They do. But I'm not one of them.'

'Tell me what this is about, Rafael.'

'It would be better if you just accepted what I have to do.'

Naqi swallowed. 'If you kill them, you kill more than just an alien life form. You erase the memory of every sentient creature that's ever entered the ocean.'

'Unfortunately, that rather happens to be the point.'

Weir dropped the glass into the sea.

It hit the water, bobbed under and then popped back out again, floating on the surface. The small globe was already immersed in a brackish scum of grey-green micro-organisms. They were beginning to lap higher up the sides of the globe, exploring it. A couple of millimetres of ordinary glass would succumb to Juggler erosion in perhaps thirty minutes . . . But Naqi guessed that this was not ordinary glass, that it was designed to degrade much more rapidly.

She jumped back down into her control seat and shot her boat forward. She came alongside Weir's boat, trapping the globe between the two craft. Taking desperate care not to nudge the hulls together, she stopped her boat and leaned over as far as she could without falling in. Her fingertips brushed the glass. Maddeningly, she could not quite get a grip on it. She made one last valiant effort and it drifted beyond her reach. Now it was out of her range, no matter how hard she stretched. Weir watched impassively.

Naqi slipped into the water. The layer of Juggler organisms licked her chin and nose, the smell immediate and overwhelming now that she was in such close proximity. Her fear was absolute. It was the first time she had entered the water since Mina's death.

She caught the globe, taking hold of it with the exquisite care she might have reserved for a rare bird's egg.

Already the glass had the porous texture of pumice.

She held it up, for Weir to see.

'I won't let you do this, Rafael.'

'I admire your concern.'

'It's more than concern. My sister is here. She's in the ocean. And I won't let you take her away from me.'

Weir reached inside a pocket and removed another globe.

They sped away from the node in Naqi's boat. The new globe rested in his hand like a gift. He had not yet dropped it in the sea, although the possibility was only ever an instant away. They were far from any node now, but the globe would be guaranteed to come into contact with Juggler matter sooner or later.

Naqi opened a watertight equipment locker, pushing aside the flare pistol and first-aid kit that lay within. Carefully she placed the globe within, and then watched in horror as the glass immediately cracked and dissolved, releasing its poison: little black irregularly shaped grains like burnt sugar. If the boat sank, the locker would eventually be consumed into the ocean, along with its fatal contents. She considered using the flare pistol to incinerate the remains, but there was too much danger of dispersing it at the same time. Perhaps the toxin had a restricted lifespan once it came into contact with air, but that was nothing she could count on.

But Weir had not thrown the third globe into sea. Not yet. Something she had said had made him hesitate.

'Your sister?'

'You know the story,' Naqi said. 'Mina was a conformal. The ocean assimilated her entirely, rather than just recording her neural patterns. It took her as a prize.'

214

'And you believe that she's still present, in some sentient sense?'

'That's what I choose to believe, yes. And there's enough anecdotal evidence from other swimmers that conformals do persist, in a more coherent form than other stored patterns.'

'I can't let anecdotal evidence sway me, Naqi. Have the other swimmers specifically reported encounters with Mina?'

'No . . .' Naqi said carefully. She was sure that he would see through any lie that she attempted. 'But they wouldn't necessarily recognise her if they did.'

'And you? Did you attempt to swim yourself?'

'The swimmer corps would never have allowed me.'

'Not my question. Did you ever swim?'

'Once,' Naqi said.

'And?'

'It didn't count. It was the same time that Mina died.' She paused and then told him all that had happened. 'We were seeing more sprite activity than we'd ever recorded. It looked like coincidence—'

'I don't think it was.'

Naqi said nothing. She waited for Weir to collect his own thoughts, concentrating on the steering of the boat. Open sea lay ahead, but she knew that almost any direction would bring them to a cluster of nodes within a few hours.

'It began with *Pelican of Impiety*,' Weir said. 'A century ago. There was a man from Zion on that ship. During the stopover he descended to the surface of Turquoise and swam in your ocean. He made contact with the Jugglers and then swam again. The second time the experience was even more affecting. On the third occasion, the sea swallowed him. He'd been a conformal, just like your sister. His name was Ormazd.'

'It means nothing to me.'

'I assure you that on his homeworld it means a great deal more. Ormazd was a failed tyrant, fleeing a political counterrevolution on Zion. He had murdered and cheated his way to power on Zion, burning his rivals in their houses while they slept. But there'd been a backlash. He got out just before the ring closed around him – him and a handful of his closest allies and devotees. They escaped aboard *Pelican in Impiety*.'

'And Ormazd died here?'

'Yes – but his followers didn't. They made it to Haven, our world. And once there they began to proliferate, spreading their word, recruiting new followers. It didn't matter that Ormazd was gone. Quite the opposite. He'd martyred himself: given them a saint figure to worship. It evolved from a political movement into a religious cult. The Vahishta Foundation's just a front for the Ormazd sect.'

Naqi absorbed that, then asked, 'Where does Amesha come into it?'

'Amesha was his daughter. She wants her father back.'

Something lit the horizon, a pink-edged flash. Another followed a minute later, in nearly the same position.

'She wants to commune with him?'

'More than that,' said Weir. 'They all want to *become* him; to accept his neural patterns on their own. They want the Jugglers to imprint Ormazd's personality on all his followers, to remake them in his own image. The aliens will do that, if the right gifts are offered. And that's what I can't allow.'

Naqi chose her words carefully, sensing that the tiniest thing could push Weir into releasing the globe. She had prevented his last attempt, but he would not allow her a second chance. All he would have to do would be to crush the globe in his fist before spilling the contents into the ocean. Then it would all be over. Everything she had ever known; everything she had ever lived for.

'But we're only talking about nineteen people,' she said.

Weir laughed hollowly. 'I'm afraid it's a little more than that. Why don't you turn on the radio and see what I mean?'

Naqi did as he suggested, using the boat's general communications console. The small, scuffed screen received television pictures beamed down from the comsat network. Naqi flicked through channels, finding static on most of them. The Snowflake Council's official news service was off the air and no personal messages were getting through. There were some suggestions that the comsat network itself was damaged. Yet finally Naqi found a few weak broadcast signals from the nearest snowflake cities. There was a sense of desperation in the transmissions, as if they expected to fall silent at any time.

Weir nodded with weary acceptance, as if he had expected this.

In the last six hours at least a dozen more shuttles had come down from *Voice of Evening,* packed with armed Vahishta disciples. The shuttles had attacked the planet's major snowflake cities and atoll settlements, strafing them into submission. Three cities had fallen into the sea, their vacuum-bladders punctured by beam weapons. There could not have been any survivors. Others were still aloft, but had been set on fire. The pictures showed citizens leaping from the cities' berthing arms, falling like sparks. More cities had been taken bloodlessly, and were now under control of the disciples.

None of those cities were transmitting now.

It was the end of the world. Naqi knew that she should be weeping, or at the very least feel some writhing sense of loss in her stomach. But all she got was a sense of denial; a refusal to accept that events could have escalated so quickly. This morning the only hint of wrongness had been a single absent disciple.

'There are tens of thousands of them up there,' Weir said. 'All that you've seen so far is the advance guard.'

Naqi scratched her forearm. It was itching, as if she had caught a dose of sunburn.

'Moreau was in on this?'

'Captain Moreau's a puppet. Literally. The body you saw was

just being tele-operated by orbital disciples. They murdered the Ultras and commandeered the ship—'

'Rafael, why didn't you tell us this before?'

'My position was too vulnerable. I was the only anti-Ormazd agent my movement managed to put aboard *Voice of Evening*. If I'd attempted to warn the Turquoise authorities . . . Well, work it out for yourself. Almost certainly I wouldn't have been believed, and the disciples would have found a way to silence me before I became an embarrassment. And it wouldn't have made a difference to their takeover plans. My only hope was to destroy the ocean, to remove its usefulness to them. They might still have destroyed your cities out of spite, but at least they'd have lost the final thread that connected them to their martyr.' Weir leaned closer to her. 'Don't you understand? It wouldn't have stopped with the disciples aboard the *Voice*. They'd have brought more ships from Haven. Your ocean would have become a production line for despots.'

'Why did they hesitate, if they had such a crushing advantage over us?'

'They didn't know about me, so they lost nothing by dedicating a few weeks to intelligence-gathering. They wanted to know as much as possible about Turquoise and the Jugglers before they made their move. They're brutal, but they're not inefficient. They wanted their takeover to be as precise and surgical as possible.'

'And now?'

'They've accepted that things won't be quite that neat and tidy.' He flipped the globe from one palm to another, with a casual playfulness that Naqi found alarming. 'They're serious, Naqi. Crane will stop at nothing now. You've seen those blast flashes. Pinpoint anti-matter devices. They've already sterilised the organic matter within the Moat, to stop the effect of my weapon from reaching further. If they know where we are, they'll drop a bomb on us as well.'

'Human evil doesn't give us the excuse to wipe out the ocean.'

'It's not an excuse, Naqi. It's an imperative.'

At that moment something glinted on the horizon, something that was moving slowly from east to west.

'The shuttle,' Weir said. 'It's looking for us.'

Naqi scratched her arm again. It was discoloured, itching.

Near local noon they reached the next node. The shuttle had continued to dog them, nosing to and fro along the hazy band where sea met sky. Sometimes it appeared closer, sometimes it appeared further away, but it never left them alone, and Naqi knew that it would be only a matter of time before it detected a positive homing trace, a chemical or physical note in the water that would lead it to its quarry. The shuttle would cover the remaining distance in seconds, a minute at the most, and then all that she and Weir would know would be a moment of cleansing whiteness, a fire of holy purity. Even if Weir released his toxin just before the shuttle arrived, it would not have time to dissipate into a wide enough volume of water to survive the fireball.

So why was he hesitating? It was Mina, of course. Naqi had given a name to the faceless library of stored minds he was prepared to erase. By naming her sister, Naqi had removed the one-sidedness of the moral equation, and now Weir had to accept that his own actions could never be entirely blameless. He was no longer purely objective.

'I should just do this,' he said. 'By hesitating even for a second, I'm betraying the trust of the people who sent me here, people who have probably been tormented to extinction by Ormazd's followers by now.'

Naqi shook her head. 'If you didn't show doubt, you'd be as bad as the disciples.'

'You almost sound as if you want me to do it.'

She groped for something resembling the truth, as painful as that might be. 'Perhaps I do.'

'Even though it would mean killing whatever part of Mina survived?'

'I've lived in her shadow my entire life. Even after she died . . . I always felt she was still watching me, still observing my every mistake, still being faintly disappointed that I wasn't living up to all she had imagined I could be.'

'You're being harsh on yourself. Harsh on Mina too, by the sound of things.'

'I know,' Naqi said angrily. 'I'm just telling you how I feel.'

The boat edged into a curving inlet that pushed deep into the node. Naqi felt less vulnerable now: there was a significant depth of organic matter to screen the boat from any sideways-looking sensors that the shuttle might have deployed, even though the evidence suggested that the shuttle's sensors were mainly focused down from its hull. The disadvantage was that it was no longer possible to keep a constant vigil on the shuttle's movements. It could be on its way already.

She brought the boat to a halt and stood up in her control seat.

'What's happening?' Weir asked.

'I've come to a decision.'

'Isn't that my job?'

Her anger – brief as it was, and directed less at Weir than at the hopelessness of the situation – had evaporated. 'I mean about swimming. It's the one thing we haven't considered yet, Rafael. That there might be a third way: a choice between accepting the disciples and letting the ocean die.'

'I don't see what that could be.'

'Nor do I. But the ocean might find a way. It just needs the knowledge of what's at stake.' She stroked her forearm again, marvelling at the sudden eruption of fungal patterns. They must have been latent for many years, but now something had caused them to flare up.

Even in daylight, emeralds and blues shone against her skin.

She suspected that the biochemical changes had been triggered when she entered the water to snatch the globe. Given that, she could not help but view it as a message. An invitation, perhaps. Or was it a warning, reminding her of the dangers of swimming?

She had no idea, but for her peace of mind, however – and given the lack of alternatives – she chose to view it as an invitation.

But she did not dare wonder who was inviting her.

'You think the ocean can understand external events?' Weir asked.

'You said it yourself, Rafael: the night they told us the ship was coming, somehow that information reached the sea – via a swimmer's memories, perhaps. And the Jugglers knew then that this was something significant. Perhaps it was Ormazd's personality, rising to the fore.'

Or maybe it was merely the vast, choral mind of the ocean, apprehending only that *something* was going to happen.

'Either way,' Naqi said. 'It still makes me think that there might be a chance.'

'I only wish I shared your optimism.'

'Give me this chance, Rafael. That's all I ask.'

Naqi removed her clothes, less concerned that Weir would see her naked now than that she should have something to wear when she emerged. But although Weir studied her with unconcealed fascination, there was nothing prurient about it. What commanded his attention, Naqi realised, were the elaborate and florid patterning of the fungal markings. They curled and twined about her chest and abdomen and thighs, shining with a hypnotic intensity.

'You're changing,' he said.

'We all change,' Naqi answered.

Then she stepped from the side of the boat, into the water.

The process of descending into the ocean's embrace was much

as she remembered it that first time, with Mina beside her. She willed her body to submit to the biochemical invasion, forcing down her fear and apprehension, knowing that she had been through this once before and that it was something that she could survive again. She did her best not to think about what it would mean to survive beyond this day, when all else had been shattered, every certainty crumbled.

Mina came to her with merciful speed.

Naqi?

I'm here. Oh, Mina, I'm here. There was terror and there was joy, alloyed together. *It's been so long.*

Naqi felt her sister's presence edge in and out of proximity and focus. Sometimes she appeared to share the same physical space. At other times she was scarcely more than a vague feeling of attentiveness.

How long?

Two years, Mina.

Mina's answer took an eternity to come. In that dreadful hiatus Naqi felt other minds crowd against her own, some of which were so far from human that she gasped at their oddity. Mina was only one of the conformal minds that had noticed her arrival, and not all were as benignly curious or glad.

It doesn't feel like two years to me.

How long?

Days . . . hours . . . It changes.

What do you remember?

Mina's presence danced around Naqi. *I remember what I remember. That we swam, when we weren't meant to. That something happened to me, and I never left the ocean.*

You became part of it, Mina.

The triumphalism of her answer shocked Naqi to the marrow. *Yes!*

You wanted this?

You would want it, if you knew what it was like. You could have stayed, Naqi. You could have let it happen to you, the way it happened to me. We were so alike.

I was scared.

Yes, I remember.

Naqi knew that she had to get to the heart of things. Time was passing differently here – witness Mina's confusion about how long she had been part of the ocean – and there was no telling how patient Weir would be. He might not wait until Naqi reemerged before deploying the Juggler killer.

There was another mind, Mina. We encountered it, and it scared me. Enough that I had to leave the ocean. Enough that I never wanted to go back.

You've come back now.

It's because of that other mind. It belonged to a man called Ormazd. Something very bad is going to happen because of him. One way or the other.

There was a moment then that transcended anything Naqi had experienced before. She felt herself and Mina become inseparable. She could not only not say where one began and the other ended, but it was entirely pointless to even think in those terms. If only fleetingly, Mina had *become* her. Every thought, every memory, was open to equal scrutiny by both of them.

Naqi understood what it was like for Mina. Her sister's memories were rapturous. She might only have sensed the passing of hours or days, but that belied the richness of her experience since merging with the ocean. She had exchanged experience with countless alien minds, drinking in entire histories beyond normal human comprehension. And in that moment of sharing, Naqi appreciated something of the reason for her sister having been taken in the first place. Conformals were the ocean's way of managing itself. Now and then the maintenance of the vaster archive of static minds required stewardship – the drawing-in of independent intelligences.

Mina had been selected and utilised, and given rewards beyond imagining for her efforts. The ocean had tapped the structure of her intelligence at a subconscious level. Only now and then had she ever felt that she was being directly petitioned on a matter of importance.

But Ormazd's mind . . . ?

Mina had seen Naqi's memories now. She would know exactly what was at stake, and she would know exactly what that mind represented.

I was always aware of him. He wasn't always there – he liked to hide himself – but even when he was absent, he left a shadow of himself. I even think he might be the reason the ocean took me as a conformal. It sensed a coming crisis. It knew Ormazd had something to do with it. It had made a terrible mistake by swallowing him. So it reached out for new allies, minds it could trust.

Minds like Mina, Naqi thought. In that instant she did not know whether to admire the Pattern Jugglers or detest them for their heartlessness.

Ormazd was contaminating it?

His influence was strong. His force of personality was a kind of poison in its own right. The Pattern Jugglers knew that, I think.

Why couldn't they just eject his patterns?

They couldn't. It doesn't work that way. The sea is a storage medium, but it has no self-censoring facility. If the individual minds detect a malign presence, they can resist it . . . But Ormazd's mind is human. There aren't enough of us here to make a difference, Naqi. The other minds are too alien to recognise Ormazd for what he is. They just see a sentience.

Who made the Pattern Jugglers, Mina? Answer me that, will you?

She sensed Mina's amusement.

Even the Jugglers don't know that, Naqi. Or why.

You have to help us, Mina. You have to communicate the urgency of this to the rest of the ocean.

I'm one mind amongst many, Naqi. One voice in the chorus.

You still have to find a way. Please, Mina. Understand this, if nothing else. You could die. You could all die. I lost you once, but now I know you never really went away. I don't want to have to lose you again, for good.

You didn't lose me, Naqi. I lost you.

She hauled herself from the water. Weir was waiting where she had left him, with the intact globe still resting in his hand. The daylight shadows had moved a little, but not as much as she had feared. She made eye contact with Weir, wordlessly communicating a question.

'The shuttle's come closer. It's flown over the node twice while you were under. I think I need to do this, Naqi.'

He had the globe between thumb and forefinger, ready to drop it into the water.

She was shivering. Naqi pulled on her shorts and shirt, but she felt just as cold afterwards. The fungal marks were shimmering intensely; they appeared almost to hover above her skin. If anything they were shining more furiously than before she had swum. Naqi did not doubt that if she had lingered – if she had stayed with Mina – she would have become a conformal as well. It had always been in her, but it was only now that her time had come.

'Please wait,' Naqi said, her own voice sounding pathetic and childlike. 'Please wait, Rafael.'

'There it is again.'

The shuttle was a fleck of white sliding over the top of the nearest wall of Juggler biomass. It was five or six kilometres away, much closer than the last time Naqi had seen it. Now it came to a sudden sharp halt, hovering above the surface of the ocean as if it had found something of particular interest.

'Do you think it knows we're here?'

'It suspects something,' Weir said. The globe rolled between his fingers.

'Look,' Naqi said.

The shuttle was still hovering. Naqi stood up to get a better view, nervous of making herself visible but desperately curious. Something was happening. She *knew* something was happening.

Kilometres away, the sea was bellying up beneath the shuttle. The water was the colour of moss, supersaturated with micro-organisms. Naqi watched as a coil of solid green matter reached from the ocean, twisting and writhing. It was as thick as a building, spilling vast rivulets of water as it emerged. It extended upwards with astonishing haste, bifurcating and flexing like a groping fist. For a brief moment it closed around the shuttle. Then it slithered back into the sea with a titanic splash; a prolonged roar of spent energy. The shuttle continued to hover above the same spot, as if oblivious to what had just happened. Yet the manta-shaped craft's white hull was lathered with various hues of green. And Naqi understood: what had happened to the shuttle was what had happened to Arviat, the city that drowned. She could not begin to guess the crime that Arviat had committed against the sea, the crime that had merited its destruction, but she could believe – now, at least – that the Jugglers had been capable of dragging it beneath the waves, ripping the main mass of the city away from the bladders that held it aloft. And of course such a thing would have to be kept maximally secret, known only to a handful of individuals. For otherwise no city would ever feel safe when the sea roiled and groaned beneath it.

But a city was not a shuttle. Even if the Juggler material started eating away the fabric of the shuttle, it would still take hours to do any serious damage . . . And that was assuming the Ultras had no better protection than the ceramic shielding used on Turquoise boats and machines . . .

But the shuttle was already tilting over.

Naqi watched it pitch, attempt to regain stability and then pitch again. She understood, belatedly. The organic matter was clogging the shuttle's whisking propulsion systems, limiting its ability to hover. The shuttle was curving inexorably closer to the sea, spiralling steeply away from the node. It approached the surface and then, just before the moment of impact, another misshapen fist of organised matter thrust from the sea, seizing the hull in its entirety. That was the last Naqi saw of it.

A troubled calm fell on the scene. The sky overhead was unmarred by questing machinery. Only the thin whisper of smoke rising from the horizon, in the direction of the Moat, hinted of the day's events.

Minutes passed, and then tens of minutes. Then a rapid series of bright flashes strobed from beneath the surface of the sea itself.

'That was the shuttle,' Weir said, wonderingly.

Naqi nodded. 'The Jugglers are fighting back. This is more or less what I hoped would happen.'

'You asked for this?'

'I think Mina understood what was needed. Evidently she managed to convince the rest of the ocean, or at least this part of it.'

'Let's see.'

They searched the airwaves again. The comsat network was dead, or silent. Even fewer cities were transmitting now. But those that were – those that had not been overrun by Ormazd's disciples – told a frightening story. The ocean was clawing at them, trying to drag them into the sea. Weather patterns were shifting, entire storms being conjured into existence by the orchestrated circulation of vast ocean currents. It was happening in concentric waves, racing away from the precise point in the ocean where Naqi had swum. Some cities had already fallen into the sea, though it was not clear whether this had been brought about by the Jugglers themselves or because of damage to their vacuum-bladders. There were people in the water:

hundreds, thousands of them. They were swimming, trying to stay afloat, trying not to drown.

But what exactly did it mean to drown on Turquoise?

'It's happening all over the planet,' Naqi said. She was still shivering, but now it was as much a shiver of awe as one of cold. 'It's denying itself to us by smashing our cities.'

'Your cities never harmed it.'

'I don't think it's really that interested in making a distinction between one bunch of people and another, Rafael. It's just getting rid of us all, disciples or not. You can't really blame it for that, can you?'

'I'm sorry,' Weir said.

He cracked the globe, spilled its contents into the sea.

Naqi knew there was nothing she could do now; there was no prospect of recovering the tiny black grains. She would only have to miss one, and it would be as bad as missing them all.

The little black grains vanished beneath the olive surface of the water.

It was done.

Weir looked at her, his eyes desperate for forgiveness.

'You understand that I had to do this, don't you? It isn't something I do lightly.'

'I know. But it wasn't necessary. The ocean's already turned against us. Crane has lost. Ormazd has lost.'

'Perhaps you're right,' Weir said. 'But I couldn't take the chance that we might be wrong. At least this way I know for sure.'

'You've murdered a world.'

He nodded. 'It's exactly what I came here to do. Please don't blame me for it.'

Naqi opened the equipment locker where she had stowed the broken vial of Juggler toxin. She removed the flare pistol, snatched away its safety pin and pointed it at Weir. 'I don't blame you, no. Don't even hate you for it.'

He started to say something, but Naqi cut him off.

'But it's not something I can forgive.'

She sat in silence, alone, until the node became active. The organic structures around her were beginning to show the same kinds of frantic rearrangement Naqi had seen within the Moat. There was a cold sharp breeze from the node's heart.

It was time to leave.

She steered the boat away from the node, cautiously, still not completely convinced that she was safe from the delegates even though the first shuttle had been destroyed. Undoubtedly the loss of that craft would have been communicated to the others, and before very long some more of them would arrive, bristling with belligerence. The ocean might attempt to destroy the new arrivals, but this time the delegates would be profoundly suspicious.

She brought the boat to a halt when she was a kilometre from the fringe of the node. By then it was running through the same crazed alterations she had previously witnessed. She felt the same howling wind of change. In a moment the end would come. The toxin would seep into the node's controlling core, instructing the entire biomass to degrade itself to a lump of dumb vegetable matter. The same killing instructions would already be travelling along the internode tendril connections, winging their way over the horizon. Allowing for the topology of the network, it would only take fifteen or twenty hours for the message to reach every node on the planet. Within a day it would be over. The Jugglers would be gone, the information they'd encoded erased beyond recall. And Turquoise itself would begin to die at the same time, its oxygen atmosphere no longer maintained by the oceanic organisms.

Another five minutes passed, then ten.

The node's transformations were growing less hectic. She recalled this moment of false calm. It meant only that the node had given up trying to counteract the toxin, accepting the logical inevitability of its fate. A thousand times over this would be repeated around Turquoise. Towards the end, she guessed, there would be less resistance, for the sheer futility of it would have been obvious. The world would accept its fate.

Another five minutes passed.

The node remained. The structures were changing, but only gently. There was no sign of the emerging mound of undifferentiated matter she had seen before.

What was happening?

She waited another quarter of an hour and then steered the boat back towards the node, bumping past Weir's floating corpse on the way. Tentatively, an idea was forming in her mind. It appeared that the node had absorbed the toxin without dying. Was it possible that Weir had made a mistake? Was it possible that the toxin's effectiveness depended only on it being used once?

Perhaps.

There still had to be tendril connections between the Moat and the rest of the ocean at the time that the first wave of transformations had taken place. They had been severed later – either when the doors closed, or by some autonomic process within the extended organism itself – but until that moment, there would still have been informational links with the wider network of nodes. Could the dying nodes have sent sufficient warning that the other nodes were now able to find a strategy for protecting themselves?

Again, perhaps.

It never paid to take anything for granted where the Jugglers were concerned.

She parked the boat by the node's periphery. Naqi stood up and removed her clothes for the final time, certain that she would not need them again. She looked down at herself, astonished at the vivid tracery of green that now covered her body. On one level, the evidence of alien cellular invasion was quite horrific.

On another, it was startlingly beautiful.

Smoke licked from the horizon. Machines clawed through the sky, hunting nervously. She stepped to the edge of the boat, tensing herself at the moment of commitment. Her fear subsided, replaced by an intense, loving calm. She stood on the threshold of something alien, but in place of terror what she felt was only an imminent sense of homecoming. Mina was waiting for her below. Together, nothing could stop them.

Naqi smiled, spread her arms and returned to the sea.